ALSO BY JESMYN WARD

Let Us Descend

A Novel

JESMYN WARD

SCRIBNER

New York   London   Toronto   Sydney   New Delhi

Scribner
An Imprint of Simon & Schuster, Inc.
1230 Avenue of the Americas
New York, NY 10020

First Scribner hardcover edition October 2023

For information about special discounts for bulk purchases, please contact Simon & Schuster Special Sales at 1-866-506-1949 or business@simonandschuster.com.

The Simon & Schuster Speakers Bureau can bring authors to your live event. For more information or to book an event, contact the Simon & Schuster Speakers Bureau at 1-866-248-3049 or visit our website at www.simonspeakers.com.

Interior design by Jaime Putorti

Manufactured in the United States of America

1   3   5   7   9   10   8   6   4   2

Library of Congress Cataloging-in-Publication Data has been applied for.

ISBN 978-1-9821-0449-8
ISBN 978-1-9821-0451-1 (ebook)

This book is for Brandon, who saw me and loved me, even when I could not see or love myself, and for Joshua, the first to show me that love is a living link to the dead.

"When they sold her, her mother fainted or dropped dead, she never knowed which. She wanted to go see her mother lying over there on the ground and the man what bought her wouldn't let her. He just took her on. Drove her off like cattle, I reckon . . . That was the last she ever knowed of any of her folks."

—"INTERVIEW WITH ROGERS, WILL ANN," FROM *BORN IN SLAVERY: SLAVE NARRATIVES FROM THE FEDERAL WRITERS' PROJECT, 1936 TO 1938*

There was a ship,
the *Henrietta Marie*,
breaking against the furious water,
and there were shackles
and the woman on deck
her legs open in the hiss of a scream.
. . . and I was there too,
unfurling with them all . . .

—"SHARK BITE," FROM *THE WORLD IS ROUND* BY NIKKY FINNEY

. . . Dear singing river full
Of my blood, are we as loud under-
Water? Is it blood that binds

Brothers? Or is it the Mississippi
Running through the fattest vein
Of America?

— EXCERPT OF "LANGSTON'S BLUES," FROM *THE NEW TESTAMENT* BY JERICHO BROWN

Let Us Descend

CHAPTER 1

Mama's Bladed Hands

The first weapon I ever held was my mother's hand. I was a small child then, soft at the belly. On that night, my mother woke me and led me out to the Carolina woods, deep, deep into the murmuring trees, black with the sun's leaving. The bones in her fingers: blades in sheaths, but I did not know this yet. We walked until we came to a small clearing around a lightning-burnt tree, far from my sire's rambling cream house that sits beyond the rice fields. Far from my sire, who is as white as my mother is dark. Far from this man who says he owns us, from this man who drives my mother to a black thread in the dim closeness of his kitchen, where she spends most of her waking hours working to feed him and his two paunchy, milk-sallow children. I was bird-boned, my head brushing my mother's shoulder. On that night long ago, my mother knelt in the fractured tree's roots and dug out two long, thin limbs: one with a tip carved like a spear, the other wavy as a snake, clumsily hewn.

"Take this," my mother said, throwing the crooked limb to me. "I whittled it when I was small."

I missed it, and the jagged staff clattered to the ground. I picked it up and held it so tight the knobs from her hewing cut, and then my mother bought her own dark limb down. She had never struck me before, not with her hands, not with wood. Pain burned my shoulder, then lanced through the other.

"This one," she grunted, her voice low under her weapon's whistling, "was my mama's." Her spear was a black whip in the night. I fell. Crawled backward, scrambling under the undergrowth that encircled that ruined midnight room. My mother stalked. My mother spoke aloud as she hunted me in the bush. She told me a story: "This our secret. Mine and your'n. Can't nobody steal this from us." I barely breathed, crouching down further. The wind circled and glanced across the trees.

"You the granddaughter of a woman warrior. She was married to the Fon king, given by her daddy because he had so many daughters, and he was rich. The king had hundreds of warrior wives. They guarded him, hunted for him, fought for him." She poked the bush above me. "The warrior wives was married to the king, but the knife was they husband, the cutlass they lover. You my child, my mama's child. My mother, the fighter—her name was Azagueni, but I called her Mama Aza."

My mama set her spear down, stood with her palms open. They shone silver. "Come, Annis. Come out and I will teach you." I started to crawl forward, her blows still stinging. "Don't forget your staff," she said. I inched back before dragging myself up and out, where I stood on the tips of my toes, one foot in front of the other, ready to run. Waiting for her to hit me again. "Good," she said, looking at my feet, my swaying dance. "Good."

I have grown from that night to this one. I am tall enough to look down on my mother's head, her dark shoulders, beautiful and round as the doorknobs I polish in my sire's house. My mother has a few gray hairs, but her fingers are still sure as daggers, and she is still upright, slim and straight in the full moon's gloom. We come here, to our secret clearing with the burnt tree at its heart, only a few nights out of the month, when the moon shines full so we don't need a fire. My mother inspects my hands, pressing each callus, massaging my palm. I may be bigger and thicker than her now, but I stand still as the gap-toothed child I was and revel in her touch, unfurled to her tenderness.

"Your fingers long." My mother taps the center of my palm, and my fingers close fast. "You practice with my staff, tonight."

"Here," my mother says, digging out the weapon Mama Aza left her. She runs her grip down the long, thin limb, stained black and warm from the oil of her hands, and Mama Aza's before. Mama Aza taught my mama to fight with it, determined to pass along this knowing taught to her by the sister-wives across the great ocean.

Mama tosses the weapon to me and picks up her childhood staff, jagged as lightning. I sweat, fear spiking my armpits. My heart thumps in my ears. Mama whips her spear, and we begin to spar: with every spin, every strike, every stab, my mother becomes more fire, less herself—more licking, liquid flame. I don't like it, but then I don't have time to like it, because I must parry, block, jab. The world turns to one whipping, one humming, and us spinning with it.

When we return to the cabin, Nan and her two oldest children are asleep. Nan and her family share the cabin with us. Her youngest two are awake, and they cannot stop crying. They hold each other in their blankets, breath hitching from sobbing, while their mother and siblings doze. Nan has always diverted her love for her four children. She throttles it to a trickle, to an occasional softness in her orders: *be still, hush, don't cry*, and the rest of her care is all hard slaps and fists. She won't love what she can't keep. My mother reaches out to me, and I grasp her hand as we tuck into our bedding. Mama has always been a woman who hides a tender heart: a woman who tells me stories in a leaf-rustling whisper, a woman who burns like a sulfur lantern as she leads me through the world's darkness, a woman who gives me a gift when she unsheathes herself in teaching me to fight once a month.

THE NEXT MORNING, MY mother wakes me before the sun; she smells like hay, magnolia, and fresh game meat from last night's midnight sweat. I'm exhausted. I want to roll over in our blanket, yank it over my head and eat more sleep, but Mama runs a firm hand down my back.

"Annis, my girl. Wake up."

I pull on my clothes, tuck my blouse into my skirt as we walk toward my sire's house. Can't help the sulkiness dogging my tucks, dragging my steps. My mother walks a little ahead, and I punch down my resentfulness. Mama is almost running: she has to get to the oven, needs to light and stoke the fire within it, heat it so that she can do the morning baking. I know she is ordered to the house just as much as I am, what with all I have to gather and deliver and clean for her, to aid her in this morning, but I am short-tempered and tired until my mother begins to limp, a little stitch in her walk. Last night pains her, too. I trot to her, slip my hand through the crook of her elbow, and rub her arm. Look on the soft down of her ear, her woven hair.

"Mama?" I say.

"Sometimes I want something sweet," she breathes, tapping her fingers on mine. "Don't you?"

"Naw," I say. "I want salt."

"Mama Aza always said it wasn't good to want sweets. I'd hunt them and eat so much my hands'd stain red and blue." Mama sighs. "Now having a bit of sweet is all I can think about."

My sire's house hulks, its insides pinned by creaks. My mother bends to the stove. I gather wood and haul water and take both up the stairs, peeking into my sire's daughters' rooms. They are my half sisters; I have known this since my mother first taught me to fight, yet envy and distaste still burrow in me every morning when I tend to them. They sleep with their mouths open, pink scraped across their cheeks, their eyelids twitching like fish who swim in the shallows. Their red hair snarls in knotted threads. They will sleep until their father wakes them with knocks on their doors, far past the first blush of dawn. I tamp my feelings down, closing my face.

My sire is at his desk, in his dressing gown, writing. His room is stuffy with cold smoke and old sweat.

"Annis," he says, nodding.

"Sir," I say.

I expect his eyes to glaze over me as they do every morning, like water over a smooth stone. But his gaze snags on me, square, then trails me around his room as I fill his washbasin, gather his clothes, grip his chamber pot. He appraises me in the same way he studies his horses, his attention as sure and close as his touch on a long-maned neck, a muscled haunch, a bowed, saddle-worn back. I keep my eyes on my hands, and it's only when I descend the stairs that I realize they are shaking, his mess sloshing in the pot.

I take care to hide from his gaze. It is something that I have always known how to do: I seal my mouth silent. As the day lengthens, I walk on tiptoe through the wide, dim halls of my sire's house. I set buckets and basins down softly, ease the metal to the floor in a ring. I stand very still, just beyond the doorway of my pale sisters' schoolroom, and listen to their tutor read to them beyond the door.

The stories I hear are not my mother's stories: there is a different ringing, a different singing to them that settles down into my chest and shivers there like a weapon vibrating in struck flesh. These girls, sallow sisters, read from the texts their tutor directs them to, ancient Greeks who write about animals and industry, wasps and bees, and I listen: "*Bees seem to take a pleasure in listening to a rattling noise; and consequently men say that they can muster them into a hive by rattling with crockery or stones.*" The youngest sister's voice falls to a mumble and rises. "*They expel from the hive all idlers and unthrifts. As has been said, they differentiate their work; some make wax, some make honey, some make bee-bread, some shape and mold combs, some bring water to the cells and mingle it with the honey . . .*" I breathe in the pine halls and repeat the most potent words: *wax, honey, bee-bread, combs*.

"Aristotle refers to the heads of the hives as kings," the tutor says, "but scientists have found they are female: actually queens. In ancient Greece, Artemis's priests were known as 'king bees.' Bees, too, were credited with giving the gift of prophecy to her brother Apollo." The tutor gives a dry laugh. "This is blasphemous superstition. However, Aristotle's advice on those who labor and the fruits of that labor are sound: leave a hive with too much honey, and a beekeeper encourages laziness," he says, his voice high and soft, nearly as soft as those of my unsure sisters. I know he is speaking about bees but not—that he is using the bees and the old Greek to speak on all of us who labor. I know he's talking about my mother making biscuits and stews on the stove in the attached kitchen, about Cleo and her daughter Safi and me, who tidy rooms, beat dust from rags, wipe their floors until they gleam like burnished acorns.

I hurry downstairs to my mother, who reads me as quickly as the tutor reads his passages.

"You've been listening again?" she asks.

I nod.

"Have care," she whispers, and then bangs her spoon on a black pot. The kitchen is thick with salt meat. "He wouldn't take kindly to knowing."

"I know," I say. I want to tell her more. I want to tell her that I envy my sire's twin daughters, their soft shoulders, their hair pale and thin as spider's silk, their lessons, their linens, their cream-colored, paper-thin dresses. I want to tell her that when I listen at their doors, I am taking one thing for myself, one thing that none of them would give. I say the tutor's words in my head again, trying not to feel guilty at my mother's worried frown, the way her anxiety makes her stab her spoon into the pot. *Wax, honey, bee-bread, combs.* How to apologize for wanting some word, some story, some beautiful thing for my own?

"I'm sorry, Mama," I say as I retreat outside to gather more wood.

A lone bee meanders through the kitchen garden: plump, black striped, beautiful. It lands on my shoulder, soft as a fingertip, and I wonder what message it brings, from what spirit worlds. They are *queens*, the tutor said. When the bee rises and disappears into a nodding yellow squash flower, wind beats through the trees, and I think for a moment I hear an echo drifting down through the branches: *Queens*.

WHEN I TURN DOWN my sire's bed, he watches from beside the cold fireplace. Normally, he is downstairs, sipping amber drinks and visiting with other planters, all buttoned-up vests and murmured conversation punctuated by bluster. Tonight, he sits in an upholstered armchair, part of his dead wife's dowry. At dinner, he complained of fever and congestion, and asked my mother for a remedy: a mixture of mushrooms and herbs. It is this I set before him in a ceramic cup. He holds the cup with two fingers, his legs long before him, his boots caked with spring mud. His eyes shine with the light of the candles, and I look at my hands: smoothing, plumping, folding. I will myself to move faster so I can get out of this room and into the moonlit night.

"You're taller than your mother," he says. Where the tutor's voice is high and breathy, my sire's voice is deep, grating. I can't help but startle, dropping his quilt. "Come," he says. "Remove my boots."

I have never done this before. I stand away from the bed, looking down at my own beaten shoes, so worn at the sides that I can see my toes. I can't move.

"You heard me," he says. His red hair glints. It is not a question.

My mother has told me the story of how my sire violated her. Of how he came across her, alone in one of the upper hallways of the house, outside of an empty bedroom. How he shoved her into that bare room and bore her down to the floorboards. How he flayed the softest parts of her. How he raped her that time, and then another time at the river, and another, and another, until she stopped counting and became pregnant with me. Years later, he married the white woman, yellow haired with thin wrists, who would later die in the bearing of his twin girls.

As I kneel at his feet, I wonder if my mother felt her heart beating as quickly as the heart of a rabbit hunched in a field at twilight, shying from the shadow of the hawk. I pull at his laces, as far away as I can be from him, so that I have to reach. My arms burn with my awkward cowering, but I unknot and shuck his boots as quickly as I can. His socks smell of overripe cheese. He raises one arm, makes as if to palm my head, grab my hair, pull me toward his lap, but I rise and lurch away from him and am out of the door before he can touch one curl. Still, I see the way he seems fixed on my mouth, my mane, which falls dense and shiny, so resistant to braids, and reflects his own copper glint in its strands.

I would shave it all off, every bit.

THE YOLK OF THE moon is high in the sky by the time my mother wakes me and we creep from the cabin, from Nan and her children grinding their teeth and talking in their sleep. We walk barefoot to the clearing, making as little noise as we can, stepping on the balls of our feet carefully in bare dirt patches. I sweep our footprints behind us with a tree branch my mother twists from a pine. Ever since I've been old enough to remember, my mother has asked me to tell her. *Tell me*, she says, *if anybody ever touches you.* It's what she said to me the first time she told me the story of how my sire stalked and violated her. *Please, Annis*, she said. I want to tell her about my sire before we spar, but she digs out the spear and staff so quickly, tossing them through the silver-washed air, that I cannot do more than swing my staff up to block hers, and then we are whirring and whirring, shuddering to a stop before attacking each other again. With every block, every strike, every jab, there is a coil in my chest, and it winds tighter and tighter before it begins to burn. *What is the point of this?* I ask myself. What is the point of this if I cannot use it?

The moon rises, and I am wrung dry, the fury of our fight leaving behind only a slick of resentment. I jab at her and try to forget.

"What was Aza's mama's name?" I ask.

Mama bids me swing, and I squirrel through her defense and touch her stomach.

"Don't know. Mama Aza never told me. Say when her father took her off to give her as a wife to the king, her mama followed them into the morning. Trailed them for miles 'til her father stopped and argued with her mother, saying it was an honor for

Mama Aza to serve, that she would be fed and clothed and revered: a king's wife. Say her mama took her face in her hands and kissed her on each cheek and her forehead, tried to whisper something to her, but couldn't talk for crying." Mama pushed my elbow lower. "Mama Aza say once her and her father got to Dahomey, where the king live, the spear became her mama. The cutlass her daddy."

Mama frowns, her face wrinkled as a tablecloth.

"The warrior wives had servants. But all the wives was servants, too. Had to train and parade. Had to move at the king's direction. And warriors couldn't have a family, couldn't have no babies. Was against the king's law."

I stop, digging Mama's staff into the dirt, beaten hard by our feet.

"Tell me about my granddaddy, please," I say, looking at my toes, our feet the same shape. Mama stops. She's told me this story many times, the first when I was a girl, in one of our earliest lessons.

"Mama Aza loved a soldier who stood guard outside the castle walls and took him as a lover." She frowns. "The king sent her and the man who loved her to the coast. They was walked to the white men, to the water that don't have no edge. The whites made her walk through a door to a beach, and then put her down in a ship." My mother reaches out, pinches my shirt, and tugs before letting go. "They stole her. Bought her here." She tugs again. "Why you ask?"

I shrug. Her second toe longer than her big toe. My second toe longer than my big toe. Shoes always hurt our feet.

"Mama Aza knew the power of men before she got to that boat. When her daddy brung her to the palace, the king tell her father: I take her for my wife, but she bound to the cutlass, the bow, the axe. Mama Aza said there were hundreds, hundreds of wives, and one king."

Mama swings, and I block it.

"No other men allowed to live in the palace besides the king," Mama said.

There wouldn't have been any other men there with the power to weigh and measure Mama Aza, to appraise her like my father did me. No man but the king: stout, jewelry laden, finely clothed. Perhaps his *tononu*, master of the house and eunuch, at his ear.

I wonder what the royal household saw in my grandmother. If they saw something in her that spoke of power, that told them she could bear more than the weight of her frame. When my mother tells Mama Aza's stories, I see her in my head, lean and long like my mother. But sometimes I think I'm wrong, that the royal women looked at Mama Aza and saw a girl like me: gangly, water muscled, cup hipped. Maybe Mama Aza had learned to hide her fierceness so good, all the women and the king saw was a thin girl with a spindly line running from head to toe that pulled her upright, defiant.

When the king designated Mama Aza an amazon, did she feel relief? Joy at knowing she wasn't beautiful enough to be one of his true wives? That she would not have to submit beneath him, to bear him on her body and then deliver him blood, babies, and breast milk? Was she happy to know that she would learn how to satisfy his other desires, for blood and loot? That she would serve him in battle, hunting elephants, with a knife and spear? That she would bear bundles for him that contained heads instead of infants? Or did it grieve her that she was bound by another invisible rope, had to surrender herself in this palace full of women in thrall to one man?

"I don't understand why Mama Aza wouldn't share her mama name. She taught me that the ancestors come if you call them. That if you having trouble, you pray to them, and they give help," Mama says, swinging again. I miss the block. "Maybe she think her mama should have tried harder to keep her, and she carried the pain of it, still." Mama jabs, and I parry. The night quiet of people, loud with bugs around us. "Some think those that die come back if they die in a bad way, a way so awful Great God turn they face. Fon believed spirits come for you no matter the why, no matter when, if you call. You swing now," Mama says. I swing and she blocks and swings. I barely knock it away. I am breathing harder than I should be. Mama steps back and holds her spear out, ready. "Don't think of me like that, you hear? I always come for you. Beyond this time, into the next. Always." She steps close, so near our knees almost touch, and wipes wet from my face: half caress, half swipe. "Now, why you ask for Mama Aza's story again?"

I tell my mother, haltingly. The words crowd one another as the panic I felt in that room froths up out of me, and I have to close my eyes to speak, to get the story out.

"He was," I say.

Mama nods.

"Watching me like a hound," I say.

She blinks.

"His shoes. His feet."

She settles, still.

"Grab my head," I say.

When she is sad, my mother presses her lips into a thin crease and turns her head away, her cheek a drawn curtain; I saw it first when I was young enough to climb in her lap whole and be held by her, after I had fallen while running and cut a long gash in my calf. When she is angry, my mother folds her arms across her stomach, as if she could hold in her fury; I saw it when my sire crushed his daughters to him in their finest black dresses as they lowered his wife into her grave, knew it was because he spent the week before throwing every dish my mother set on the table at the floor, the wall, the ceiling, in his grief. My mama and me spent them days on our hands and knees, scrubbing, scrubbing. My mother holds her stomach now, her spear in the V of her elbow.

"Why," I ask. "Why we do this if we can't do nothing with it?" I let my staff drop.

My mother closes her eyes, sets her spear aside, and crouches on her haunches. I sink down next to her, let my arm rub against hers.

"Mama Aza taught me this," Mama says, looking up to the roux-dark sky, her arms still tight around her stomach. "Was about the only thing she could teach me. This and gathering."

I rub her arm with a finger, all our hard strikes gone from this clearing.

"This place, these people, this world," she sighs, "was new to her. She ain't know how to move through it. Didn't know the order of it. Just a few short months after the ship, she found out. The old master come into the cabin after she birthed me, and he laid claim to me, me wet with birthing blood and bawling. This owning from birthing to the grave, and on down, through children—this world overwhelmed her."

I grip the soft sliver of meat under my mama's armpit, one of the few tender, fatty pieces on her.

"This place horrified her," Mama whispers. "When I got older, I thought I knew. Thought I understood how wrong this place was, but I didn't." Mama squeezes her middle. "I didn't understand how wrong until you came squalling out of me."

In that one place, my mama's flesh is soft as pig stomach, the pale plush of intestines.

"Teaching Mama Aza's way of fighting, her stories—it's a way to recall another world. Another way of living. It wasn't a perfect world, but it wasn't so wrong as this one."

Mama squeezes my fingers.

"Best we don't forget," she says.

The trees wave and whip their fronds above us. The ruined tree creaks.

"You remember what Mama Aza did first as a king's wife?"

I nod.

"She ran," I say.

Mama snorts.

"He come at you again, you run," she says. "Knowing when to stand and when to go, when not to fight, well, that's a part of fighting, too. Knowing when to wait and bide and watch and duck. You got to know that, too."

We sit in the clearing until just before dawn, both of us too anxious to do more than lean into each other, hugging, blinking and slipping into sleep in little nods. When we rise and bury our blunt weapons, I pour the last palmful of sand over the wood, and the wind silences. Everything is quiet, until there is a buzz at my ear, a brush of sound. It is an inky bee, drifting in the dregs of the night, in this fighting clearing. Mama and I walk back to the cabins with our arms locked and linked. Her leaning on me, me bearing her up.

WE GLANCE PAST THE silent cabins and walk directly to my sire's house.

"We start early," Mama says as she lights the kindling in the stove, blows in its belly. "Mayhap we finish early," she says, and I know why. She thinks to hurry our work so I do not have to kneel at my sire's feet again.

"Yes, Mama," I say, and set to hauling water.

But the hours unspool anyhow. My sallow siblings want extra water to wash. The tutor wants me to clean and polish the shelves in the nursery turned schoolroom, complaining of dust. My sire wants fresh bed linens, tells me that fever made the ones I'd turned down the evening before reek of sweat. When evening falls, I still am not done. When the family's bedtime approaches, I find myself sloppily tucking and folding my sire's linens on his bed, kind Cleo and sulfur-eyed Safi already gone downstairs. When they left me to finish, I wanted to call after Safi, beseech the thoughtful girl who has always run to hoist too-heavy buckets with me, has always been quick to grab the opposite edge of a bedsheet so we could fold its length together. She would've known I needed help. But my voice has withered. My breath rasps. *Run*, I say to myself. *Mama said run.*

My sire trips into his open doorway: he has hurried here. I jab the last corner under his mattress, rise, and stand, balancing on the balls of my feet. I take a step toward the door. *Run*, my mama said, *run. But I ain't got nowhere to go*, a little voice says. I take one breath, and then another, the air cool in the room but burning down my nose, and I know I can't surrender to what he wants to do to me. I know that I don't have my mother's self-control, know that I will struggle with him, that I will use my elbows like hammers, my legs like staffs, that I will make my knees fists. I think of Mama Aza squatting in the cabins, infant in her arms, afterbirth still in her, and this man's father, my grandfather, standing over her, and how it must have rung through her head: *This is wrong wrong wrong*. I hear it now. How the knowing sink in my stomach.

"Annis?" my mother's voice sounds from the hallway beyond the door. She has opened the door, and stands in the open palm of it. "We done." Her arms band her stomach. Her head is down, but then she raises it and I know that eyes can be weapons, too, that they can glitter like small knives, like them used to gut a fish. I have never seen anyone look past my sire as my mother does now, him a buzzing gnat, unworthy of notice, of even a waved hand. "Come," she says.

My sire has his own signs for anger, but I don't look for them. I edge past him to my mother, her bladed hand, the long, dim hallway, the creaking stairs, the quiet kitchen, the murmuring garden, the loud night. We walk past the cabins, past the fields, into the forest to the clearing. We walk as far away from my sire's house as we can. We do not dig out our weapons. We make a bed in the soil we have beaten soft with our feet and pillow our heads with our arms. My mother curls around my back, her breath soft on my neck.

"There are herbs," Mama says. "I'll look for them tomorrow. We should have them." She circles my stomach and pulls tight.

"He won't stop. Every time after the first, I grabbed this," Mama whispers. She pulls something out of her braided hair that looks like a white awl, thin as a needle.

"What's that?"

"It was Mama Aza's. A piece of a elephant tusk. She got it on one of her hunts." Mama puts it in my hand, and it is smooth and warm as her skin.

"Once I got myself past the feeling of hitting him with it, right here"—she touches my neck, below my ear, where my heartbeat thrums—"I tried to remember that I still had plenty inside he couldn't take."

The shoulders of the trees shake with wind.

"Mama Aza said bringing down an elephant is a good way to teach somebody small how to beat somebody big. How you have to be cunning, have to be smart. If you not, you don't live through it." Mama slips the ivory awl back into her hair. "You remember that, too, you hear. You don't need this ivory or them spears. In this world, you your own weapon."

The moon blanches the sky; she is nearly set before we sleep.

In the hour before dawn, there is a perfect silence. I wake, my mother's snoring hushed in my ear. I slide my hand up her forearm to the muscley meat before her shoulder and squeeze, hard enough to feel the push of her flesh under my fingers, soft enough not to wake her. I turn on my back so I can see her face: her open mouth, her cheekbones fallen with ease. The moon has set behind the trees, but its light still suffuses our clearing: milky glass. Some nights I steal these moments for myself; what my mother demands in fighting, I take back now. My mama's face is slack as a child's; her limbs are so close, they could be my own. I put my hand on her neck, feel the rush of blood there, the red river that binds her to me. I feel as I only can with her.

A buzzing hiccup sounds from the ruined tree above us, and suddenly, the clearing fills with a grating whisper. I squint against the sky and see trailing garlands of black dots rising from the trunk in a humming chorus. I rub the down of my mother's arm. It takes moments more, each one stretching thick as honey, to decipher the dark rising, the sibilant singing: a beehive has taken root in the tree, and now they wake and go forth with the dawn. *A little more*, I think. I will let my mother sleep a little more, drift skyward in the place of dreams, before rousing her, waking her, pulling her back here.

One breath more, I think, feeling my mother's heart in her neck. *One breath*.

MONTHS LATER, WHEN I see the Georgia Man standing at the head of the trail leading from the cabins to the fields, my sire beside him, pointing at me and my mother, I dig my nails into my mother's hand to stop her.

"Mama, no," I say.

"Come," I say, echoing the first time she roused me to fight.

"Please," I say.

I turn back toward the cabins, the woods, the far clearing. I pull my mother's arm, try to rouse her to run, but she will not. She stops still and grabs me by my collar. Tears are already leaking down her face, and she does not try to wipe them, to hide the glaze of her sorrow. The sky is thick with clouds, the air heavy with coming rain, the smell of water cloying. My mother has eyes for nothing but me, only me. She smooths her hands over her hair and then does the same to mine, and something sharp knifes my scalp: the ivory awl sliding into place. And then I feel only the press of her palms on my cheeks, my ears, as she holds my face to look at her.

"Annis, my Arese," she says, her voice fluttering. "I love you. I love you, my little one." One of the Georgia Man's men walks toward us and grabs my mother by the same soft meat of her arm as I have done so many times. Cries rise from the people around us; a bolt of summer lightning flashes in the distance. The Georgia men are grabbing men and women and children on their way to their labor. The Georgia men are separating those to be sold. They have come for their goods to march to New Orleans. There is a sinking at the heart of me, a whirlpool sucking down and down. Surely the earth is opening to us. Surely this terrible world is swallowing me. I grab my mama's wrists, sinewy as corn sheaves, and howl.

"Mama," I say.

"I always be with you," my mama says, and *No she not*, I think, *no she not*, as the closest Georgia Man, broad armed and dirt faced, wrenches her away. Pulls her back. My sire done chose her for the markets.

"No," I say.

One more, I think, and yank my mother from the man, whip her like a spear to me. He grabs her again and pulls, and we are three of many, tussling in the path, until the Georgia Man standing next to my sire pulls a gun from its holster and fires it in the air. Panic stills us but cannot calm my love, my frantic need to keep my mother here, here, here. I fall to the dirt, wrapping myself around her legs.

"Mama," I mouth into her skirts. Her free hand finds my scalp.

One more breath, I think.

CHAPTER 2

Walking Ropeward

I can't sleep after my sire sells my mother. Cleo moves into my mama's place in the kitchen, the stove her great iron elephant now. The cleaning and upkeep of the house, the servicing of the kitchen and waiting at the table, fall to me and Safi.

For weeks after the Georgia Man leads my mama away, south to the markets of New Orleans, I can't even look Safi or Cleo straight. Don't care to listen at my sisters' nursery doors. Slosh water from buckets; polish with a fast, light touch; launder clothes so quickly they never lose my sire's stink, my sisters' rot. Finish all my work so quickly, I ain't never alone in a room with the man who sold my mother. Can't even sleep in the cabin with Nan and her children. Instead, I take to the woods at night, to our clearing, the black, bee-choked tree. In all things, I run.

Even with the summer in full bloom, nights in the clearing are cold. I wrap myself in the blanket I shared with my mother. I lie in the roots of the tree, on my side, mouth my forearms, feel the chill running from my neck down my spine, over my bottom to the dimpled backs of my knees, and know I ain't never been so cold. That this what it means to live without my mother spooning my back, draping her arms over me, cupping my stomach. This what it means to be alone. To sleep without safety is to lie awake. To cry so much, spit runs from my mouth and puddles beneath my face. To feel the bees that I have come to think of as my own descend in the night to land on my wrists, my feet, and then alight back to their hive; this makes me wonder what bitter nectar they collect from me. This makes me wonder where they taking my sorrow. This makes me wonder if my sobbing is a soothing call to them, and why they the only witness to my grief. To sleep without my mother is to walk to my sire's house before the unveiling of the dawn, to sit in a corner of the kitchen while Cleo wrestles with the stove, and not care that my hair is matted with dirt, my face smeared with mud.

One day becomes another. One night becomes another. Heat leaches from the earth, leaves brown and fall, and sun and moon are pale lights in the sky. There is no warmth anywhere. I don't dig up our weapons. I huddle into the earth under the wind's firm press in the clearing. I look through my sire, through my sisters, through Cleo, through Safi, and know only grief in this new world. I don't see anyone until one day I see Safi, who kneels before me on Christmas morning, wet rag in hand, and lifts my chin. I don't see anyone until Safi kisses her palm to mine and pulls me up from my corner, leads me off to the laundry vats, and there, peels me out of my clothing.

"It's me, Annis. It's me," Safi says, and then she dumps cups of warm water she's heated over my head and starts to scrub me.

"You here," Safi says, and my face breaks.

I let her clean me like a child. When she bids me to sit, I slump before her knees, and she detangles my hair with the comb of her fingers, shank by shank.

"What's this?" she asks, pulling the long ivory needle from my scalp. I have not touched it since the day the Georgia Man took my mother.

"Something my grandmother bought from across the ocean. She give it to my mama. My mama give it to me." I hunch forward. "When they took her."

Safi sets the ivory on her thigh before she washes and rinses and oils my hair. When she leans forward and begins to braid it to my scalp, she pushes down with just as much pressure as my mother, twines the hair with just as much tension as my mama. Safi's legs less strong, but the feel of them just as tender. I keep my mouth shut but cannot stop the salty tears that run my face. When Safi is done, she slides the ivory needle back into place, hiding it in my scalp.

I feel warm.

•   •   •

AFTER WE FINISH THE work in the house, I walk back to the cabin, wrapped in a scrap throw that Safi wound about me, shoulders hunched to my ears. I am chill again, empty. My feet feel cold as frost. In the cabin, I sit in a corner while the wind scrapes the logs of the walls, fidgeting in the warmth of the small fire, in the glow of Nan's children singing play songs to one another. I wonder where my mother is in the world. I wonder if there was some small holiday treat for her—a sliver of chitterlings, a knob of pigs' feet, a taste of warm broth and salt meat. I massage my temples, try to knead the sore wondering away.

When I step out of the cabin to go to the clearing, Safi is there, her shawl pulled tight against the bitter cold of the night air. There is no full moon tonight; I have lost track of the waxing and waning, only feel the deepening freeze of the year: my grief's due. I would brave the chill tonight, even though I am clean, even though the silky memory of heat follows me like a bothersome cat, because part of me wants winter to enfold me in its freezing hand, to squeeze all the heat and sorrow and presence of me out, out. To leave the shell of me in the roots of the trees. I wonder if I would fly off, my spirit, and range south. Find my mama down below, somewhere.

"You was leaving?" Safi asks, looking up at me through the puff of her hair, braided across her forehead. The plait is even, fine, and her eyes are as liquid, as dark, as my mother's. I look off in the direction of the clearing I shared with my mother and nod.

"It's cold," Safi says. She tightens her shawl and frowns. Her face is always so calm, so smooth when we are serving or hauling or cleaning; it is strange to see it fold. "Could I stay here with you, tonight?"

Protests froth up, bubble in my throat. The cabin is crowded. Nan and her children are loud, even in sleep. And the sharpest, quietest rebuttal: the bedding is dirty from my nights spent in the clearing. It doesn't smell like my mother anymore. But I don't say this to Safi. I look down at the step I stand on, and I think of the heat of the laundry, the bath, the tepid brush of the rag Safi wielded, and I can't say no.

"He say he want my mama there," Safi says, "in the big house."

I turn and open the cabin door. I lead Safi to the stuffed mattress and blankets I shared with my mother. One of Nan's children cries out in her sleep, a formless word. I scoot closest to the wall, turn my back to Safi, make sure we don't touch. I want her to have space. She settles in next to me, her back to my back. I am awake until I am not, and when my eyes open in the darker night, Safi has scooted back on the bed, her spine a fine line on mine. Warm, sure lightning. I burrow back into her and close my eyes.

SAFI RETURNS THE NEXT night, and by the end of the week, I expect her, so I don't make myself ready to go to the clearing. Instead, I begin sitting on the cabin steps and waiting for her, the wood gouging my bottom, cracked and hard as Mama Aza's and Mama's spears, lying in the earth in the clearing.

While my mama had weapons for hands, could coax or demand, Safi is all tenderness. She fusses over her mama when we return to my sire's house every morning, smoothing her mother's hair, pushing her to eat, bringing her more water than she needs. Me and Safi clean the house together, walk side by side through the rooms, the doorways, so closely our arms bump, and I get used to the feel of her long, slender, hairless arms, her wrists thin as a bird's bones. She is a comfort, but she cannot soothe all.

I dream of my mother nearly every night, see the Georgia Man snatching her away. Hear her sobbing and rubbing at her chest. I followed her for miles away from my sire's house until the Georgia Man fired his gun in the air in a rapid beating, one shot after another, dispersing all of us trailing and begging for our kin's release.

On nights like this, grief, dammed up by the hours and the work, floods me. I hide my shattered face, my silent sobs, from Safi. I curl up tighter and tighter and cry. I try to slip my sorrow under the sounds of Nan and her children, under the tremor of the clacking, nude trees, but I can't. Safi winds her arm around my side and clasps my hand, and I hiccup at the wonder of it, of her wanting to comfort me. To touch me. She tugs.

"Annis."

I shake my head.

"Annis," Safi says, and she tugs harder.

Shame makes me flush hot. I freeze still.

"Please," Safi says, and she palms the back of my scalp, and I can't help myself. I lean into her, remember my mama cupping me the same, so when I turn over and face her, I'm sobbing.

"You don't need to hide," Safi says, her voice quiet as a mouse's scamper. "I see you."

She puts her hand over my heart, which blazes like a fire in my chest. Her fingers fine but still strong as spider's silk.

I lean forward and kiss her, and her hand leaves my breastbone, skirts up and over my shoulder, and cups the back of my neck. She pulls me closer, closer.

I am burning.

THE KITCHEN GARDEN BEGINS to bud, the trees to green, and I dream of my mother less often. The days slip from one to another, only surfacing when me and Safi meet in the dark of my bed. A kind of relief breathes through me because I believe those stolen moments with Safi have turned some deep unhappiness in me to cinder, made it float away as ash. My mother told me that some of the king's wives loved each other, caressed each other; I remember this at odd moments—with Safi's thigh wedged between mine, her licking my neck. *Oh, Mama,* I think, and then I can't feel my body anymore, my grief rising in a sort of flood. Even midkiss with Safi, I sink. On these nights, Safi uses teeth to wrench me from my shame, shame at our happiness, and afterward, when we still under the blankets, sated, I wait for Safi to fall asleep and descend again. I think of my bees, wondering if their hum rises from the ruined trunk, wondering if I could wrap myself in gauze and coax honey from them. Wonder where my mama's at, somewhere out in the dark, wide world. I know I'm not meeting Safi right, not rising to her tenderness, so when the rice grows tall and rigid in the fields and the moonlight shines through the cabin's cracks, I grab Safi's wrist.

"Come," I say.

In the chalky light of the moon, Safi is beautiful: her cheeks like plums, her mouth full as purple figs. A hot flower blooms in my chest, and I squeeze Safi's hand, but it is so much smaller than my mother's. The flower folds. I shrug against it.

"I want to show you something," I say.

Safi follows me as I lead her out of the shallow valley and into the low hills where my mother taught me to forage for mushrooms, for greens and roots and herbs, to our clearing, our tree. I wrap gauze I filched from my sire's house around her puzzled face, her long, lean arms and legs, until she is shrouded, protected from the sting of the bees. A wolf yips, and I turn, swear I see a mirage of another white-shrouded woman in the clearing, but there is no one there but me and Safi and my bees. The tutor said bees are still at night, but my bees are alive, humming and flying from their amber pyramid, riveted between the bones of the tree. The bees, my bees, are awake. Safi and I stand in the moonlit night, pinkies hooked, while my bees greet us, flush with summer. They land in kisses, busking touches, on our shoulders, the crowns of our heads, our palms. Her finger: a living link. I could weep with the sweetness of it, of knowing that there are others in this terrible world who will touch me with kindness. But all the while I know that the carved spears lie buried at the edge of the clearing charging the air as before a lightning strike. My mother. I step behind Safi's smaller frame, drape my arms over her shoulders, and stand like that, back to front. I try to blink away the missing of my mama. Feel what it might be to feel, to love again.

I let that ribbon of feeling carry me beyond the sunrise of the next day. Let it buoy me up so that after me and Safi scrubbed and rinsed and hung laundry, after we dusted and mended and bent together, I linger outside the schoolroom door. The tutor's voice, the same; my sisters' reading, still as slow and halting. The tutor is telling a story of a man, an ancient Italian, who is walking down into hell. The hell he travels has levels like my father's house. The tutor says: " *'Let us descend,' the poet now began, 'and enter this blind world,'* " and his words echo through me. I hear the sighs: the summer wind pushing slant at the house, the wood groaning, but instead of the Italian poet descending into hell, I see my mother toiling in the hell of this house. Walking down from a hot, crate-choked attic to a second floor clustered with bedrooms where my sire's children cried through keyholes after their mother died, after my mother became their nursemaid and pulled them from her breast, down to the first floor, where my mother grew sere over a burning stove, to the potato-and-onion-rank basement, cool and rat infested, down and down, to deeper basements, root cellar opening to root cellar. More hell. " *'I shall go first. Then you come close behind,'* " the tutor says. " *'Through me you go to the grief-racked city,'* " he says, his voice like the soft buzz of velvet.

"Grief-racked city," I whisper, wondering what the spirits might look like in that place. I asked my mother about spirit once, after we were done practicing in the clearing. The sweat cooling on us under the drench of the far starlight, while mosquitoes shredded my feet.

"They don't know," my mama said. "Them got to open a door, walk through a cave, go down into a valley or up a mountain to find spirit." My mama looked up to the wind tossing the trees. "This world seething with it."

"Seething?" I asked.

"It's everywhere." Mama hummed and rolled her eyes, and then frowned, serious. "When you ask, spirit answer, Arese," she said.

I am still thinking about spirit, about hell, when I meet up with Safi in my sire's room to dust and change his bedding. I want that ribbon, that buoy. My sire is never here during the day, always out, supervising the bent in the fields, visiting neighbors. I think my dirt, my grime I wore through the summer and into the winter, drove him away. For once, I am glad for my grief, but I want more than that now.

I step near to Safi when she rises from smoothing a bedspread and put my palm under her elbow, my lips to her downy neck, long and elegant as a crane's. She does not step away. *This spirit, here*, I think, *in this blind world*. She turns to me, kisses my forehead, and I hum until a thump sounds at the doorway, and Safi and I lurch away from each other, lips still wet and warm, to see my sire, his mouth wide and pink, his red hair splaying away from his head like a fan. Panic beats through me, and it rises up and out of me in a laugh, high and jagged. Safi folds her hands, looks down at her feet, bows. My laugh saws away. This hell.

Let us descend, I think, and follow Safi out of the room.

I KNOW THE COST of that kiss come two mornings after, when I see the Georgia Man. That's when I know I been walking toward this rope my whole life. All my work-run days, all my short-close nights. That I been walking to this knotted cord, frayed and black. To this white man looping and fastening me to the other women on this line. Some pull back. Some cry. Some scrabble for crying babies, rot-gutted women, soft-eyed men, shivering children clustered about us in the dim cold before dawn. To this death before death. To this selling. Nan and Cleo and my mother talked about what it was to be sold—we all did, since we heard stories about what it was like, stories carried from one farm to another, one work camp to another. *Bog bottomed,* the boy sent to trade scrap metal with our blacksmith said. *Manacle awash,* the man sent to trade livestock said. *Smoked and sunk,* the farrier sent through the rice counties to shoe horses said. *Hell,* my mother said, *and more of us marching there every day.*

Even though I heard the talk, even though I watched this man rope my mama, even though I followed for what felt like miles, I don't know until now what it means to be bound. Safi struggles next to me as another white man loops her arms in the rope that ties us to be sold.

"My mama," she cries. "My mama!"

"No," I say. The rope tightens when they are done tying Safi. She yanks at it, yelling for her mother. Her head whipsaws back and forth.

"Please," I say.

The binding abrades. Safi sags into me, but I only got eyes for my sire. He looks straight back, his mouth closed now, his lips thin and set. His feet in the dirt, the land he inherited from his father along with the rice fields, the forge, the weavers. I jerk against the rope, bare my teeth; I would bite his cheek. I would smash the flat of my hand into his nose and stab the bone deep into his face. I would circle my hands around his throat and squeeze and squeeze the spirit from this man who would call the Georgia Man. The Georgia Man who moves us south to New Orleans in the cheapest way, the old way, terrible and nasty: he chains the men, binds the women with ropes, leaving the children to walk behind as far as they can, not caring if they drop dead at the side of the road in this red-earthed place. This wide, cry-choked hell.

The line jerks. The men are already shuffling down the road, awkward in their chains. Some of the women cry out, startled, as we begin to move. I kick the ground like I would kick my sire if I ever, ever had the chance, before turning away from the man who gave me the middle mud of my skin. Spit and spite the ground of the man who sells me and Safi for stealing some life back from him. The man who violated and sold my mama.

Our line shuffles slowly into the approaching dawn until the sun floods the rolling land with light. We walk into it. We are one long snake, rooting through the trees. For the first mile, there are coughs and hiccups and crying. Eight white men on horses flank us, leading us. Two follow with a buggy at our back, guns unholstered. That is the threat that makes us move. Unbound men and women and children follow: they beg, beseech, and plead for their kin's release. Just like we did once. The white men ignore them. A quarter of a morning's travel, and my wrists already rub raw. Safi stumbles.

"Walk, Safi," I say. "Please walk."

"Annis," she says, and then says nothing, but the shake of her shoulders speaks for her. *You led us here*, they say. *You.*

The rope bites.

I quiet, and Safi lurches into the woman before her, who yelps. Guilt sinks low in my gut.

I, who, in my grief, was starved.

This is my fault.

"Safi," I say. I want to call her other names, all the other names I whispered to her after she found me and warmed me. *Sweet*, I called her. *Honeysweet*. At the end of our first night with the bees, she lay next to me at the root of the tree. We cupped each other in the dirt, still bound in gauze, and she wrapped her dark arm around my paler one and rested her cheek on my back. Us love-hungry, hurt-full children, in the dark.

WE WALK MILES BEFORE the Georgia Man pulls his gun, before he shoots it in the air, setting those that followed us to flee. At the sound of the gunshot, Safi trips hard, dropping to her knees. The Georgia Man shouts from the front of the line and whirls his crop. If my hands was free, I would pick her up and carry her as far as I could.

"Safi," I say. I grab the back of her dress and heave. My bones feel bent to break. "You got to walk," I say. "Come."

I push her to her feet.

"No," she says, but at least she trips forward as the line pulls us both, all of us women stumbling to a jog.

"Walk, Safi, or they going to make you," I say. I wish I could say this: You saved me, Safi. You cleaned me from my sorrow and saved me, wrapped me in the warmth of your regard. I want to say: I love you. But the rope is relentless.

"Hyah," the Georgia men yell. "Hyah!" they say, spurring us bound men and women and their horses to a trot.

"Please," I huff, and then all I can do is breathe, my grief-shattered muscles useless, able only to trip along. I run.

WE JOG INTO THE night. Dusk comes like the slow descent of a great bird, gliding through the air, and then settling over the tall, blue trees, sinking to the earth, all of it turning black. One of the men on the line sets his feet in the dirt, won't move no more down that road, and when he does, the Georgia Man and his boys set on him. Kick his legs out from under him and beat him 'til he's breathing saliva and blood in the soil. 'Til he's making rust-colored mud.

"You getting yonder one way or another," says the Georgia Man, to the darkening sky, to all of us. "Your feet your boat."

When we stop for the night, the white men on horses leave us bound together. They ring us by fire, four fires in a clearing, and they eat from their wagon. Us, they give hard scraps. I chew what I can, swallow it down with water from a tin bucket they pass around for us. The Georgia Man smiles, brushing his horse where the saddle rubbed its back and sides all day. The horse snuffles and munches. I wish I had my mother's spear with me now. I could knee the horses, strike the Georgia men in their mouths, set their teeth to flying.

"You sleep, Safi?" I ask.

Safi's cry comes out her in a long whistle, and I rub her back just a needle's length, round and round one of the acorns in her spine, 'til she quiets. 'Til she stutters a breath, and we can pretend for a blink we back in the cabin, Safi rubbing my scalp, my face in her neck, and us swapping stories.

"Tell me a story."

Safi hums.

I pull the rope, put my knuckles in the middle of her back.

"Tell me about weaving. Tell me about your grandmama."

She shakes her head. I want to hear her voice.

"Please," I say.

"She push that shuttle," Safi breathes.

"Yes," I say.

"It sound," she says, "like a river. Like a hush. Her mama taught her. And she taught my mama."

Down the line, the women murmur in the dark. The pain make us talk past each other. I pull my knees into my chest, try to ease the throb of the walking from my feet, the tight drapes at the backs of my legs, the swollen hinges of my knees. Safi turns on her back, speaks to the sky. I look up, trying to see what she sees, but there is only great darkness looking back at us.

"Took years for my mama to do it without thinking."

I hum and wind my knuckle around the knobs under Safi's skin.

"But when your sire moved us to the house, he told her to let it go. That she was needed elsewhere." Safi quiets. "My legs hurt," she whispers.

"Oh, Safi," I say. *I'm sorry, Safi*, I want to say, *for this*. But what my mama always told me comes out instead. "Breathe."

It's what my mama said when my arms shook from holding the carved spear up and away from me and I whined I couldn't do it. Maybe she took this same trail; I wonder if she looked up at this same black sky. If she told herself what she told me on this dark path, when she was here a year ago. *Breathe*, my mama said.

Safi stills to sleep. The smoke from the fires singes my throat. I squint through it, blink to see a white-wreathed woman in the shadows, her skin gleaming darkly in the light of the Georgia men's fires. I wonder if someone from my sire's farm could be following us, if that could be Safi's mama in the dark, trailing us, but when I close my eyes and open them again, I can't see the woman. The wind runs through the treetops like a stream.

WE RISE IN THE night. The smell of coffee and cornbread are wispy but go right to my gut and tug. The Georgia men lead us in groups by our tether to relieve ourselves, and after, pass a cup along the line so that each one may drink, but there is no sneaking a little food for breakfast, no hot potatoes baked in the coals, not even boiled corn filched from the livestock. There is water, only that, sloshing around in our stomachs as we walk through the woods, following the black mass of the men on their horses through the gloom, a darker darkness against the lightening sky. I look to Safi, but her back is a closed door. The morning fog lifts and rises. There are no murmurs this morning, no shouts or pleading. Yesterday's walking wrung us dry, and this day's walking stretches before us. I squint, try to find the woman again, but there is only forest stretching on and on, enclosing both sides of the rutted path, a mention of a road. One of the men, older with gray tufts of hair and a bald head, trips and falls. Half the line tumbles, and the rest of the men stumble to crouches.

"Get your feet together," the Georgia Man says.

The man who fell is the last to rise, but when he stands, his back is straight as a young sapling. He looks square at the Georgia Man for one long second and then down at his feet. The Georgia Man spurs his horse, shouts "Walk on" at all of us. I study the path, try to avoid ruts or roots. I don't want the Georgia Man looking at me, don't want none of his attention. Don't know if I could look at him in the face the way the older man did, straight. That look a whole sentence. The roots rise like waves on a lake. The walking becomes something mindless, like scrubbing a grate to stack tinder for a fire, or like fetching water for the people in the field.

We walk. We walk and I see only trees' knees and dirt and scraggly weeds beneath my feet. The sun rises hotter, burns brighter, and as the day enlarges, my world narrows more, becomes this: My bones pestles grinding the bowls of my joints. Becomes the rope rubbing my wrists red. When the sun is high in the sky, I realize we will not be fed midday; when Safi whimpers in front of me and water streams down her leg, I know that we will not stop to relieve ourselves, that in this, we are livestock, too. That we are expected to walk and drop filth like horses. As the sun blazes, I touch Safi's shoulder, but she does not feel my fingers through the cloak of her sorrow, or pretends not to. How we walk, all of us. My mother away from me, south to be sold. Mama Aza to the gate, the ship, that would bear her over the near-endless water to this place. Before that, the walk she took with her father to the capital, where she fell at the king's feet in the inner royal courtyard, thin as kindling.

I look up to find dusk settling. We are shuffling slowly, leaning back against our chains and ropes. The tutor's words ring through my head: *Let us descend.* The Georgia men call their horses to a stop. Safi drops to her haunches. I step closer to her and sink. My tongue feels swollen in my mouth. Safi hunches over, and she leans away; she does not want my comfort. I can't return the care she gave to me, can't clean her and warm her and give her ease.

"I'm sorry," I say.

When it is my time to drink from the cup, I don't feel any divine line running through me—just a loose rope of loss. We chew the hard food given to us. We lie down but I cannot sleep; all I can do is stare at Safi's narrow back, watch her hitch and hitch, and I think that she is crying, but when I scoot closer to comfort her, I realize that Safi is working the knots. She is rubbing her wrists back and forth against the rope. Blood wets the yarn, dyes it ruby dark.

"Safi," I say. But she won't talk to me, not on that night, or the next. Instead, she rolls over to face me, touches my cheek, once, twice. I can't help but lean into her swollen fingers, which send a cool crackle over my face. She turns away to return to her yanking, all the tenderness she spent on others set to loosen the rope, to escape.

"Safi," I say. "I could tell you a story?" I want to tell her about Mama Aza, about how she found love in orphaned grief, too.

"No," Safi whispers. Her muscles twitch like a horse's flicking flies, and her little yank tells me what she is doing.

"They can see you, Safi," I say.

She stops, turns her head. I want to yank at the rope, too. Scissor my hands, shred my wrists until I can jerk them, slick, out. I want to scoot toward Safi, put my mouth on hers, breathe in her breath for the last time, because I know her. Know that her mother, melon faced and black eyed, standing alone in my sire's kitchen, head cocked, unseeing, anchors in Safi's chest and pulls, pulls.

"She got nobody, Annis."

I want to say: *I ain't either*, but then shame submerges me. A wind whips up and for one breath, two, it presses hard before breezing away.

"Sweet," I say, and I don't know if I'm apologizing or begging her to forgive me for wanting to fall into her, to follow my own sinking line of happiness to her. The trees around us brush the black leather sky. I doze to a relentless itch in my scalp, the peeling burn of the scabs on my wrists, the grind of my bones in their sockets, the rub of my clothes against my arms and waist, raising my skin to red welts. We have been walking for five days. Sleep is no relief.

THE NEXT DAY, I am a dragging plow: stuck in steps and routed by roots. Safi's neck flashes with the sun that cuts through the leaves: fresh-cut wood set aflame. How soft her tendons were beneath my tongue, how salty, but I look away, ashamed. I wonder if the Italian man felt like this on his downward walk, wonder if his mind snagged on everything the upper world that ever bought him ease and pleasure. Wonder why all I can think of beyond the pain is Safi's mouth, my mother's hands.

After we are settled for the night, I reach for the tender bridge of Safi's ribs. I pull against the rope, and though the woman at my back says, "Ain't they enough yanking on the walk?" I still, my fingers barely brushing Safi's dress. There's a wash of muslin fog beyond our line, stark against the fire's glow, in the shape of a woman. *Who*, I think, but when I focus, she is not there. Instead, the Georgia Man is standing before us. All else looms at his back. He has come for Safi.

"You, girl," he says.

Safi and I both sit up.

"You," he says.

"Me, sir?" Safi whispers.

The fire crackles. The smell of smoke, of the dinner the Georgia men ate, hangs in the air. The overseer bends and unties Safi.

"Quiet," he says.

He pulls her free by the wrists. With my mother's spear, I could slam the wood into the backs of his knees, then slash clean across the flesh over his ankles.

Safi stumbles and leans back against his hold. The wind stirs in the trees. I hear a whisper then: *Little Annis*. Safi and the Georgia Man disappear in the dark, away from the men and their fire. I curl into myself, tuck my neck into my chest, my knees into my stomach, thankful for that small mercy: these Georgia men will not share her. But I hear Safi, crying out in the dark. I don't cover my ears. If she must bear it, the least I can do is bear witness.

AFTER THE GEORGIA MAN ties Safi to the rope and leaves, I grab her arm. She whimpers, and I know he bruised her inside and out. The night flickers. I wish I could see better, maybe touch Safi's skin where it ain't split, some piece of her that's whole. Safi shakes her head, pushes her crown in my chest. Her breathing sounds wet in the dark.

"I'm sorry," I say. My fingers burn like it's me that dragged her out into the black beyond the fire, like it's me that flayed her. "I'm sorry," I say, and I mean it, mean it as I huff it into her hair, as I kiss her thin, weaving fingers, mean it even as I stop, dumb, because the Georgia Man done made a mistake. The Georgia Man done bound Safi too loose in his haste to get back to his bedroll, the crackling fire, and Safi has slid her thin wrists, her twiggy fingers, out the rope. She looks at me, both of us startled still, and a smile flitters over her face like heat lightning, and it's so wide and white in the dark, pleased as my mama the first time I jabbed her in the ribs with the spear, the first time I made it through her whirring defense, that love rush through me like a fire. I startle, pulling back from her, and blink, and Safi is free of the rope, brown and beautiful and lined with moonlight in the dark, just as we were in the blanket of night, wrapped in gauze, awash in my bees in my clearing.

"Safi," I whisper.

She puts her hand over my mouth, pulls my roped hand up to her face, shakes her head, and I know what she means. I know. The rope gnaws my wrist. Safi's face is wet. She tugs the knot that binds me, tries to stick her fingers through the weave. The Georgia Man's horse shakes its head out in the darkness, and Safi stops, dropping to a crouch. Her hands ribbons of red, running with blood. But she free. She free.

"Go," I whisper. "Go."

"No," Safi says. "Come with me."

She turns her head into my palm. Sorrow sinks at the heart of me, heavy as soaking bedclothes, heavy as the cauldron that cooks

47

the clothes. But there is love there, too, beating through me like a drum for Safi, Safi who was the first to touch me with kindness after my mama left. Safi who wore the kiss of my bees like fine lace. Safi who leaned into me, parting the curtain of my grief, always.

"Go," I say.

She kisses my palm, and my skin is so callused there, I hardly feel her lips before she crouches away into the darkness, away from the men's fire, away from the Georgia Man, his smell still thick on her, away into the wood. The forest takes her in with a whisper that sounds like what my sire and most everyone called me: *Annis Annis Annis*.

I turn sideways in the dirt and lie still. I listen for Safi, for the chatter of her running, but I hear nothing beyond the echo of the trees' murmur, feel nothing but the absence of her, of Safi, in the air curling around my back, whistling along my damp front. I lick my palm and taste blood and the salt of Safi's tears. Close my eyes when I hear a woman's voice, a misty calling under the shush of the trees. At first I think the person calling me is Safi, come back to work the rope, to free me. And then, when Safi doesn't slink from the whispering dark, I think it's my mother, that she done came for me like she said, because I called to her spirit, because I call, because every breath, every lurch, every cutting eye, every blink, is me saying her name since she was took from me: *Mama*. But the voice murmuring from nowhere, from the dark every-where, it is not my mother's voice. It is not soft Safi's. It is a bad wind, pushing through the seams of windows, rising through gaps in the floor. It would flatten green saplings in fields. It would knock a man from a horse. It is a high howl that simmers to a low groan.

My heart judders: with fear, with want. Part of me don't care who this voice belong to, because I realize only I can hear her: no one else wakes and peers into the woods, asks "Who goes there?" The Georgia men snore and snuffle, and the chained men and the roped women are prone in the night, flattened by the day. I hear her calling me by my true name, the name my mother gave me before my sire flattened it to Annis. *Arese.*

Arese: *She came in at a good time.*

CHAPTER 3

✻

Line of Loss

The Georgia Man don't realize Safi's gone until milky light seeps through the morning fog. He cusses and swipes the women of the line with his crop, and we huddle together, bow our heads, and hunch our shoulders. The crop stings: a thin streak of fire. Our line is a panting, tangled knot.

"How," he hisses. "How?"

We shuffle until he tires, and then he ties a new woman in front of me, and the rest of the men untangle us, pulling our line straight. The new woman before me has a crooked nose, broken and smashed to a hook, and the cower of someone used to being beaten.

"How," she says. "How?"

She turns her head to me, her hair, like all of ours, tangled around her cheeks and forehead from a week of walking. Unable to wash herself or rub fat on her skin, her creases have gone scaly,

51

angry, cracking. They bleed. How the miles done wore us down, peeling us away piece by piece. I wonder if Safi hears the Georgia Man cussing his men from high on his horse, pointing them off into the woods, knitted dense, around us. I don't answer the woman in front of me. As far as everyone else reckon, I know nothing.

"We ain't got time to spend. Meet us in Alabama," the Georgia Man spits. The two who had the night's watch ride off into the muffled morning, angry faced and lank haired. The Georgia Man checks the men's chains, our rope, knotting the cord tight to our wrists. Our limbs are starting to swell: our arms, our hands, our feet, tight and hot with blood from the previous days' walking. I learned remedies from my mother that could bring the swelling down. But I can't get none of it, no yellow weed or red oak. The line pulls to a shuffle. Soon, our feet will split.

I don't know how I would answer the woman's question even if I could. *Georgia Man mistake*, I could say; that would account for the loosened rope, but not the bruising and blood on Safi when he led her back to the line. *Luck*, I could say; that would account for the cover of night, but not for Safi alone in the wild, running toward a nothing sort of freedom. *Her fight*, I could say, and that would be as close as I could get to the answer of how Safi got out her bonds. It was her fight that drove her out into the dark, away from me. *Honeysweet*. I stumble and jerk upright, pain a sharp knife in my leg. I won't be the one to bring us all down in a pile. Not this morning when the Georgia Man would beat us back up. Us walking cattle, us goats. Us made to be a herd, but we not. We not.

THE FIRST LESSON THE older warrior wives taught Mama Aza was this: *Run.* I repeat the word as I look down and see the woman in front of me, the one who took Safi's place, dragging her feet down the path. Every time she lift her foot, it flashes red. I try to walk on tiptoe, but it hurts worse than flat-footed, so I fall into the rise and descent of however my legs want to stride. I wonder if Mama Aza did the same. I recollect Mama's stories about Mama Aza and the sister-wives so I can forget the ache of me, how every step feels like bone studding the ground: not flesh, not foot.

"When Mama Aza met the oldest of the king's warrior wives, that warrior woman thought she was weak and put her to the back of the line. And then they strapped a stick long and heavy as a sword to Mama Aza back and bade her run. Mama Aza and her sister-wives ran until they bled. And then they ran through it," Mama said. "Left footprints in the dust. And that's all they did. For months. Until they feet healed, flesh thick. Tougher. Ran through the countryside until they felt like they sides was going to burst. Like the air was cleaving its way down they throats. You feel pain like that long enough, you wake up one day and find that it hurt a little less, and a little less. Until it barely hurt at all, and you can block it up like a mosquito bite.

"Mama Aza thought because it was all women, it would be more like a family, that the other wives would be her sisters and mothers. But then they came across the elephants. She hadn't ever seen an elephant up close. She watched the mamas wrap they trunks around the babies, watched them link they tails to the noses and walk through the world, eating and napping and playing, saw how the females was the bone of the family, always at the center, just like her mama. Was then Mama Aza found out they was sent to kill the males, the ones with teeth, that the hunting of the elephant would teach them how to fight. Because if they could slay an elephant, they could kill a man. But she didn't want to kill none of them. She said it to the girl next to her when they camped for the night. Asked her if she wanted to slaughter them, if she wasn't a little afraid. The girl, who had teeth big and wide and white as tusks in her mouth, ducked her head and whispered. Said it was her honor as a wife to the king. Looked up at the leader, who Mama saw was watching them, her sword in hand. And that's how Mama knew wasn't no family she'd been given unto. It was an army. And she wasn't nothing but a body."

WE'VE WALKED THE SUN high when the woman in front of me stumbles. Her every breath whistles. She lands on her knees, and we stop. The woman in front of the fallen woman, tall with a scarf tied over her hair, pulls her up, sets her on her feet, but the poor woman drops again. Her eyes look worm-ridden: yellow and dry.

She keeps blinking, can't stop, even when the Georgia Man rides over and the solid woman drops her.

"Get up," the big woman whispers, but the fallen woman does not hear.

"Let's go, gal," says the Georgia Man.

He flicks his riding crop. I start praying to Mama: *Mama, please let her rise. Please let her stand.* I shuffle back until the line between me and the fallen woman is tight. I melt into the crowd: wax puddling in a candle well. I don't want to be singled out by him, like Safi, like the kneeling woman.

The fallen woman shakes. The big woman steps back and pulls her own rope taut. The weak woman is stuck there: a worm on a hook. She groans.

"You know how I ride this horse, gal? I dig my spurs in. Pain make anything move." He flicks his riding crop again. "Get up," he says.

I lean back and pull. Use all of me to move, the way my mama taught me to. The big woman looks over at me, sees the line yanked tight, and leans back too, slowly, slowly. The fallen woman rises an inch. The Georgia Man rubs his crop over his horse's flanks, and I see long, thin scars all over the animal's hindquarters. Old wounds from the Georgia Man cutting it to run. The horse dances, its breathing heavy, shortening to panic. I pull harder. The big woman jerks. This seems to wake the kneeling woman only for a second, and that's enough.

"Yes," she gulps, "sir," spitting the second word out. The fallen woman stands slowly, her knees locking, then giving beneath her. She bobs in the air. The rope eats at my hands, but she stays upright.

"Get," the Georgia Man says. We unspool. The weakened woman lurches against the rope that we pull tight, but she stays standing, wobbly-walking. There is a flash of white through the trees: the phantom of the woman is back. I see her clearly, sharply enough for one moment to know she is not Safi. She is too tall, too thin. And her dress billows: a foggy ball gown that bleeds and darkens with every knife of pain in my feet. I cut my eyes at it, desperately, hoping against hope that this could be my mother, escaped from the line a year before, like Safi. Wandering and waiting for me to walk south. I can't help it: I whip my head to look at the woman straight, and she is not there. Hope gutters to smoke. The sky spits rain. Water burns my wrists.

IT RAINS FOR TWO weeks. One day is drizzle, the next blinding wet, the next fitful coughs of wind driving the water sideways, the next a fog dense enough to keep us soggy, the next the deluge returns, and then the weather circles back again. We wear pants of mud, which slur our steps. On lighter days, clouds of mosquitoes whirl about our line; but we cannot scratch. There is no sign of the strange woman who appears and disappears, nothing to distract me from the sink of hunger, the competing pains shooting through my swollen limbs, my head, my stomach and feet, so I do what I can: I remember.

Mama Aza told my mama the warrior wives ran for so long, the young wives collapsed at the end. The older warriors would poke and rap them with the butts of their spears, chastising them.

"Rise. Only the dead lie," the warrior wives said.

Mama Aza said their endless runs led them to the elephants' paths: the lands where the great animals beat the grass flat. The brides spent hours watching the elephants from a distance, observing the old, the weak, the sickly, the young. The elephants were playful and angry. They fed and stroked their young, and they cared for their old. Mama Aza began to tell them apart, and she couldn't resist naming them: He Who Charges, She Who Sings to the Moon, the Little One Who Trips. These she whispered to herself. When the warrior wives designated the old bull they would kill, Mama Aza said, her blade and spear felt loose and heavy in her hands, so that her fingers almost couldn't hold them. The bull's hide was dull and wrinkled with age, but he had beautiful marbled tusks, pearly as goat's milk. Mama Aza said each of the older warriors pointed to a younger with her rifle and said: *Earn your bridehood.* If they didn't rush the elephant, they would earn their disgrace, and after the march home, their death, because what good is a king's bride who won't fight for her king? Who won't risk her life for him in serving?

Mama Aza said the older warriors tied antelope horns tightly to the young brides' heads, and they all crept through the tall grass. Those who ran first to the animal were swiped and gored, tossed skyward, and fell. Mama Aza leapt over the girl with the big teeth, who lay dead on the ground, her eyes wet globes, open and open, to the clouds. Mama Aza aimed for the animal's eye, its neck, its belly, all the soft bits of it, chanting one of the first things the warrior wives taught her: *Hard weapon soft target, hard weapon soft target.* The bull spun, feinted. Dug in. Struck out. But there were too many wives, and only one elephant.

Mama Aza said when the bull fell, the females of the herd wailed and roared and two charged, and she wondered if they were the bull's wives or sisters or daughters. The older warriors, who had muskets, shot in the air and frightened the cows away. Then the wives set about butchering the elephant: packing the meat, slicing the hide, securing the tusks. That night, Mama Aza found the needle of shattered ivory, a palm's length and thin as a pen, that she would later give Mama. She hid it in her clothes, as the wives were not to take any of the king's spoils for themselves. The elephants followed the warrior women for miles as they carted the old bull's carcass back to the king, near to the walls of the city. The cows were stormy, trumpeting clouds in the distance; then silent dark rumbles, and at the perimeter of the houses, the elephant herd melted away.

The skin that rims my raw wounds is rough, raised, and as leathery as Mama Aza's elephants' hides. At least Safi will be spared this. For all her running, the beat of her heart in her throat, her spiky panic as she flees north, back to her mother, to hide and live in the wooded borderlands around my sire's plantation. If she can get there—*she can*—at least she will be spared.

AFTER THE RAIN PASSES, the sun dogs us for days. It burns me red. The wind scrapes my face, blowing incessantly for a week. Its rush is strange and loud, and so relentless that I miss the sound of flowing water; we are all startled by the Georgia men telling us to halt in a sudden clearing. There's a green hill, trees all around us in an overturned bowl, a waterfall tossing down into a pool the same deep green as the trees around us. It's so beautiful I feel a turning in my chest, my heart a small bird stirring in its nest. For a moment, I don't feel bound. I forget what holds me. But the ache of me, through wrist and hip and thigh, tunnels me back down into my body, along with this rope. I yank when we stop, pull the wire of it with my arms, just so it can beat back that beauty. I want it to turn my awe to bitter.

The Georgia Man makes his men set up camp. When their fires are high, the two men who were sent after Safi return, their horses winded, their ropes useless. The Georgia Man cusses so loudly we can hear him over the waterfall. We roped women and chained men look everywhere but at the yelling man; the big woman who helped me pull up the ailing woman puts her chin to her chest to hide a smile. On most nights, the women of the line are only able to whisper to each other before the Georgia men are on us, bidding us to hush, riding crops swinging. But after they have settled, we can speak under the rush of the falls. The water swallows our murmurs. The cloudy, wind-worn sky rumbles. Tonight, the chained men sit a body length away from us. A hunched older man speaks, lines like spiders' legs at the corners of his eyes, his cheeks high and firm as walnuts in the light of the fire.

"It's most rock here," he murmurs. He moves his hand, and in the dark, the chains clink. "But not in some places. On the other side of the river, further up. Look like it's not. Got some clay there, mixed with sand."

"You been here before?" another iron-clad man asks him, this one with narrow shoulders, his hair grown long in this month on the road. He shakes it out of his eyes, which shine bright in the dark.

"Naw, I ain't. But I logged. Ran them logs down rivers. Sometimes we used to dig in the banks, make caves so we could sit out the hottest part of the day."

"Wouldn't they fill up with water?"

"Not if you build them right," he says.

"Don't seem like no way to build it right," the narrow man says. He breathes hard in the dark. "You always going to drown."

"Naw," the older man says. His smile flashes. "You got to measure. Got to have two times as much earth above the hole as the size of the hole. Got to dig in and make a turn, and then shore it up with sticks. We ain't have no nails to waste, so we broke limbs, dug them into the walls, held everything up that way."

The narrow man looks over at the Georgia men, says, "I almost ain't hungry today," as if to convince himself.

I know his stomach, like mines, like all of ours, is eating his center. Hunger gnawing on him like a scavenging dog. I can't stop myself from grinning, and it hurts. The older man turns to me and smirks. He also knows the other man lies.

"You knew the girl who ran?"

"Her name Safi," I say. I peer into the forest's dim trunks, half hoping to see her face, half not. The smart part of me don't want her nowhere near here; the smart part of me know she's not. But there is a ripple in the air, a flash of roiling robes and long, thin limbs, and I know someone is out there. I know a woman follows us: not Safi, but someone who hides in that bad wind.

"I knew Safi mama," the older man says. "She was famous for her weave work." He looks off into the trees, too, where the path we will walk tomorrow leads south. Us like a little bird going down a hot, wet gullet, swallowed by a snake. The night pulses. The man don't smile no more, and glancing at him, I wonder how he ever did. All the spiders' lines on his face crease down. "Even so, she had the softest hands." Something about the warm burr of his voice is too tender, reminding me of my mama, whispering in the dark.

"You knew my mama?" I ask.

"What was she called?" he asks.

"Sasha," I say.

"She had a skill?" he asks. He means weaving or sewing, some skill that would make her famous across counties. I want to say: *She could flip a spear so fast it would disappear, and when it cut through the air, it sound like the rasp of a hummingbird's wings. She was short and slim with muscle, and strong as a tree-climbing snake. Mama's hands wasn't plush, not with the cooking and lighting and lining and cleaning and laundry she did, but her touch was.* But that story ain't for him. It's mine, and it's the only thing keeping me upright.

"No," I say.

"I don't recollect her," the older man says. He slumps, and the narrow man next to him sighs. Their cuffs clink. I look up. Bats dart over us. I work the hardtack in my mouth. I have to let my spit wash it soft, and with each bite, my gums protest, tender. *Please, Mama,* I pray, *tell Safi's daddy watch over her. Keep her safe.* I wonder why it hasn't begun to rain, even though the water in the gathering storm presses down on all of us. We slump under it. I make a pillow of my arm, wish there were more meat on my bone, and close my eyes.

MY JAW ACHES. WHEN I wake, my teeth are loose in my mouth. I yawn and my bones click. I lie still, listening to the dark, hear snoring loud as cutting saws and dreamy yelps. Hear the up-cry

of the insects, their rising hiss and tick. I need to sleep but can't.
Worry for Safi worms through me. Wondering about my mother,
whether she lay in this same clearing, roped and sorrowful, blankets me. I turn on my side, stare into the night that rings the clearing. My longing for my mother spreads over me in a great fishing
net and tightens, so whole I can feel it from my head to my middle
to my feet. Wild hope surges in my chest: What if my mother is
the lurker? What if she freed herself as Safi did, and what if she has
been making her way back to me this whole terrible year, and has
finally found me on this descent?

"You said you would come if I called," I whisper, words hidden
under the waterfall's rush. "You said, Mama," I say.

There is movement in the trees: skirts as flouncy and full as
any my sire's children wore, except these writhe. The woman who
wears them is brown as my mama, slender as her, too, and a sudden
terror freezes me. I want her to come for me, to untie my ropes, but
I do not want these men to catch her. The word rings like a bell in
my head; I could not bear to see these men rope my mama again.

Yet the woman who might be my mother, who must be my
mama, is not afraid. She steps out of the forest upright, sure, more
graceful than any woman I have ever seen, and it is then that I
realize it's not her. She looks like my mama in the set of her eyes,
the pull of her mouth, but my mother never walked like that, gliding almost, shoulders arced back. My mother never wore a dress
so fine, gray and layered, so gathered and bustled: my mother's

skirts never billowed as if alive. I swallow and look about at my fellow roped, my fellow chained, at the Georgia men rolling over and twitching in their bedrolls, but they are all sunk into sleep. This woman must be some other sister, wife, mother, caregiver; disappointment breaks in my throat and drains downward. I try not to feel it, but still: this woman could mean freedom for someone else here—but not me.

The woman stops a tall man's length away from me, near enough for me to see the black sheen of her eyes, to see that there is something wrong with her skirt, with her top. What I took for silver thread woven into the fabric, glinting in the firelight, is electric, lightning slithering over her garments. Her skirts are not silk, not cotton spun fine, but are obscure and full as high summer clouds, towering in the sky, boiling toward breaking. What I thought was a cape is tendrils of fog draped over her shoulders, yielding curtains of rain down her arms.

"Who are you?" I ask.

She looks at me like it's a mistake she came across me here, like it was somebody else she was expecting to find laying on the earth, someone else she thought she'd find, shivering in the chill wind that carries from her dress. I raise up on my elbow, careful of the tug of the rope. Something about the tilt of this woman's head, her smirk, makes me wish I could rise and stand like my mother taught me to prepare myself before the first blow: light on the broadest part of the foot, heel off the ground, toes spread. But the rope, the sleepers, make it impossible for me to do anything but tremble, every bit of my body shaking so hard I can't hardly breathe.

"I," she says.

"Who you come for?" I say.

"I come for you." The lightning cuts her face in two.

"What?" I ask.

"You called me," she says.

"No," I say.

"I come to deliver you," she says.

This spirit is taller than my mama, darker, and where the mist of her hair settles, it falls in ropes all around her.

"You called me," she says again. The way she gazes at me, wide-eyed and searching, stern about the eyebrows, reminds me of the one who sold me. She makes me feel weighed and wanting.

"Did my mama send you?"

The woman's cloak undulates like a nest of snakes in the breeze. Her smile splits and she laughs. The worm-ridden woman bound before me in the line startles awake and sits up, swiping her eyes in the crook of her elbow. The woman with the strange skirts is closer to her than me, but the yellow-eyed woman does not even glance at this figure wreathed in black clouds and silver lightning.

"It's cold," the weak woman says. "Do you want me to lie closer to you?"

I shake my head, and the bound woman settles back down, pulling her wrap tighter around her shoulders, rocking herself back to sleep. It's then that I know that this woman wrapped in storm is no woman at all.

"No," the spirit says. "I come in my own time, when I am called." She points at me. "You called me."

"I don't know you. I don't know your name," I say.

This world thick with spirit, Mama said, and if you call it, you should gift it: trinkets of shells and cloth made only for their beauty, nose-pinching herbs and ripe fruit. I got nothing but my split feet, my skin growing to the rope, and my blood in the sand. I got nothing but myself.

"Call me Aza," she says.

"You my grandmother?" I ask. "You my grandmother's spirit?"

When my mama told me stories of Mama Aza, there was a sharpness to her, ground into her by the march, the running, the whir and beat of spear and sword, the press of the warrior wives' feet, the way the king looked through her. But there was tenderness at Mama Aza's heart, too, in how she woke my mama, always with a rubbing hand to her back, a murmuring in her ear: how softly she bought her into hard days. But I don't see any of that in this being, not in the marbled black of her eyes, not in the predator's tilt of her head.

"You not," I say. A panel of the spirit's skirt flutters out in a sleeting wind and wraps around me, binding me.

"You have grown," this Aza says.

The cold tightens, and I cannot breathe. The sky shakes. Thunder claps and a torrential rain begins, running over us all in a great river. The spirit has disappeared; the storm has come. The men and women around me struggle upright, backs curled to the downpour. My body is one great bruise. I groan, roll over on my stomach, and retch. I scuttle as well as I can away from the sick, but the rope tenses, so I crouch on all fours like the others, trying to inch out of the muddy ground. The sky bellows over us. I bow my head to the deluge, to the pain ricocheting through me, to the wonder of that storm-borne spirit, and do not sleep.

CHAPTER 4

Rivers Wend South

The Georgia men wake everyone in the drenched dark. The pain of the march simmers through me, and I wipe at my mud-soaked clothing, swipe at the threads of soil in my wounds—all of it futile. We are tired. Even though the Georgia men threaten and harass and whip, we chained men and roped women plod. *Aza*, I say, sounding the name of the spirit who wore lightning: *Aza*. Every step jolts up my leg, my spine, my head. Every step, another beat of her name: *Aza*.

Why did she take Mama Aza's name? There are no answers in this footprint or the next. No deciphering in the dirt. The storm the spirit bought with her has muddied everything the color of rust: my hands, the endless trail, the sky through the spiky, upright pine trees. Them with needles sharp and straight as little knives. If I call Aza's name, would she come to me now on the march? Would she bring a cool calm with her storm cloud? Even though she presses like the heart of a hurricane, her windy skirts and light-ning-wreathed face are a relief. A break in this walk. The miles grind down as the sun arcs across the sky, and it becomes harder and harder to recall her: to feel how her coming, strange and new, made me forget the rope and my wounds.

WE WALK, EAT, AND SLEEP. Aza doesn't return the next day. She doesn't return the next week, or the one after, as we make our way deeper south. This land is wet, veined with rivers and marshes. At the next river, terror suffuses me like scum in the rice fields. We've forded a few, picking our way across where the water ran the narrowest and shallowest, balancing on boulders or digging our toes into rocky bottoms, the cool a moment's balm. This far south, the river's muddy water churns, black at its center. We stand on the bank, hoping for the Georgia men to remove our ropes, our chains, but they do not. A few charge the water with their horses, who carry them to the other side. The rest wait with us, and they whistle at the line of women, crowding us with their tall beasts.

"Go on," they say. "Go." We shuffle toward the water, and the first women on the line wade into river, their skirts rising. The rope yanks, and I step in behind them, minnows darting around my ankles. The water burns the gore on my toes, is acid in the small cuts all over my legs. The chained men, who follow us, stand close together, looking at us with no words. The woman in front of me, her hair framing her gaunt face, breathes hard, pulls back.

"I don't know how to swim," she whispers.

"If the water picks you up, kick like you running," I whisper back. This another thing my mama taught me. "It's another way of walking," Mama said, putting her arms around my stomach and holding me up in the river's cold water; she made me kick and swing my arms until I could keep my nose and eyes dry, until I could angle through the water like a snake.

"Kick," I tell the woman, but even I panic in the middle of the river when I feel the water pick me up. The women who entered first are already rising out of the river on the other side: they know the current drags, so they brace their feet in the brush and pull back, trying to help us along. The woman who can't swim is before me, head bobbing with her kicking, but the wet crown of her hair disappears and reappears and sinks, and she sputters up water when she surfaces before descending below again. I swim as best as I can: I am more like a cork than a snake. My feet hit sand underwater; I wrench the rope across my waist, pulling the woman behind me up so she can surface, can breathe. When I stagger out of the river, the woman before me is vomiting water, the woman behind me coughing and lurching ashore, all of us roped women kicking sprays of hot, powdery sand as we make our own huddle and look back across the river, at the chained men on the other side. We only swam for a few feet, in the black vein at the river's center, but it felt longer. I sob for breath, knowing one more way to die on this walk.

The first of the men hop into the water. Taller than us, they try to bounce across the bottom of the river, through the deepest current, but their chains drag heavier than our rope. It takes more thrashing and kicking for them to cross. The water froths as they struggle. Silt turns the river to sludge. On the banks, the Georgia men pace and yell. "Hyah!" they say like they are spurring their horses. "Hyah," they shout, and laugh.

A rumbling like thunder sounds in the sky, and I look for Aza, almost think I can see her at my shoulder, her hair writhing like wind-whipped rain, but I don't see nothing but one of the big red horses the Georgia men ride, pawing the sand. Water streaming down its sides. Eyes rolling: tonguing the bit.

WE COME TO DREAD the rivers. In the shallow ones, our feet sink down in the bottom, and the walking that was hard on dry ground becomes a searing struggle. In the deeper ones, we fight drowning. The women who can swim, the women who successfully cross, pull the others, the gasping ones, the thrashing ones, through. They stretch wider and cut lower until we come to the worst so far: dark brown at the sides, black in the middle, a middle that stretches the span of at least two wagons. Eddies feather across the top.

When the women wade into the water, the first drops and disappears at the black heart of the river before surfacing and gasping for breath. When I wade in, I walk to the edge of the inky current and pull back when my forward foot hits nothing. That dark heart is a ledge. The woman in front of me struggles, her hair floating like a waterweed. I don't want to kill her. *Breathe*, my mama said. I step again, and the world disappears.

The water is dark as the night, and it burns everywhere. The bubbles tickle up my cheeks, over my scalp, and when I close my eyes, I can imagine it's my mama's hand all over me, closing me up, cradling my whole body. Sometimes after our monthly sparring sessions, we'd settle in to sleep and she'd run her fingers over my scalp with a touch as light as this, as caring as this, and for one moment, I want to open my mouth wide, want to let the air stream from me, from my chest, want to breathe in this wet caress and let it take me down, down, to the black bottom. I wouldn't never have to walk no more.

"My little one," Mama would say. She'd speak so softly it was nothing but a breath in my ear. "You going to fly in your dreams? Where you going to go?"

"To the woods, Mama," I'd say.

"And what next, Arese?" she'd say, coaxing a story from me.

I wonder, if I die in this moment, if I could stay in this memory. If after I let the last air bubble ascend, I would rise and be there in our clearing with my mama again, listening to her stories. Wonder if I'd get to hear her say: *My little one: Arese.*

But then the rope grinds into my wrists, and I remember the yellow-eyed woman who sags under the weight of our days. I remember the woman behind me who whines low in her throat every time we come to a new river. And I know it won't just be me dragged to the bottom by the current, drifting downstream, turning to silt. It would be them, too. I kick and there, in the silty wash, is the touch of a warm arm. I rise, gasp, and see the top of the worm-ridden woman's shoulders bobbing before me, and the head of the woman behind me kicking and jerking to stay aright.

"Aza?" I gasp, and then there are many arms, as many arms as there are currents, and they grip me all at once, and I swallow as much air as I can and sink down through the water. The underside of the river is murky and ill lit, shot through with yellow. I thrash, fighting against the current, but look down too, to see a river within the river, a current in the current, a knot of swirls that, for one fast, blurry blink, makes a face: flat nosed, deep eyed, wide mouthed, which, with the popping of a bubble, speaks.

I could swallow you, this river says.

The line yanks.

Hold you. The river's voice pops in my ears as the water pulls down, as the line yanks up. I kick toward the surface, the light. Breath burns my throat. The multitude of the river's arms grip and drag me to the darker deep.

Remain, the river says.

Her voice: the muffled clink of submerged boats and chains.

Beyond them above, beyond them below. Here.

Her voice: the thud of fallen trees on the dark bed of the river.

I could give you quiet.

My lungs flutter.

I would ever hold you.

They slap.

My current would be easier for you. That storm spirit would be worse.

My lungs snap and bellow.

She would rend you with her winds.

They ignite: white flame.

I would keep you whole.

Silt on my tongue. Rotten bloom in my cheeks.

I could give you ease here.

There is no pain in my feet. No pain in my arms. No pain in my legs. Only the center, burning for breath. I could breathe. I could breathe. Still feet. Still teeth. Open. Open.

You could be free.

I suck. The rope yanks me back into my arms, my chest, my legs, and all at once, dragging me up, up. There is mud in my mouth.

On the surface, the day is terrible and bright. The river's grip is slick, grasping, but all the women on the line are pulling, pulling from the bank. I sink, rise, and gasp. Sand abrades my knees as I stumble on the bank, women hacking and vomiting all around me. There is water everywhere: igniting my nose, streaming down my eyes, pouring from my throat. The women on the line shriek and pull. My mama always said this world seething with spirit. She was right.

Across the water, the chained men shuffle down the bank, looking sideways at the Georgia men. Their iron clinks and sinks in the muck.

"Hyah," the Georgia men say. "Get!" they scream. They let the commands loose like shots. Each shout, I flinch, scrambling up the bank, crouching to pull, pull the last of our line from the watery rush.

The river speaks in a little murmur, laps the air: *Come*, she says. *Come.*

The first linked man walks into the water and when he pauses at the dark underwater ledge, he jumps, trying to build up momentum, but it is a long time before his head crowns the river, and he only gets one breath before he sinks again. The man behind him is yanked into the water by the pull of the chain, and each man with him, until the last, a narrow-shouldered man, stumbles into the shallows. This last man, I realize, cannot swim. And he is short, shorter by a head than all the other men. I recognize him; he kept the kitchen garden at my sire's house. Even in the winter, the little man made it bloom green. He balks, but the metal pulls.

"No," I whisper, but no one can hear it over the men's struggle to cross the river. Not the women gathering themselves on the ground around me, not the last of the Georgia men fording the water with their horses, and not the chained men, who are being dragged downstream with the current, the line of their sinking and surfacing heads angling like slack fishing string down the river. The last man sits and leans on the bank, digging his heels into the earth, but he slides sideways and forward, closer to the ledge.

"Damn it," the Georgia Man yells, and then his men scramble from their horses and down the bank and into the water, where they grab the chained men by their arms and pull hard, trying to save them from disappearing downstream.

The last man falls sideways into the water, down into the midnight heart of the river. He makes only a little splash, and once he's down, there is no froth from his kicking.

"Hyah!" the Georgia Man yells. "Pull!" His men yank, wrestling with the chained men, who rise from the river one by one, choking, gasping, hollering and hoarse. The older man who sat near me after Safi left vomits water. The young one is coughing so hard he can't breathe, his face buried in the sand.

"Come," I say, against the river's murmur, to the sky, to the sunken gardener. The white men heave. The half-drowned men stand and pull against their chains, too, and fresh blood runs from their wounds to circle their wrists, trickles down their arms, but when the last man, the little gardener, surfaces, he floats, his face to the dark deep, his back to the gray, cloud-occluded sky. The woman next to me lets loose one sharp sob. The chained men sit on their haunches, their mouths open, gasping breaths, while the white men cuss. The Georgia Man lashes his horse, and it spins in a circle, crouching on its haunches, its eyes rolling white. The little chained man cuts the water easily now; in death, he is straight as a snake.

When the Georgia men unlock the gardener from the chain, they let his body float downriver. I watch until I can't see him anymore, until he disappears around a bend in the river, eclipsed by green. Sorrow: bees stirred by a strong wind shaking their hive. Despair: the queen at their center. Great-bodied, pulsing, pushing. Still.

WE SMELL THE SWAMP before we see it. It reeks like the rice fields at first: black water, mud on the bottom, plant and animal turning to sludge in the deep. That scent of the dying giving way to the living. When we walk, our feet sink. Our wet clothes won't dry in the hot day, and all of it pulls us down. We lean into the rope and slog. The Georgia men lead us around the edge of the swamp: the water reaches in every direction, duckweed bright and green, floating on the murky wet. Cypress, fresh with rain, shimmers.

It's hard to stay upright. On the bigger trails up north, I walked half asleep, half awake and half not, but I can't here. The trail grows spines and sends up sharp-rooted teeth. The bugs swarm the swamp in clouds, so dense they turn the air gray as they swirl around each other, rejoicing at all there is to eat in this world, but when we women walk through their frantic gathering, we drag them behind us in a fine, stinging net. The Georgia men range ahead and behind, capping our lines at both ends, because the trail is so narrow.

The bugs hiss and click. The yellow-eyed woman in front of me looks back, and I realize she's talking.

"They got a swamp like this up where I come from." She trips and rights herself, then half turns to me again: I figure she want me to know she talking to me, so I nod. "They call it the Great Dismal Swamp."

"Big as this?" I ask.

"Bigger," she says. "Person walk in there, they disappear."

"What people?"

She looks back at me and smiles. Her lips closed over her teeth, the corners of her mouth turned down just a touch, fishhooks here and there, and I know her answer as clear as if she'd said it. *Us people.*

"Where you from?" I ask.

"Upper North Carolina. That swamp so big it go up in Virginia, too."

I step on a splintered root and hiss, surprised I can feel anything through the bloody, leathery mess of my feet.

"What's your name?"

"Phyllis," she says.

"You been in that swamp, Phyllis?" I ask.

She don't smile this time.

"Naw. I heard stories. Some people I know went." Her whisper comes so low I can hardly hear. "My uncle. My nephew." With each word, each step, her shoulders curve more, and her head sinks. She is studying the ground but I read shame there, too. "I was too scared. They say it got sinkholes and snakes and boars." She stumbles and catches herself. "Hard to walk in. Harder to walk out." Her hair catches in the wind, swings with the gray moss on the trees around us. "I ain't want to go that way."

I squint at the fingers of the swamp laying its hand on the earth. At the vines and the moss obscuring it all. A whole family of alligators, sunning themselves in a row on a log in a bright spot, a gap underneath the tangled foliage. Turtles clawing their way along the lip of the path. One of the alligators flicks its tail and there is a savage grace in it, like Mama's arm swinging her staff.

"What's your name?" Phyllis asks.

"Annis," I say, spitting the sweat that pours down my face.

"Nephew came back once."

"What he say?"

"Said panthers prowled the swamp. That he saw mamas and cubs all through there, and that when the sun set, the males hollered like cats caught at the tail. Said that there was black bears, too, that you had to run your food up trees. Said the bugs was so thick that sometimes they turned the sky gold."

"Where they lived?"

"They built houses."

"Houses?"

She glances back.

"Out of wood."

"Them two did all that?"

She looks crosswise at me then, and shakes her head.

"That's where they go. Somebody disappear, that's where," she whispers.

I gape at her and snap my mouth shut to duck under a spider-web with a yellow spider in it, big as my hand.

"They got islands in them swamps." Phyllis looks ahead again and tosses the rest over her shoulder, the words landing on me, light as salt. "You got to find them."

I study the murky jungle, the knit of trees. It's hard to imagine anyone out there, beyond the wall of cypresses, fences of vines, past the animals seeking sun and food, over the water. I can't imagine islands, dry risings, in this sunken place.

"He asked me to go with them." Phyllis says the rest so low I strain to hear. "I said no." She breathes wetly and then she is quiet, the only sound the suction of feet in the mud.

"You can't swim," I say.

"No."

"You was scared."

Phyllis hiccups and passes her bound hands over her face.

"Better than this," she says. She barks a laugh, and it's the sound of something breaking.

"Phyllis," I whisper, and she snaps her mouth shut, but still her shoulders shake as we pick our way through this ever-reaching dusk, this never-ending wet wood.

I ALMOST DROP WHEN we get to the next river. It's wide and brown, at least five wagon lengths across. Ain't no crossing this. We'll all drown. Phyllis laughs until she sobs. I don't want the Georgia Man to look at her, so I get as close as I can in our little huddle and lean into her.

"Phyllis, look," I say. I point with my chin even though she can't see me. She's breathing too fast, too hard, and she trembles with her whole body. "Breathe," I say. Phyllis can't stop and won't hear me, so I touch her at the top of her back where the bones of her spine rest like little pebbles under her skin.

"Look," I say.

"What?" she says.

"There."

There are boats moored along the edge of the river, all tied to the trees bending out over the water. There are pirogues, canoes, and skiffs. All of them roughly carved, the skiffs lashed together haphazardly. There is a rope running from one side of the river to the other, and a little white boy with hair the color of fire is using the rope to pull himself across the current, his pirogue only big enough for him. None of the boats is big enough to take all of us at once, and my heart lurches, flush with hope. They'll take the ropes off.

The Georgia Man doesn't say anything when he walks over to us, the women, first. His hair is plastered to his head, and even though he wipes his face with his handkerchief, gray with use and coming loose at the edges, his face glistens.

"I'm going to untie you now," he says to all of us, to none of us, because he looks over our heads, off into the forest. He gnaws a twig, and it mangles what he says, but we understand him. "Y'all know what this water will do. Best be careful." The other Georgia men come over then, and they are loosening our hands, and my arms, my arms feel light as wings, so light my hands rise, and for one moment, I could be one of the swamp bugs, zipping above the choking trees, the damning water, up into the clear sky. My shoulders fist. I look down at my split feet. The absence of the rope loosens longing in me, and I could weep for it all: my bees; our sandy clearing; our lightning-burnt tree; the woods far away from my sire's house where we foraged for mushrooms and plants; the sure knowing of that land, of what it could give and what it could withhold; the high, clean smell of the air on the first cold morning of the fall; Safi's tenderness; my mama's hand curled around mine on my staff: *Arese, my little one.* We roped women are all still, all quiet, stewing in our loss.

"Come," the Georgia Man says.

It's hard to walk without the rope, my body familiar with the jarring pull of the line. Behind us, the other Georgia men cough orders at the chained men as they prepare to remove the links. The Georgia men hold their guns ready: one across a thigh, another over a shoulder, yet another loosely in a hand. The threat of them as present as if they were pointed and cocked. There is no sand at the edge of the river, just the swamp reaching all its green fingers to the water. Cypresses arch skyward, their knees breaking the shallows. The boats bump them. The red-haired boy smiles; he's missing most of his front teeth, his mouth gaping and pink as a baby's.

"Go on," the Georgia Man says.

Phyllis steps on the first skiff. The lashed wood bobs in the water. She grabs my hand tight and I move to the middle of the raft. My hand aches from her grip's desperate need, but I don't snatch it away. The women crowd the boat until it starts to tilt.

"Stop!" one of the conductors, peppered with freckles, yells. "Dumb as sheep," he mutters, his voice round with some sort of accent, not one I've heard. The conductors push off. I wonder what the foul man would think if I told him that my mother taught me everything I know about foraging, tutored me to identify dozens of mushrooms. I learned every single one, and I was young and soft mouthed as his little flame-haired boy, younger even, but I could go out by myself and hunt food for me and my mama, and I never bought home nothing that made us sick.

Alligators float on the top of the water in the shallows, and over the rush of the river, they hiss at each other. Under their slithering, clicking sounds, the old river speaks in a language I cannot fully understand, but I catch words: *To freeze*, it says, *to ice. To rest*, it whispers. In the forest on the incoming bank, Aza blinks into being. She is waiting for me. I'm weak as a wrung-out rag, but still I want to spit into the water, want to speak over its murmur, over the hiss of reptiles, and tell the pale, hairy men: *I ain't no animal. I ain't no sheep.* The second conductor, short and hairy chested, smiles at the freckled man and says: "No food for the gators this time!" The freckled conductor laughs.

Phyllis lets go my hand and leaps, graceful as a soft-hided deer, to solid ground. I know it hurts when she lands, know what the grinding walk has done to her feet, legs, and hips. I look for Aza, but she has disappeared. Phyllis frowns. I gather my own ground-down bones, breaking dusty at the joints, and follow.

THE GEORGIA MEN BIND us as soon as everyone has crossed the great river, loop the ropes around our wrists and chain the men tightly. We walk until dusk. The trees blot out the stars, blacken the world, and the insects are deafening. When they stop us on the trail for the night, the Georgia men light great fires at both ends to protect us from predators. They are afraid of what lurks in the marshy darkness. I wait for Aza. I will her to come, to eat all the light of the fire, but she does not appear. I curl my legs and arms into my clothing, hide my face in my hands, but the mosquitoes still prick me until I drift off to sleep.

When I wake, Aza is bending over me, her face framed by the smoldering fires, which burn low in the night. I roll on my side, but she hovers, still as stone. I try not to tug on the line although everything in me wants to stand and walk away from her, this spirit wreathed in black fog. I envy how she comes and goes, and I have to swallow my anger; even though she says she comes when called, when I need her she does not appear.

"You sleep long," she says.

"You left," I whisper.

"I am with you," Aza says, "even when you cannot see me."

"Why?"

"I walked with your mama," Aza says. She looks down the long line of us, at the Georgia men rolling to their feet, rising and spitting.

"To New Orleans?"

She smiles. Instead of teeth, her mouth shines with the flash of lightning.

"Yes, and before. Her whole life."

"I ain't never seen you." The touch of her wind reminds me of the rivers' currents; I tamp down a lick of panic. "She never told me about you."

Her smile collapses.

"I am with you even when you cannot see." Aza reaches out an arm, and a ribbon of breeze ruffles my coiled hair. "Just as I was ever with her. Now I walk with you."

She says this as she rises and recedes into the trunks of the trees, where she stops, floating, her face smooth as swamp water, ending the conversation. But she does not disappear. Instead, she remains, just far enough away that I cannot raise my voice and speak to her. The Georgia men grunt awake and begin barking at us all. By mid-morning, we are circling a lake so large I cannot see where it ends. The questions I want to ask Aza crowd my throat. She has floated near, wreathed in storm clouds. Her voice sounds like rain coming from a distance.

"Your grandmother," she says.

I nod.

"She came across an ocean."

The rope digs.

"That water spread from horizon to horizon. And all the stolen ones with your grandmother, them all packed head to feet, side to side, in the ship."

I hold my hands out straight and down, but it does not ease the pain.

"The men who sailed the boat raped them."

One of the Georgia men whistles.

"They dumped the dead. They let the water have them."

My ankles feel packed with rocks.

"Your grandmother prayed in the dark. To her ancestors. To the spirits her mother taught her. She woke and prayed. She drank when they watered them and prayed. She went to sleep praying, her lips bleeding."

Every jarring step is a bruise.

"One day, the two women flanking her died."

Every lurch is a stabbing in my hip.

"I came across them on the great sea. My dancing rocked that boat deep and high. The waves tossed your grandmother with the dead, bathed her in blood, vomit, and shit. She stopped praying."

I tuck my elbows in tight, try to sink back into the mindless walk, but the pain persists.

"That night, she beseech the storm. She don't know it, but she called to me. She say: please, please don't take me. She say: I know you here. You hear. Please."

I am swimming in ache.

"I know your power, she said. I know you."

I let the rope tug me along: All of us women groaning. Our chorus telling me I'm not alone.

"The others still alive was crying. Timid as ants. But your Mama Aza was insistent. Loud."

I try to remember there is more than pain, even as my bones round in my sockets, grinding the dust of the grave.

"Her call stopped my dancing over the waters. I knew all them gasping like fish in the hold, crying so the water run in their mouths."

My wrists bleed.

"I spared them because of her. Because she called to me."

We leave the lake, but we have not left water. Our soles sink and sting raw.

"I spared them because your Mama Aza called me."

The bog gives way to land, and the trees fall back on either side of us.

"You understand?"

We are on a tiny rise, and the Georgia men's horses are snorting and dancing in circles in the grass. The sound of dogs barking carries high on the air.

"She knew me."

There are small wooden buildings, sitting high on stilts, above the bog.

"Your mother called me, too, like her mother before her. When he violated her, and she begat you."

In the distance, there is a smudge of dark squares, too uniform to be a forest, wreathed in fog instead of foliage. It is a city.

"You called me."

A great black river worms along its side.

"You all call me."

The Georgia Man steadies his horse, rides it to the front of the line.

"Here we are," he says.

The city shimmers on the horizon. The tutor's voice sounds in my head: *"I am the way into the city of woe, I am the way into eternal pain, I am the way to go among the lost."* Aza holds her hands out before her as if she is reaching for the crackling flames of a warming fire, her face lit with the golden hour and a half smile, pleased.

"That place calls for me loud as you and your line. It's all beseeching. All prayers. All yearning," Aza says. She's grown large, so I have to look up at her, the storm swirling below her face. "City of the living, city of the dead, city of all between." The clouds boil over her mouth, her cheeks, her eyes; her a pillar of storm, and all I hear is her voice. "New Orleans."

CHAPTER 5

City of Woe

We walk down into New Orleans, and each step is a little falling. We leave the lake and the stilted houses behind; the trees reach, swaying and nodding on all sides, and us in the middle of a green hand. When the hand opens, there is a river, a river so wide the people on the other side are small as rabbits, half-frozen in their feed in the midmorning light. Aza disappears. The boat that carries us over this river is big enough that all the women fit. There is no reprieve from our rope here. This river is wordless, old groans coming from its depths. After we cross, there are more houses, one story, narrow and long, and then two stories, clustered close together, sometimes side to side, barely space for a person to stand between them. The grandest are laced with wrought iron and broad balconies: great stone palaces rising up and blotting out the sky. Long, dark canals cut the city at every turn. The air smells of burning coffee and shit.

People crowd the streets. White men wearing floppy hats coax horses down rutted roads turned to shell-lined avenues. White women with their heads covered usher children below awnings and through tall, ornate doorways. And everywhere, us stolen. Some in rope and chains. Some walking in clusters together, sacks on their backs or on their heads. Some stand in lines at the edge of the road, all dressed in the same rough clothing: long, dark dresses and white aprons, and dark suits and hats for the men, but I know they are bound by the white men, accented with gold and guns, who watch them. I know they are bound by the way they stand all in a row, not talking to one another, fresh cuts marking their hands and necks. I know they are bound by the way they wear their sorrow, by the way they look over some invisible horizon into their ruin.

But some brown people look like they ain't stolen. Some of the women cover their hair in patterned, shimmering head wraps, and they walk through the world as if every step they take is their own. They are fair as I am, some of them even fairer, as milk hued and blue veined as the white women in their bonnets and hats. I slide close to Phyllis, lean away from the caravan of wagons rumbling past. A handful of women snake past; their head wraps are bright and glittering as jewels, and they look everywhere but at our bound line: stooped, bleeding, and raw from the long walk.

"They're free," I tell her.

"Who?" Phyllis asks.

"Them." I point with my chin.

Phyllis sneezes and wipes her nose on her arm.

Three boys, heads shaved, follow behind an olive-skinned woman in a cream head wrap. The boys stare at us, their eyes wide and wondering, and the woman, who must be their mother, grabs the closest by his shoulder and herds the boys in front of her.

"*Non*," the woman says. She hurries them to a trot that matches the horses pulling the wagons. "*Allons-y.*" One of the boys trips, but she bears him up with her hand on the back of his collar.

Phyllis watches them until they disappear around a tree-lined bend. I try not to, but I still search for more head wraps, more quick walkers with averted eyes who wear deep, brilliant colors. More who are free.

"Move," the Georgia Man says, shouting us deeper into this warren of a city until he stops outside a wooden fence high as two women standing on each other's shoulders. Haphazard roofs, tiled and patched, show over the top. There is a gate at the center of the fence, and as it swings wide, the sound of someone wailing in the enclosure swoops outward.

"In," says the nearest Georgia man.

We walk in a knot through the door. I look back at the two-story houses and stone businesses. A white man with a bushy moustache stands on the porch of a home, his hands shoved in his pockets, watching us being herded. His face as blank as the windows.

"In, girl," the Georgia Man says. The man across the street rubs one hand down his black-vested chest and tips his hat. The gate closes with a rasp, ill-fitting wood scraping, and we are inside.

WE ENTER INTO A courtyard clustered with buildings: Two are tall and whitewashed brick. The rest are short and windowless, their bricks as dark as the river. The ground beneath us is beaten to dirt and sand, nearly as even as a wooden floor. But there are footprints in it, so many footprints: the dimples of five toes, the smooth ball of heels, sometimes ringed by the mark of a horse's hooves. The Georgia Man enters one of the tall buildings, and his men dismount their horses and lead them to a stable. Laughter echoes from inside the buildings. Dogs yip and bark at the noise.

"Come," says one of his men, short and burnt red at the forehead. His hair snakes below his collar. We women follow to one of the long, low, dark brick buildings while a white man leads the chained men to another building—this shack's twin. We women stoop to enter, and when I stand, my hair brushes the ceiling. The taller women stoop and shuffle into the close darkness. There are no windows, and the only light comes from cracks between the bricks. The man takes his time untying us; the first woman he unbinds limps to the furthest corner of the room and sits. One woman drops to her knees right as the rope is taken off. Another hunched woman holds her hands in front of her like she has an offering, listing side to side. Phyllis slides down the closest wall. When my length of rope falls, I step backward, slowly, as I did with my bees on days when it took time for the smoking moss to calm them. For a moment, the longing for my hive feels so strong it makes me stumble to remember: the clearing, the old char of the tree, the honey, amber and heavy.

"Annis," Phyllis says.

The Georgia Man closes the door. I sink to the floor next to Phyllis, lean my head back against the brick, close my eyes, and try to recall how beekeeping taught me to hold myself still, my mirth muted. How once, in my breathing, there was joy.

WE SLEEP HUNGRY, WRAPPED in rags. Phyllis's rasping breath has turned to a hard, hacking cough. Some of the women snore, but most of them are still and silent as fallen trees. I wonder if this where my mama came, if she slept on this floor, too. If she laid in the close, hot darkness and thought of me. I scratch my scalp and imagine the press of my fingers as my mama's the last time she washed my air, oiled it, and braided it. I scoot so that my back grazes Phyllis's, and for one minute, I let myself pretend she's my mama, warm and whole.

A tendril of smoke winds through the crack of the bricks, gathers to sooty coils under the seam of the roof. Aza takes shape in a darker black.

"You came back," I say.

"Others called."

"Did you follow my mama here? To a pen?" I whisper.

Lightning rings Aza's neck before sizzling to darkness. She does not descend to the floor.

"Yes."

"What happened to her?" I ask.

The lightning arcs across her head in an electric halo. She frowns before speaking.

"The same that will happen to you," Aza says. Her face changes. A softening around her eyes could be sympathy, but then it is gone, fast as the zip of a flitting hummingbird over her cheek. "You will sorrow. One will come and take you away."

"You know?" I ask. "You know where my mama went?" Hope foams up my throat, and I do my best to swallow it all down.

"Out of this place," Aza says. "She was taken away, north and inland."

The feeling, the hope, is a heavy cream now, and it sinks down to my stomach.

"Did you follow her?" I ask.

Aza finally descends in a blanketing mist.

"She was ill, but she wouldn't call me." I reach out a finger. At the edge of Aza's smoky garments, there is a pepper of cool rain. Her face is placid, still water. "Spirits need calling," Aza says. "That's the last I saw of her."

I ball my hand into a fist and rub it against my stomach: it aches with cold.

"You knew she needed you," I say, and wish I hadn't. My hope gone rancid, bubbling up to eat at the back of my tongue like acid.

What I don't say: *You did nothing.*

Aza is sharp and beautiful in the darkness. She looks away from me, beyond the brick walls, and her profile, for one perfect moment, is my mother's. She seems near, near in the night, and longing clangs through me.

"Yes," Aza says. "Sleep."

I turn to my side, wondering how cold can soothe one moment and sear the next.

THEY MAKE US WASH in a trough before they dress us in sack dresses, all the same color brown. They take the first woman away midmorning while we are crouching in the low, dark building. When the first woman returns, she stumbles into the room before slinking into a dark corner. She refuses to speak, even when the other women crowd her, asking after her. Men come to the door and take us away, one at a time, calling us by name: *Sara, Marie, Elizabeth, Aliya, Annis.*

When the white man, featureless in the blotted-out doorway, calls me, I follow him into the bright, hot day. The slave pen is dusty and barren, but over the gate that separates us from the outside, the treetops lining the street sway. Clouds, with the underbellies of doves, float in the sky. The horses roped to poles shuffle and neigh. Men's voices tangle into one rope, loop around me, squeeze. I can't breathe. The white man leads me through the door of the grand building that the Georgia Man entered yesterday, but the Georgia Man is gone. There is a fireplace and a mantel inside, candlesticks to light the room, glowing before mirrors edged in gold. There is a desk, a table with ornate scrolling at the corners, and high-backed wooden chairs. There are five white men, clean clothed, their hair smashed flat in indents left by the hats they've hung at the door. They are white whiskered, tall and short, paunchy and lean, pale. They wear watch fobs. Their teeth gleam in the candlelight.

"Come here, girl," says the shortest and paunchiest of them. He is red at the edges: his hands, his hairline, his cheeks, all mottled red, as if he has slashed some animal's throat and been splashed with blood. Another white man, lean and bald, stands next to him.

"Good gait," the short man says. "Bright eyes."

"She looks healthy enough, given you feed her," says the lean man to his paperwork.

"As I will," the short man says.

The lean man scribbles and talks over his shoulder.

"Take her in."

"Yes, sir," a voice says, and it is only then that I notice the brown woman, her hair covered and wrapped, her eyes on the floor, who stands from her seat and walks toward us, her shirt and skirt loose and plain. She puts out her hand to me but doesn't take mine, and she turns, expecting me to follow her, before disappearing through a small door. The men are all watching me, but they say nothing. There is a low table there with a stained cloth on it. I don't want to go anywhere near it, but she points and says, "Please, sit." I perch on the edge so the wood cuts into my legs.

"That's the doctor, and he's going to examine you. Ensure you're healthy and if something wrong, he'll treat it." She talks, but she looks beyond me, as if there is another me behind me, floating midair, ascending through the ceiling. *Aza*, I think. *Aza, you said you would stay.*

"You understand? Nod if you understand."

I look at her, right at her: the splash of freckles across her high forehead, the mole at the side of her nose, the crooked set of her canine teeth.

"You understand," she says.

Aza, I say. *This woman free. Who spare her?*

The doctor walks in.

"Undress," the woman says.

Aza, look, I say. *Look at her.*

I pull my sack dress over my head. I swallow a small sound when the air touches my skin with a chill hand.

Aza. There is a shimmering at the side of my eye.

"He's a doctor," the woman says. She glances toward me and her eyes stick for a moment, and then she looks away. Shame like a frown on her. "He'll ... examine you," she whispers, and she looks past her folded hands and down to her feet.

Aza, I say, *please*.

The waxy string bean of a doctor walks in and measures: height, hands, feet, waist, legs, arms, and head. He looks in my open mouth, my ears, peers into my eyes. I jump when he palms my skull, presses down onto the plates of my head, rubs across my closed eyes. I keep them shut when his hand works its way from my crown to my neck and crawls downward, a walnut-knuckled, pale spider.

"Delicate features from some admixture. She bears no marks from childbearing. Slender waist," the doctor murmurs. "And wide hips." The head-wrapped woman scribbles his notes, her gaze fixed to the page. "Would probably sell best as a fancy girl," he says. I imagine myself like Aza, floating above the head-wrapped woman, above the doctor, above the little worms of pain burrowing into me with the doctor's fingers as he works them over me, into me, into sleeves and pockets ever more tender, even softer. But knowing that my mama endured this, and worse, snaps me back, back into my body. For all the fighting she knew, she prized, she could not rebuke this.

Oh, Mama.

ONE OF THE MEN leads me back to the low brick building. It is hot and close, and I want to warn Phyllis before she follows the same man back out, tell her of the woman, the thin doctor, his stabbing hands. But I can't. I sit next to her and hug myself, every part of me wet: my head, my face, down the middle of my shoulder blades, my stomach, my wrists, between my legs where the doctor probed, and down to my red open feet. I lean into the wall. I squint against the sharp threads of daylight coming in at the seams; there are etchings in the brick. Some letters. A shape that looks like a sun. And further down, a straight long line with a little triangle across the top. I touch it, trace it; it looks like a spear. I wonder if my mother might have carved this, put her mark here since she could never write her name, since she had no staff.

I wonder if she left this for me.

When Phyllis returns, she tilts to a fall next to me. Her sobs, soft as they are, come out of her like pulled teeth. I wait for her to still, and then I take the ivory awl from my hair, from where it is hidden in my scalp, from where I have worn it every day since my mother was taken, and I scrape into the wall next to the mark that could be my mother's. I scratch a circle, draw a straight line down the center of it, and then draw a little oval on one side of the back, and on the other side, another: wings. When I squint, it could be a bee.

ALL OF THE WOMEN are asleep, holding themselves or each other. All of us throbbing and bruised from the walk and the doctor. After my mother was sold and before Safi cleaned and warmed me, when my grief was a hot, fresh deluge, I'd wander to the clearing when the air turned orange, when the rabbits sought their last feed of the day, and the owls and coyotes came to hunt them. I would take out the ivory awl my mama gave me and walk the forest, tooth in hand, feeling a hair less helpless, yet knowing myself for a fool. Didn't Mama say I was my own weapon? That I was always enough to figure a way out? But I feel weaponless now, all aching softness. Aza descends and wreathes me.

"Why?" I whisper. "Why you didn't spare my mama that? Why not me? You could take us out of this place."

Aza's hair is a living thing: scudded clouds, the setting sun lighting them on fire. She leans forward and a breeze blows from her. Feels like the slap of a freshly washed linen on my face, snapping in a cool wind.

"My rain cannot wear the lock. My wind could break it, perhaps, but there are too many men here. Too many dogs. They would follow, and they would find you, fast."

"There have to be other ways. You ain't never tried?" I say.

Aza's wind is brisk, nothing of the tender mother in her. She glares at me with her black eyes, her lightning irises.

"I followed your Mama Aza after I spared her on the ship. Was something about her, some sound. A thin whistle, like the high wind birds ride before a storm." Aza's fog flashes purple; one of the women moans. "I followed her through the market. Saw how tightly your Mama Aza was bound in this land, as surely as she was bound on the ship. Saw her all the way to your sire's home, when she began to swell with your mother, the baby she carried inside of her from across the water. Wasn't no escaping then."

I slip my hands into my armpits. Clench my thighs and my stomach.

My breath frosts for one exhale. Phyllis shivers next to me.

"Aza," I say. I hold up both palms, fingers blanching violet. "We're freezing."

Aza turns dark gray, velvet as a coyote's belly. I look away from her storm-flushed face and curl into my own heat.

"I left your Mama Aza. She was full and fumbling. But I thought about her when I returned to the roaring, moon-etched sea where I first saw her, to the whales rising to blow from the deep." Aza looks away from me, seems to look through the walls of the building, through the city, over the miles. "There were so many ships, so many of your people in their holds, but none beheld me like her," she says. "I returned to find your Mama Aza bearing your mother."

Aza's hair settles sleekly to her scalp: dozens of dark rivers winding to the ocean, before sprouting again.

"The water that come out of your grandmother when your mother reached her way into the world was purple. She came out so fast, buoyed on all that water; she slipped through the midwife's hands and hit the dirt. Your grandmother laughed, and the midwife tried to shame her. She wouldn't have it, even when the baby screamed. That baby had it in her. Veins of lightning. Spear-straight. High song."

Aza lets her fog roll over my legs, my middle.

"That's all we want." Aza turns the color of a fine morning mist: a pale, cool gray. "To be called. To be beheld. Your mother beheld me. First word your mother spoke was her word for me: *Storm*, she said. Tongue so thick and her mouth so small, studded with teeth, it sounded like the hiss of a small green grass snake." I tuck my chin into my chest. "But when she grew older, your mama lost the little snake in her words."

The women around me murmur and burrow into one another, away from the cold, away from our pain. They leave me and Aza alone.

"Mama Aza never asked you to help her run?" I ask.

Aza's skirts drag over us. The women grip each other's dresses tighter.

"She never spoke of it, but I think this land, these people, was too strange to her. It set her to spinning, and when she stopped, she couldn't set herself to rights. She was shocked, overwhelmed. She'd lived the crossing, but the world that she landed in was merciless. She figured there was no returning to the elephants. To her mother. The ocean was too large. Only thing she still had to keep her upright was her fighting."

"What about my mama?" I say. "She ain't never asked for your help escaping?"

Aza's breeze is as brisk as the first cool day of the fall. A herald of the dying to come. I trace the spear on the wall with my fingers. It is grooved, thin.

"Your mother closed her eyes to me. Last time she spoke to me was the night your grandmother died, burning with illness. My water could not cool your Mama Aza."

Aza blinks slowly in remembering.

"Some spirits can leach sickness, but I could not," Aza says, and it is the quietest I have ever heard her speak. "When your Mama Aza rose, I buoyed her up from her body. I told your mother I would take Aza's name, so it would live."

Aza waves her hand from my crown to my feet. An icy flutter follows, runs in a downpour over my forehead, my nose, my mouth, my neck, my shoulders, my stomach, my thighs, to drench my soles.

"But your mother fell on Mama Aza's chest in her grief, wailing, and never beheld nor spoke to me again."

What a blessing to feel no pain. To feel nothing. How weightless Mama Aza must have felt.

"She blamed you?" I ask.

"Yes," Aza says. She answers quickly, whooshing down. Aza wraps the clouds of her garments around me, from feet to thighs to hips to ribs to shoulders. She looks at the other women on the floor, and I wonder at how quickly she replied. I wonder if she is telling the truth. How easily this story exonerates her.

And then I can't think because her cold is everywhere. It numbs my raw feet, my shredded wrists. I am frozen as I was in the months after my mother was sold. How bitter to know I have only the detritus of my mother's life, the leftovers of her leaving: her ivory awl, her lessons on fighting, her stories, the recollections of her hands, her care. I only have what Mama salvaged from her own mother's death, but I cannot make the choice she made. I do not have the strength my mother had, the will to turn away from this spirit for failing me, for perhaps lying to me. I am too lonely, too cold. Instead, I take what Aza can give.

"Your Mama Aza went to the Water," Aza says.

"The Water?" I ask.

"It's a place beyond this place, where all spirits issue. Tomorrow," Aza says. "This world so much more than you know. Sleep," Aza murmurs, and my eyelids rasp closed.

WE ARE AWAKE WHEN the next white man comes to the squat building, unlocks the door, and directs us into the courtyard, where he lines us up before the seller, the short blotchy man laden with gold over his big-knuckled hands. The doctor stands off to the side with the woman who looks like us. Phyllis, next to me, crosses her arms over her stomach, as if she could protect her soft parts, those parts not bound by bone. The woman at the end of the line is short, shorter than most of us but muscled where the rest of us are thin as ribbon. The seller stands in front of the first woman and reaches out, grabbing her face.

"You a full hand. If a buyer asks, you say 'yes, sir.'"

The doctor writes.

"Don't, and you'll be lashed. Understand?"

The woman trembles, shivering like a horse run too long. Then she nods.

The seller moves down the line, studies each woman's arms, fingers, legs, and back before speaking. *You a lady's maid*, he tells a woman with one drooping eye. *You a prime hand*, he tells the big woman. *You a sick nurse*, he tells another who lurches with a limp. *You a child's nurse*, he tells another with knotted hair falling down her back. *You a cook*, he tells the one who the walk didn't pare to nothing. *You a seamstress*, he tells Phyllis. She doesn't even nod; her chin falls into her chest.

"And you . . ." He brushes one knuckle up my arm. "You don't speak," he says. "The buyers'll know." He echoes the doctor, telling me that I am a fancy girl, my only worth between my legs.

A finger of fog curls over his head, encircles it, and grows fat. Aza rises from it. She shines in the sun: river water lit from above. Her arms hang loosely from her sides, and her mouth moves.

"See," Aza says, and points to the seller's back, where there is a flame, narrow as a candle, in the air. The thief moves to the next woman, speaks to her, but his words are muffled. The flame blooms to a fire. A molten head rises from it, then shoulders, then a torso, then a blazing gown. The face turns dark, and a nose appears, then a mouth, and then eyes. The spirit's hair is a conflagration. Her head and shoulders crackle with definition, her visage a log fire, banked and blackened. Hovering over the man, over all of us, is a smoldering cloud of a woman, a burning spirit.

"See," Aza says. "She Who Remembers."

The seller steps to the next woman in our sad line and tells her how she will be sold.

The blazing spirit flexes her arms, which have turned black as her face. The seams in the wood of her forearms curl and move, form lines, form script. The fire at her heart slides into words. These words flow up her arms, over the hills of her shoulders, and into the valley of her black, black mouth.

"She is the witness to your suffering, to all suffering," Aza says, "She witnesses and remembers. That is her power."

The other spirit crackles and spits embers as the accounting scrolls up her arms, over her face, her whole body, only to disappear and make way for more as the women of our line nod at their narratives.

"This world makes us all anew. Calls new spirits, feeds the old. Gives us followers, offerings," Aza says. "Us a piece," she says. "I tried to tell your Mama Aza that us a family."

I clench my hands, as if I could choke the seller's words back into his mouth, back down his throat. I look over the other women in the line, past Aza, to the spirit who remembers. She looks back, her gaping mouth swallowing the last word, and smoke rises from her. There, the smell of an old fire, an ancient fire, a fire prodded and fed and blazed and stoked for generations. I wish I could speak; I want to ask Aza: *What she going to do with it? What her remembering going to do?* Aza's fog obscures her hands, her arms, her gown, her neck, until all of her is wreathed, and with a crack, she disappears. She Who Remembers looks down at me, and her legs disintegrate, then her hips, her torso, her arms, and last, her face, all of it raining ash.

I would bury the awl in this short man's eye.

The spirit's remembrance is not enough.

CHAPTER 6

Surrender

I wake to a woman sobbing. I can't make out who it is, but I squint into the night's darkness.

"Mam," the woman calls. "Mam." She calls out again, the sound muffled as if her mouth is covered with her hand or her forearm, the sobs running out of her like water from a tipped bucket.

I wonder if the spirit who burns witnesses this too, the private pains, our crying in the evening hours, or if she only writes and remembers public suffering. The kind of suffering my sisters' tutor said abounded in the Italian's hell, with its suicides turned to trees, eaten by harpies, or its heretics burning in flaming crypts. I wonder if She Who Remembers floats now, unseen above us, watching us cry for our mothers. My mama knew the world was sopping with spirit, that you didn't need to go to heaven or hell to witness it; she knew it was all here. And now I know, too.

I roll on my side; scoot up close to the wall, away from the others; and take my little awl out of my hair. It glows. I feel the marks on the wall with one hand, and then I etch. I cannot see well enough to draw my bees. I carve one spear, then another, and another. My mother's mark. Wish she were here so I could ask her whether I am right in believing it is hers. Wish she were here so I could ask her about Aza, about the stories Aza intones. Wish she were here so I could ask her why she never told me about Aza, why she told me the world was wet with spirit but never told me about the one she knew. Wish she were here so I could ask if I should trust Aza. Once, when we were out foraging for the herbs and roots that would end a pregnancy and for mushrooms to eat, Mama told me this: *You good at finding, but you too quick to see good. You got to see all. You got to see the danger, too. You quick to trust; don't.*

Phyllis touches her back to mine in her sleep. I smell smoke in the air, know that the men in this place are waking, starting woodstoves for food.

"Aza," I whisper, and wait for her storm to gather, wait for the bronze burn of her face to show. Phyllis mumbles. I still and listen.

"Mam, no," the woman who cries in the dark blurts before quieting.

Without Aza's coolness, the tenderest parts of me are all spiky pain.

"Aza," I whisper again, but the air remains stale, the only movement the dust stirred by the women asleep on the floor. I cover

my face and try not to cast about for Safi, but I do. She could be
anywhere between here and home. I see every person she could
be: Her shivering in the whitening day. Her dug into a riverbank,
safe. Her arms locked around a tree trunk, bark gouging her tender biceps, hounds baying below. Her caught and bound, loaded
into a ship headed here, south to New Orleans. Her still, soulless,
eyes shriveled to pale raisins, bone surfacing from her skin like
rocks when the tide recedes: dead. Her spirit, where? I press my
face hard, pushing the weeping that burbles like a brook back, but
the tears come anyway, and I see not Aza, not my admonishing
mother, not a rotting Safi, but the bloom of stars.

NEW ORLEANS IS A hive, and us the honey. This what I know
when the brown woman comes in the shed handing out clothes,
long, dark dresses, dark caps, and aprons the color of butter. "Put
them on," she says, and then after we are all clothed: "Rub this oil
in your skin." She passes out corn cakes so dense with fat they leave
a gummy residue in the mouth; we wolf them down anyway. The
clothes are rough, abrasive as a cat's tongue on my open wrists.
There are darker spots on the dress, blood from some other woman
penned here, outfitted for sale. The head-wrapped woman leans in
and looks at me for the first time.

"Speak," she whispers, so low I can hardly hear her, her lips
stiff. "Tell them who you are. You more than lying on your back,"

she says, and there is a memory in her words, something that explains her freckles, the blondish cast of her hair that winds out of her tignon. Some wound of her mother's, maybe, or her grandmother's. Some wound every woman in this shed knows.

Her words set a shaking in me. I try to still, pat my hair for the bit of ivory I slipped back inside: my one piece of armor. The tignoned woman ducks her head, moves to the next of us, Phyllis, who sways in an invisible breeze. I watch her move down the line as she whispers to the others while straightening their bonnets or plucking their skirts or retying their aprons.

"Some sell in the auction houses. This man sells outside the pen. You will stand, and you will wait." Then the woman who works for our captors bows her head and whispers: "*Que le seigneur vous bénisse et vous garde*," and then she says louder: "Come."

We follow the woman's straight back out the low door, through the dusty courtyard, and out the front gate to the street. The cloth tied around her head looks like a flower, soft, washed purple, in the half light of the overcast day. The chained men are already there, all lined up in a row facing the road, staring at the horses and the people who pass. The tignoned woman stops us and lines us with our backs to the fence, our faces to the sky. When drizzle begins drifting down, nearly as silky and light as pollen, I look up to the gray, scanning for fire, for cloud, for She Who Remembers, for Aza. And when I see none of them, I feel the shadow of my mother's hair, wispy and light, on my cheeks.

When I was a very small child, after my mother's long day of work, when she was tired and hungry, she carried me to the cabin in the dark. Her hair my veil. *My little one*, she'd murmur. I open my eyes to the gray shock of this day, to sorrow. When I was small enough to be carried, how those walks lasted seconds. How every moment without her, this damned waiting without her hair, her song, her face, lasts years.

IT IS ONLY AFTER the morning has waned into afternoon that I realize our baths, our oiling, and the fatty cakes were meant to mask the horrors of the long walk and make us easier to sell, but it is all futile. The wounds on our wrists are barely healed over. Phyllis has spots that look like raw meat on her neck and cheeks. One of the women at the end of the line stands but leans over her leg, favoring one foot; beneath the skirts we wear, her ankle blooms, a bulbous, mottled onion. When the first man stops to assess us, he asks the seller about the worth of the woman with the bad foot, whether she can clean well, but when he sees her bad ankle, when she gives a little limp, he swipes one hand over his tobacco-stained beard and leaves. When the second man, clean-shaven, tall, and pale, stops to inquire about the big woman, he startles me: I stutter-step to nowhere, my hips canted beneath my bowed back, my aching legs. The afternoon stretches, and by the time the tenth man stops, I don't move at all.

The day's drizzle slows and dries, and my stomach feels as if it tumbles end over end inside of me, hungering and thirsting. When a big, round-bellied man in a satiny suit stops in front of the line of women and begins asking us what we do, I breathe through the hunger pains in my stomach and look straight ahead. Fool myself into thinking, for one moment, that if I look through him he might look past me. But then he's leaning over me, looking down his nose, blocking the street, the horses, the houses, the journeying people, the day. Him wearing all black, him like a descending night, and I got to look.

"This one," he says, and it is only then that I notice the seller standing beside him.

"This a fancy one," the seller says.

The man hums. He smells like cologne: spicy fruit souring in alcohol. He grins.

"Fine stock, by the look of her," he says.

"She has no marks of childbearing, but she ripe for it," says the seller.

My mother bore the marks of childbearing. My marks: four black lines that spread like oil from her belly button, across her hips, and over to her bottom. Two black threads on the bottom of each breast.

"No," I say. The word is a stone bouncing off the big man's suit, dropping and creating waves. The women around me lean away; their flinch is the ripple.

"I'm a housemaid," I say. The seller is swatting at his face with his hands, annoyed at the insects circling his head, and me, opening my mouth, countering his assessment.

"I wash, I iron, I sew, I start and bank fires." I swallow panic. "I cook." The sun catches the tall man's whiskers, burns them red, and for a blink, he looks like my father, and I know I am failing because now I'm plump and learned as a well-trained mare to him, and him ready to mount. He grins.

"You got yourself a prime, here," the tall man says to the seller. His eyes black as iron, black as my grandmother's blade she ran with, slew with, slaughtered with. Black as my mother's carved spear. Black as the weapons they couldn't draw, couldn't swing to protect themselves from the men that would sell them, buy them, rape them.

"I know plants," I say. "Berries, herbs." I spit. "Mushrooms."

The big man takes a step back. His body has moved without him, and it's only when he's rocking back on his heels on the stones that I think he realizes why. He knows a little of mushrooms, too. Knows that there are brown mottled ones, black ones, bright yellow ones, orange and rust-colored ones, and that those tender stalks can be delicious or deadly. I don't know who taught him, but my mother taught me in time we snatched from my sire. She passed along what she learned from Mama Aza, who learned it from an older woman of the Original People who lived in the Carolinas before us, and who traded with Mama Aza and later took to the mountains to hide from removal. I can't stop myself from frowning in the big man's pale face; my mouth tastes bitter, like burnt cabbage. We sway in our line along the pen's gate. I don't know if I done damned myself or saved myself. The big man spins and leaves us, weaving down the stone, hugging the road, disappearing around a corner.

When the sun is near to setting and the air has turned heavy and soft as a quilt, more than a handful of men have walked down the line, one who spat questions out of his mouth like sunflower seeds, another who asked no questions but squinted at each of us as if we were writing he could not read. I know the seller has his own answer for what I have done. I am not surprised when we return to the pen, to our shed, and when the woman comes with food, she hands none to me. Her mouth frowning, her eyes apologetic.

I look for Aza, but she is not there.

I lay on the floor among the women, murmuring and turning in their sleep, and part of me wants to curl my forehead down into my stomach and close my eyes, but I know if I do then all I will feel is hunger. All I will feel are my bruises, my cuts. I trace my bee sign, my mama's spear, all the little spears I have carved into the crumbling brick. I look up at the ceiling and call the spirit.

"Aza," I say.

Aza does not come. I wonder if she is clear as the air, floating above me, refusing to speak like my father's god, like the seller's god. I wonder if she is choosing her silence, her hiding, like she done for most of my life. I wonder if my need is not great enough, or if there is some other revelation she wanted me to understand that I have not. Or perhaps she knows that to me she is like one of my mother's bad mushrooms: velvet and vibrant on the cap, some trace of hidden poison in the middle. Or perhaps Aza thinks nothing of me and is instead drunk with worship in this watery city. Perhaps she is intent on finding others like her, gathering a multitude of spirits, and they are damning and burning and saving and bestowing everywhere else but here, here in this hot, close building of ragged women mewling like kittens in their sleep, worming their way across the dirt ground, searching, searching even in their dreams for something like a kind body, a soft voice, a lifting hand that will enfold and say, *Rise, rise, come away—I have a place for you.*

We seek and find nothing.

THE MEN WHO STOP and inquire blur to one after a week. The only thing that shines clear when they hesitate before me is that which tells their cruelty. A riding crop rapped against a leg. A quick grin when one of the women falls to her knees on the paving stones, borne down from long hours standing. The hard glaze of an eye as another inspects and questions, as he demands we open our mouths and show him our teeth. The digging fingers of another as he assesses us for mating, brags about his bucks, about the fine 'ninnies we can make, about how much each would fetch, his words a steady bad wind carrying the stench of an animal carcass slaughtered and left to rot in the woods.

The men come like grubs from a rotting log and peel the women from the line, one by one. They pare us away, leaving a handful of us standing. Every time another pale man approaches, I know all the ways he will sink me further into this purgatory, and I let him know what I am capable of. That I know how to seek mushrooms that grow in the darkest seams of the woods, that I know how to gather them, that I can bring them to his table. I don't say it, but they know it: I know of the running of a house, of a kitchen—I can hide them in his food.

Soon me and Phyllis are the only sleepers in the shed.

When we came to the pen, I never thought I could feel more grief, but at night, I know a familiar weight in the musty, empty shed: sorrow and loneliness, fresh as what I felt after my mother was taken from me. It crowds the low-ceilinged room. I can't sleep. I don't feel safe enough to close my eyes. After Safi washed me, on nights I couldn't sleep, I would forage. I figured since I wasn't sleeping in the dirt and mud of the clearing that I would become visible to my sire again. I figured he would come for me. So under the dim light of the quarter moon, I set out to find the roots and herbs that my mother said would prevent a baby from forming in me. Some nights, Safi woke, and even though I bade her to sleep, she followed, clutching a bunch of my shirt. Both of us bleary eyed, blinking in the gloom; I wanted better light, knew that the plants would be easier to find under the light of a full moon, but I also knew that I couldn't wait, that one day, my sire would reach and grope. That he would cover my mouth so his scarlet-faced children wouldn't hear us over the tutor's drone: *"There is no greater sorrow than to recall our times of joy in wretchedness."* That he would flay me as he did my mother. I knew that after nine months or so, I could bear an ill-conceived baby.

"Mama Aza always told my mama she should talk when she was gathering," I told Safi as I stooped and dug. "That everything, the creatures and spirits and animals, just want to be spoken to. Want you to open your mouth and say thank you, or hello. Said it was like calling to like."

Safi knelt next to me and put her hand on the small of my back. Pieces of her hair that had escaped from her hair knot brushed my temple. She was close enough to kiss, and I fumbled in the dark, startled by the soft puff of her breath, the near down of her skin.

"She gave y'all so many stories," Safi said.

"Your mama didn't tell you none?"

"She tell me about people she knew here when she was younger, how they all lived for the holidays at the end of harvest, how that one day they ate their fill and danced, the ones who worked in the field, at least, since they could rest. But none from her mama."

"Why?" I asked.

"When my mama's mama was stolen, she stopped talking," Safi said. "Mama said it was a old hand that told her that her and my grandmama come over together, and when the thieves put them on the ship, my grandmama was crying, yelling, talking so fast the words ran together. Sound like one long sentence nobody could understand. They chained her, and the hand said she just stopped. Like they'd cut something in her. That her mouth kept opening and opening, and no sound came out."

Safi put her cheek to the back of my shoulder, and I stopped pulling at the root so we could sit still in that moment. Us, our light. Us, speaking in that night. I twisted and pulled, and the root I'd been digging came out, hairy and dirt flaked. It smelled of soil given to hiding the gathering of life under the rotten leaves. Safi ducked in close and kissed me. Her lips soft, plummy. Even now, I feel a bone-deep pull to the blunted edges of that memory in the night, to the fragment of Safi's narrow back and worn, skinny hands, her fingers fibrous and uneven as roots, but so tender.

I turn my face to the shed's dirt and breathe in, but this bad soil here, soaked through with sweat and piss and vomit and feces, the acid of despair and fear. No life here, no soft touch but in recollection, recollection that floats high above the dreamers, churning with sorrow, with remembrance. It deepens in the quiet.

THE NEXT NIGHT, AZA finally returns. She gathers in one corner, a deeper darkness; she inks to being in an eye, cloud-roiled hair, a dusky neck, one kicking leg, and then another. She grins to life, her nose spreading like my mother's when she smiles, and for a terrible breath, I hate her for being here when my mother is not. She smooths her long-limbed arms, and I hate her for being here while Safi is not, for all that I would not want Safi to suffer in this place. I hate this afterlife so much I want to curse Aza, want to turn away from her as she said my mother did, and never, ever speak to this faithless spirit again. And then deep down, I hate that a small part of me is glad to see her, this spirit who proves there is more than the offal stew of this dirt, the misery of this hell.

"You left," I say. I turn on my side even though it means smelling the ruined soil.

Aza drifts from the corner, floats on a changeable wind. It is as if she's let herself come unmoored from the ceiling, and she is as drunk as my sire, clutching the walls on his way to his bedroom, sweating with drink.

"This city calls to so many, spirits and people. There are so many who beseech, who beg, who offer," Aza says. She rumbles, a sound deep in her throat that betrays pleasure, like Safi when I would touch the inside of her thigh, the tender skin no one ever saw with a soft brush but me. How worship feeds Aza. I want to ask her why she leaves again and again if there is something so special about our line, about me and Mama Aza and Mama calling to her. But I won't. These terrible long days of selling have taught me this: Aza is inconstant, giddy with her own godly allure.

"But I didn't leave to seek them. I sought another spirit. She is of a family of spirits who sees afar, like the scouts atop ships. My people are storms; we spin and rend. We dance chaos. But this spirit and her ilk—they view the world from afar. They are navigators. They can plot a way out of no way."

"Why do you need her?" I ask, even though I want to bury my face in the dirt and pretend to sleep. I would mouth the ill floor to avoid asking her, beholding her. I am beginning to think my regard is an offering.

"I found that farseeing spirit with her fortune tellers and her spiritualists: with those who worship her, who catch glimpses of her and attempt to read time through her." She scoffs. "Infants," she says. "But her—she has true vision. I traded her a gathering of my skirts, the threat of a storm; it rustled up fear and cowering and regard—so much regard. This I gave to her, and she cast for me, about you. She said that tomorrow, a woman comes."

"Who?" I ask as Phyllis mumbles in her sleep.

Little flashes of light arc along Aza's arms, sizzle at the ends of her hair.

"A woman comes. A little woman, pared to the point of a knife. The spirit who foretells says you must let yourself go with her." Aza roils to a stillness, like the moment before the first raindrop falls. "You must let her buy you."

"Why?" I ask. Awareness sizzles from my crown to my feet in a hot wash. *Aza seeks from me, too*, I think. She, like the man who owns this pen, who does his selling on the lip of the street outside, wants me to sell myself. But why?

"I—" Aza shimmers and blackens in waves. "I am not all-knowing. That is for the Water."

Aza closes her mouth as if to stop speaking, but she looks back at my face in the dark, and she rolls like a fog in the air.

"What is the Water?" I ask.

"You must understand something more of this spirit," Aza says. "And you must understand something more of time, of the universe, to begin to know the Water. The spirit speaks in riddles because that is how her and her kind see. The universe is no straight line, no narrow road. The universe *is* a riddle, a slant gathering of places, of voices, of happenings. But she who foretells sees a path, the most likely path, for you to be free. And that way is for you to let yourself be sold to this woman, to be whatever she needs so that she buys you, takes you out of the city and away. It is only after you have left this place that you may rise."

"What?" I blurt. Phyllis rouses and burrows further into my back. I wait until she stills to whisper, "You say the spirit speaks in riddles, but so do you."

Aza reaches out an arm that is not an arm, and it turns solid and brown in the reaching. She runs a finger along my shoulder.

"The Water is all spirit. Before you and me, before anything, there was the Water. We come from the Water. We return to the Water. Only the Water knows all, but the Water does not speak."

Phyllis shivers.

"Those Who Foretell, who see far, they read what they can of the ways of the Water. They would have seen your people crowded in the holds of the ships that carried your grandmother and her brethren over the water. They would have heard your grandmother and those she was chained to calling, beseeching, as I did. But more than that . . ." Aza stills. She has never been this placid; for one breath she does not seem as if she will burst the room at the seams, blow apart its sloppily mortared walls and low, haphazard roof. For one moment, she seems of a piece with this world, wrung still by its rules, and it is then that I know that Aza, too, is bound in her own way, limited in her power.

"Only Those Who Foretell would have known that your people who were thrown overboard, who leapt overboard, who sank to the bottom of the ocean, would become one with the deep, and after that sinking, that they would sing. Only they would know that your people's voices would rise from the deep, that their spirits would rise like water bubbling to air in the heat of the sun. Only Those Who Foretell would know that your people would be like the vapor of my skirts. That they would transform to storm. That they would come into power and freedom."

All I saw before this moment: my own rope.

"You must leap. You must do as your people did. You must sink in order to rise. Those Who Foretell see this. They read the Water," Aza says.

The Italian wrote about this. After the tutor and my sisters came to the end of the man's journey through the depths of hell, the guide led him up and out of that sunken place by the *sound of waters*. They followed a rivulet of sound, up and up, back to the upperworld, the *shining world*, climbing until they saw "*the lovely things the sky above us bears. Now we came out, and once more saw stars,*" the tutor said. I worry that phrase like I worry my mother's awl, over and over, for its beauty, its promise: *Lovely things the sky above us bears. Now we came out, and once more saw stars.*

I want to rise. I want stars. But I cannot do what the seer says. My hope, my desire for freedom, is too great an offering. I don't trust Aza, even if she does admit to limits, to desires. Even if she is bound by rules. I cannot sell myself; I can't erase myself to silver chalice, crystal goblet, lace table linen. The wrongness of it sits in my chest, fat as a bee grub, white and wet and glistening, turning, rooting for honey, for more than this life. It thumps with my heart. Beats with my blood.

"No," I say. The dust of the floor puffs and settles in powder on my lips: residue of bones. "Is this what you told my mother to do? To sell herself, to go off lame to some fresh hell so she could rise, too?" My words, the dirt I lay in: all bitter. It sucks the water from my lips, my mouth. Grits me dry. Grinds me silent. "Give me water, Aza," I say. This Aza can deliver. This I trust her to give.

"You must do this," Aza says.

"Water," I say.

Aza gathers her storm to her, rolling in her skirts, tucking her clouds.

"You must trust me," she says.

I don't.

"You must," she says.

I don't.

"Mother," I say. "Where did you lead my mother?"

The question sits between us. Aza failed her. Will she leave me too, pass like the storm she is and leave me adrift in the ocean, under the heart-of-flame sun, the merciless day? She says she heard Mama Aza and spared her, but didn't she leave her to this wretched afterlife? She says she followed my mother to this place but my mother refused her help, so she left my mother; why didn't she save her?

"Your mother," Aza roils, "was her own storm."

"Water," I say. "Give me water."

"As your Mama Aza asked," Aza rumbles, "I give."

A cloud blankets the room. Phyllis groans and sighs at its wet coolness. I let Aza's cool dew gather in my mouth, slide down my throat. My tongue plumps like a flower.

"Believe me. And if you cannot, believe the one who foretells."

Aza's wet reach eases me, runs dust in rivulets, but then it turns dense. I can't breathe. Aza is smooth as a placid cloud.

"What happened to my mother?" I ask.

Lightning runs over Aza in an electric veil. Phyllis startles and grabs me, rooting closer in slumber; she would bear me up in Aza's storm, even in sleep.

"You will rise," Aza says. "You will all rise."

"My mother," I grit. "Did you fail my mother because she wouldn't see you? Wouldn't beseech you?" I bare my teeth.

"Your mother chose her own way. She would not go where I told her, with who I told her to go. She wouldn't even look at me! She cut her eyes to the ground!" Aza is on me, a downpour, a torrential eclipse in the full heat of summer. "I would follow your line to the end of the world. I would usher you through the depths, down past the riffles and holes, down so you can come up."

"Did my mama die?" I ask.

Aza reaches out, her lightning crackling on my cheek. I swipe it away.

"She did not do as I told her."

I spit out Aza's water, even though it hurts every part of me to do so.

"Did you leave her to die?"

Aza's skirts undulate, but her face is frozen with remembering.

"Yes," Aza says.

"Leave," I say, covering my face with my hands. I can hardly speak through the howl, sudden and ragged, that shreds through me. "Go."

"Annis?"

"You can't ask me to drown on the promise of freedom."

"You can be delivered," Aza says, her voice soft like thunder thudding from far off. Now she beseeches. I face her square.

"*Through me you go to the grief-racked city*," I spit, the Italian's words vomiting from me. "*Through me to everlasting pain you go. Through me you go and pass among lost souls.*" I don't want to break in front of Aza, but the pain of knowing my mother is no longer in this world rends me. "You misery," I say, rolling on my side to push my forehead into the sleeping Phyllis's and grab her limp hand to feel less alone, but there is no comfort here. Everywhere, hot knives of pain. Aza flashes heat-lightning orange, spreads her skirts and presses, presses, squeezing my ears. Phyllis squeals. Aza smashes us like the blueberries my mama mashed and cooked to jelly for my sire's table. *This how you get to the sweetness*, Mama told me. *This how you get it to set, to do what you will.* But there is no sugar here; there is only searing, virulent grief.

Aza disappears.

ON THE SIDE OF the street, at the bottom of the world, the New Orleans air is hot and dense and close; over the long weeks of walking and the wait in the pen, spring has settled to summer. Phyllis lists. I try to grab at her hand, to help her steady, but she turns to me, unseeing, her hair wrap askew.

"Annis," Phyllis says, before her knees bend, and she puddles to the pavement like a soaked piece of laundry. She has fainted.

A small white woman steps over Phyllis. This woman is as thin as me and Phyllis, and every bit of her is covered, from her capped head to her gloved hands to her stockinged feet. The seller graced in gold watches us from his slouch along the fence, his mouth puckered over a pipe. His smoke carries, harsh and grating.

"Do you launder?" the woman asks.

I don't want to say a word to her, not one thing. Me and Phyllis are wet as if we'd waded in a river before letting it swallow us whole. There is no sweat on this little woman. Her pink face is dry. The skin of her temples wrinkles paper pale. Her eyes are the blue of a sky that ain't never seen a storm like Aza. I clench my teeth, but then Aza's tendril snakes around the woman's neck, knots itself in a phantom scarf, and tightens. The woman frowns and coughs into her gloved hand. I look for Aza's roiling hair, her deep sea eyes, but I don't see nothing else of her storm but that tendril. This *is* the woman Aza told me to look for.

I frown and say nothing. The woman leans in closer.

"Do you launder?" she says, ploddingly, loudly, as if I might be unable to hear.

I lean away from her.

She looks to the seller, who approaches us.

"Is she mute?" the woman asks him. "I already got one serving in the house who can't talk. I don't need another."

The seller exhales a perfect circle, and the woman waves it away. It smells of fire singeing a throat dry. Of flame desiccating chests.

"I think she waiting for a man to come along," the seller says. "I think that's more to her liking."

Surrender, the Italian said.

"No," I blurt. "I cook. I sew. I launder."

My words feel like a sinking. I had to let my bees be in winter, had to let them alone as they slid out of the honey-making, egg-laying frenzy of summer to the slow creep of cold. How it felt like a losing every fall when I pried my last bit of honeycomb from the hive. It feels like that now, inside, when I make myself answer this woman, this woman with her sand-dry face and sky-dry eyes, in this place that will never know snow. Despair when I tell her what she wants to hear. But I will not let that man sell me to lie under others. Will not let him decide to take me for himself once I chase away every other man who would buy me.

"You know any herbs?" she asks. "Any medicine?"

I nod.

"Mushrooms?" The woman squints.

I shake my head.

"You answer me with 'No, ma'am.'" The woman smiles, closed mouthed, thin lipped.

She turns and walks to the seller, who glares at both of us. They haggle. One of the seller's men hauls Phyllis up from the ground. I wish I was in a dead faint for all of it, that I didn't have to answer the woman, to rebuke the seller, that they didn't all lead me to fall into Aza's plan. I wish I fainted to sleep like Phyllis under the bright anvil of the day, under the sun burning molten in the sky. Aza wisps her breeze across my cheeks, under my jaw, but I look away from her cool hand and watch the men carry Phyllis, soft faced in slumber, her mouth half-open, back toward the pen. I hope Phyllis dreams. I wonder if I've damned myself.

Surrender, the Italian said.

I have.

CHAPTER 7

✻

Marvel of Mere Dark

I follow the wagon that carries the thin woman. I am not alone. Four of us shuffle behind the lady and her manservant, a twig-necked, dark, one-handed man named Emil. After we left the dishonest seller and his pen, the lady led us through the pitted, sulfurous streets to another pen, and then another, where she found a man with yellowed eyes and a hump at the back of his neck as a stable hand, another woman who walks with her fists clenched as a prime hand, and last, a child with a swollen mouth. This child, the lady says, will work in the sugar refinery.

After the lady has collected us all, she directs Emil and the wagon out of the city and into the bristling wild, bursting with summer green. For miles, the swampy forest swallows us. Several hours into the journey, the trees open to a clearing; the lady's house sits at the heart of it, a columned building that rises skyward, elegant and vicious as an ornamental blade. It is twice as big as my sire's house. Emil lets the lady out at the grand front porch and then leads us down a winding road that meanders to the back of the home, where barns and butcheries and smokehouses and an ironworks cluster. The people in the buildings pause in their tasks, glance at us, and then turn back to their work. Their clothes are more threadbare than my mother's, than Nan's and Safi's and mine. Far fields spread beyond the kitchen gardens like the white from the yolk of a great egg.

"Sugarcane," Emil says, nodding at the fields before he spits in the dirt. Knee-high green shoots reach from the black earth, hungry for the sun. From where we are standing, the land rolls in one long sweep down to far woods. I have never seen so much land razed of forest and bent to growing. Cabins clump in narrow rows at the far edge of the fields, looking like scattered toys. The path around the house to the back buildings is mostly dirt, but some of the bowls in the road are lined with white, crusty shells, large as my palms. They slice fresh wounds in my feet, and each nick makes me hate Aza and the slaver and the small white woman more.

"Them's oyster shells," the prime hand says. "Taste like tides and waves." When she looks up, I know she sees beyond us to where she comes from, to the people who were home. Her face goes soft, the eyes black as a cooling coal: fire dying at the heart.

"You was a cook?" I ask.

She nods.

"You left people?" I ask.

"A girl," she says. "I thought if she had skills, if she could fillet and knead and baste." She looks down again, breathes hard, and I know she's trying to push the feeling out of her, fast. How that love, with nowhere to go, aches: wind snagging ragged over frosted winter rocks. "I thought I could teach her something that could save her from this. But all's I did was make it easier for them to send me."

I hum past my own jagged hurt.

"She tall as me now—" The woman inhales wetly, stumbling, and I steady her. Her elbow is hard in the meat of her arm, and I wonder if my mother walked down this same road, if she talked to another woman, a stranger, about me. What a small mercy, short as a breath.

"What's your name?" I ask the woman.

"Camille," she says.

"Your girl's?"

"Temple." She says the name so low silence eats the end.

"That's a good name," I say. "Temples is places for spirits."

"Ain't no gods here," she says, her words a hatchet buried in the tree trunk of her wound.

Aza whirls in the darkness, tossing mossy branches. I want to tell Camille that spirits are here, even in this sulfurous place, rooting through sunlight and shadows. *They here*, I could tell her, *but they want too much*. I grip Camille's elbow with what could be comfort and try to swallow the burn of my resentment at Aza's request, the one that led me here: it is acid in my throat. *You gots to let it go,* my mama told me once, *so it don't choke you.* Camille looks through me to her child. I squeeze and let her go as Emil leads me down into the kitchen, where the cook, Cora, sets me to little tasks, testing my know-how. She is tall and wide hipped where my mother was not, but she has a kindness in her that echoes my mama. I lose myself in the tedium of carrying and scrubbing and emptying long into the night.

WHEN I WAKE, I lie in the roots of the lady's great house and look for Aza in the dark. The coming day: a coyote hunched in undergrowth, wet at the mouth for food. A heavy pain slithers through the center of me, twines around my stomach and shoulder blades, and hugs. I don't want to rise. I let myself lie there, feeling the full press of nothing, heavy as the house in whose dark belly I curl.

I get up when Cora and the two housemaids do, before the sun has fully cracked the sky. The housemaids are all scrawny as me, looking like they just stepped off the trail. The women roll up their pallets in one of the pantry rooms where we slept, and I follow. We make our way through the maze of storage rooms to the kitchen, whispering names to each other in the dark.

"Esther," the housemaid with slim shoulders says. "And that's Mary." Esther points, and the last woman, long necked, hair braided to a twisted crown, nods. They both look around my age, not yet in their twenties. "She don't say much."

"Annis," I tell them, giving them my nickname; Arese is only for my mama. Esther hands me a pole and two buckets before grabbing her own and leading me and Mary out of the house and down the trail. Mary swings a poker. They walk quickly into the blue wash of the coming day, elbow to elbow, matching their footsteps.

"What you got that poker for?" I ask.

"She watching for snakes," Esther says. Mary pinches Esther's side and grins, her mouth turned down so it looks more like a frown. We cut through clouds of gnats that pester us. We fill the buckets at the well. I sling the buckets on the pole across my shoulders and follow Esther. She doesn't have to look where she walks, but I do; bugs hum in the rustling leaves around us. The waking of the day cracks like the embers of a new fire.

"It's good to have another," Esther says. I breathe hard. The buckets are heavy. "Less trips. And Mary don't make for good conversation."

"She don't speak at all?" I ask.

"Naw," Esther says as she stops.

Mary runs forward to where a snake twists its way across the path, seeking the light and warmth of the sun it can feel edging into the world. The serpent squirms, thick and black, blacker than the dying night. Mary swings the poker high and strikes the snake just behind the head, pinning its skull with the metal and a little laugh, and then stomps on its head with her bare foot.

"That's what she do." Esther smiles. "She get breakfast."

Mary twists the head like a chicken's and slinks the rope of the snake over her shoulder. With each of Mary's steps, the snake writhes against the pale shirt at her back, a carcass necklace. After we deliver the water, Cora skins and guts it before rubbing some fat into the meat, a dusting of salt, and cooking it in the crowd of pots on the stove. I think something in me done died as I watch Cora fry the snake and portion it out, but I feel nothing, nothing inside me when I chew the pale meat, choking down each bite. I feel nothing when Cora tells me about the skinny mistress, how overbearing she is. I feel nothing when Esther says the mistress checks under the mantel with white gloves for dust, under the hanging eaves of the table. I almost feel nothing when Cora says the lady counts every potato, every pound of rice, every bushel of corn, every haunch of meat, everything grown on the place so she knows if we filching food.

"The best eating is alligator," Cora says, "when we can get it." I don't ask her if Mary hunts that, too. I swallow, throat thick.

When we're done, my stomach feels light, light as a feather escaped from bedding. I drink more water and eye Esther's sharp collarbone, thin as a paring knife. I look at the long line of Mary's neck, and I know all of them is starving. We work anyhow. We fold and lift and haul and darn and light and rip and set. On our trips back and forth to the well, to the river, we bring water to the fields, where the people are bent over the sugarcane. It already looks taller than it was yesterday, shooting skyward under the late flush of summer. I have never seen fields spread so far, and I have never seen so many people bending to work in them. Their backs: curved and dark as a scuttle of beetles. The air: redolent with manure. Older people and children are weeding the fields, wading through ankle-deep mud. No one looks up to the blue expanse where Aza floats and watches with her arms aloft, setting the leaves of the trees to clapping. She blows a breeze, pulling sweat from studded skin. All of the workers in the field are bare to her touch because most of the men work without shirts. Even some of the women have only a cloth bound over their chests, tied around their necks. Some of the children who run water to those in the fields are naked.

"You from up country?" Esther asks when she sees me staring at the children, mouth open. The smell of the animal dung lives like the plug of snake I ate earlier, gagging me.

I nod. "It's mostly rice and tobacco up there."

"This a good season." Esther laughs and there is no light in it. "Yellow fever ain't come through yet. Harvest time ain't here." Esther hoists the bucket further up on her shoulder. "You lucky. You live longer when you work in the house." She looks anywhere but at my face and half chuckles. "But none of us is spared the field—'specially come September and October."

One of the men stands straight when Esther says this, spies her limping toward the house, and raises his hand briefly in the breeze. Esther waves. It is Emil, the one-handed manservant, bent to weeding.

"Uncle Emil," Esther says.

He returns to the mud, and Aza stirs the hair at the nape of my neck. I do not turn to look at her. I will not look at her like a loved one, the way Esther looks at Emil, the way he looks at her.

The day passes in a blur of work for this overbearing animal of a house. The white mansion eats our labor in great gulps, hour after hour, until we are standing at attention behind the lady's table, waiting. Esther, Mary, and I are rigid, long faced, and sweating in the dining room. The lady eats a bite of food from each plate before motioning for me or Esther or Mary to clear it. Aza hovers in the window, the fog of her skirts still like a great buzzard. I ignore her. The lady has no children: her mother is the only other person at the table with her, her hair and eyes the color of snow. She is sightless. The lady's mother is a careful eater, made cautious by her blindness. She eats her food in little bits. As we clear and run down the narrow hallways to the kitchen, Esther eats the lady's untouched food. I carry the older woman's plate, but I cannot bring myself to eat from it.

When the women rise after the last course, I look Aza straight in her storm-dark eyes, and I let my loathing for her billow, tornado sharp, for forsaking my mother, for failing Mama Aza, for leading me to this place that presses, presses, so it is nearly impossible to think beyond bending, carrying, serving, lifting, lathering,

drying, putting away, folding, lighting, and dousing. On my second night in this house, I ignore Aza's whispers, the sound of rain
and wind that circles the low ceiling of the pantry where we sleep,
us sandwiched between sacks of beans and flour.

"Annis," Aza says. "Little one."

THE NEXT MORNING, AFTER we help Cora in the kitchen and
serve breakfast, Emil asks us to follow him to the barn, where he
grabs a hatchet before leading us out to the fields. A pair of older
women stand next to us in the waning dark, thick oak branches in
their hands; others, also carrying tree limbs, ring the cane. They
murmur to each other, looking out over the rows of snapping
stalks. Emil chops one branch for Esther, another for Mary, and
finally, one for me. Mary grabs her limb, strips it bare, and twirls
it in the air, almost as graceful as my mother. She hops from toe to
toe. There is a dark, living stream running through the rows.

"What is that?" I ask Esther, squinting at the dark writhing.

"Rats," she says.

"That many?"

"Yeah, we got to beat them out. First gang fertilize and harvest.
Second and third gang plant and weed. This, we weed."

Esther smiles a grim crescent. I strip my branch bare as Mary
did. It feels good, familiar, to hold it in my hands, to feel the balance of the wood, the lightness of the top where I stripped the leaves,

the heaviness of the thicker bottom. Men and women and children ring the field, all with branches and impromptu clubs in their fists. The hands shout from their horses, watching. The children run first, sprinting down the rows, beating at the black rope of rodents that scurry through the green shoots, slower for the night of feeding. The women and men trot into the fields slower, chasing the fleeing rats. Mary runs clean as an arrow through the air, and all at once, she is Safi, who was the fastest of us when we were children helping with harvest, racing through the wet rice flats, fetching water and hauling sacks. The rats fall still under Mary's flailing club. I follow her, Esther at my elbow, but the shoots are too tall, too turgid in their summer green, to see easily; we get the straggling rats, the confused, but still, it feels good to swing this knobby staff, to imagine my mother at my side instead of Esther, whipping her spear and hitting, again and again, at those who bedevil us. There is no singing, no murmur of talk now, only the thud of killing. Slight children follow the hunters and pick the rats up by their tails, holding them in bunches, like wet, brown fruit. The light rises and moves through the trees, and the hunters meet in the middle of the crop and gather their bounty.

"Can't leave them there," Esther says. She wipes an arm over her forehead to dry her sweat. "They bring buzzards and possum and armadillos. We got to gather them, burn them."

A hand hovers near us, mounted on his horse, squinting at us as we stoop and gather. The hand's horse swats its glossy tail, but the man is still. I pick up a dead rat, its tail dry and downy.

"You there," the hand calls, and everyone, even those far away from him, pauses picking up the dead rats. Esther lets out a quick breath and looks at her feet. At the far edge of the field, Emil stands tall and wiry.

"You done broke it," the hand says to Emil. The hand's moustache and beard eat his face: they cover his mouth so that his voice almost seems to come from nowhere. Aza puffs at my shoulder, huffs in my ear.

"Look away," Aza says.

I shake my head. Emil stands still as a lamppost, holding a hatchet in his hand, the metal axe head askew.

"Here," the hand says. "Now." He rides over to Emil, sidles the great dark horse next to him.

Emil's shirt gaps at his chest, and he stands still in the shadow of the animal. The hand kicks him, and the kick makes Emil's shirt yawn over his shoulder. There are grooves at his neck, his chest, his ribs. Bones overlain with skin, no flesh. Unlike everyone else, Emil looks at the hand squarely. He grips the hatchet in his hand, and his knuckles bleach in the day's harsh light.

"I ain't going," Emil says through gritted teeth. He holds his ruined arm over his stomach, clenches it and the broken hatchet to him. "I ain't."

"Take him to the hole," the hand says. Two other hands dismount their horses and come running. They are bright haired and pale as my sire's daughters. Emil plants himself, sags down with his hips, buries his feet in the black dirt. The hands drag him away from the fields, back toward the barns and the big house. His heels leave long, curling snakes in the soil. The hand on the horse clicks and spurs his horse to a trot and follows.

"I ain't," Emil shouts, "I ain't," and one of the hands elbows him across the face and wrestles the broken hatchet away. Birds caw in mourning and dip overhead. The people leave the fields, vermin in hand, and begin piling the carcasses in small mounds. Mary kicks the ground, frowning at the bunches of rats she holds by the tail.

"What's the hole?" I ask.

"Come on," Esther says as she picks up her pails of water. I follow her and Mary. We run down a dirt path under two oaks whose branches meet above our heads, their limbs tangled in an embrace. Wind tugs the moss, a peppery, gritty wind, and I know Aza is there, moving through the small room under the trees, before I see her. We stop, crouching in the underbrush, looking at Emil, who struggles against the hands again, kicking and jerking like a fish on a hook. The hand elbows him again in the face, and Emil slumps in his arms. The other hand leaves them, walks over a few feet, and kneels. He grabs at the earth and a door opens in the ground. The other hand drags Emil to the doorway and shoves him and he falls over sideways, shouting, into the dark mouth of the earth. The hands close and latch the door, and Emil is gone. Aza spins and rushes through the clearing, pulling leaves from every limb until they all tear from their stems. She arrives in a green hailstorm: a living fury. The hands cover their eyes and hunch, looking like a pair of lost ghosts.

"A storm coming," Aza says. "I gather it."

Clouds cover the sky, and earth tornadoes into the air, turning it brown as the silty bottom of a warm lake.

"You must look for it, Annis," she says.

"What?" I whisper, and Esther looks up at me.

"What you say?" she asks.

"Nothing," I say.

I squint at my feet, wonder if Emil is screaming. Wonder if none of us can hear it for Aza's whirling. She tunnels through the clearing again, and the hand on the horse hollers as the animal kicks and dances in a circle under the reach of the trees, boiling against his hold. We crouch under the wind. The hand on the horse yells but Aza drowns him out with her rushing. Mary beckons, and me and Esther follow her, ducking into the thrashing underbrush.

"You wait for me," Aza hisses, pleasure in her voice. I want to swing my stick up and at her, see if it hits her, if it drags her winds, interrupts her power-drunk whooshing.

I wonder if Emil can feel Aza's wind down there, if the soil shakes with it. Esther has tied a cream rag around her head, and I follow its dim bob through the gloom. Mary raises a bouquet of rats above her head and looks up to the sky, to Aza roiling there, and smiles wide.

Later, the wind carries the smell of burning hair from the mounds of dead rodents ringing the fields. The foul odor of them wafts into the kitchen and up into the rooms of the house. The lady's mother coughs and coughs into a handkerchief, and the mistress orders me to gather and make an herbal tea for her tomorrow, something that would soothe her throat, before directing us to close all the drapes and doors. Still, the house reeks of charred meat. Its rooms are silent and near dark as that hole must be in the earth.

WHILE THAT EMIL IS shut in the hole, the lady makes us open all the windows in the entire house, and then tasks us with laundering all the bedding, sweeping and mopping all the floors, polishing all the wood, dusting the candlesticks, making every metal surface gleam. *I want it to shine*, she says.

"The man is coming," Esther says as we haul and chop and wash. "Her husband. He stays in the city and works."

I wonder if I saw this man when the Georgia Man walked us into the city, if he ignored us standing outside the slave pen, or if he stopped and questioned us or haggled with the seller.

"What he look like," I ask Esther.

"He don't miss no meals," she huffs.

On the second day Emil is in the earth, I slow when we fetch water in the morning. Let Mary and Esther leave me so I can take the path to the trees, to the hole in the ground. I listen for Emil. He moans. Even though my armpits and my face flush with fear, I kneel next to the dark grate, and I pour water, one cup, two, in a stream through the grille.

"Emil," I whisper. "Water."

I hope he catches some of it in the cup of his palms or in his mouth.

The next morning, I return, watching for the hands, but they are never there. The door looks heavy, final. Emil never answers, but I whisper to him anyway, and I pour, thinking of my mama, wondering if she found herself in a hole like this and if anyone snuck her mercy. I try not to think about him when I'm in the house, sore muscles pulling against sore, moving without rest. I try not to think at all, but I can't help but imagine my mama in a hole, looking up to the grate, to the sky beyond, calling for Aza.

The lady tells the hands to let Emil out on the morning of the fourth day. They lower themselves down and hoist him up with a rope. They bid him to bathe, and he does so in the back garden off the kitchen. After the hands leave, he scrubs slowly with his one good hand, swiping at the dirt that cakes his face, his arms, his legs, his back round like a sickle. He pauses, stands and stares, and then a hen clucks or a rooster crows, and it jolts him back to cleaning. We watch from the shadow of the house, and Esther offers to wipe Emil's back; he waves her off, insisting he only needs her to pour water over him once he's done washing. He slowly straightens as he gathers himself in the light, aboveground. He dresses in the barn, and once he steps out, his sleeve tied over his ruined arm, he is upright as the first time I saw him, driving the lady's wagon.

Emil is sent to New Orleans and returns in the evening, the lady's husband in tow. Esther told me true; the husband is a big man. He booms into the foyer and laughs when the lady tiptoes to him, blushing and shining like a bird scattered over with diamonds from bathing in a stream. The husband's cheeks wax round as corn cakes, red-washed with fat. He curls over her and engulfs her, eating up any shadow left in the glowing room, with his gold-threaded vest, his hair springing out over his head in big blond curls. The round pork of his shoulders fills the space. He is as showy as a robin. His wife, the small bird, flutters around him.

Before the husband came, the lady kept the home dark and closed as underbrush, ordered us to keep the drapes drawn and allowed only two candles to a room; they flickered in front of their mirrors, letting off weak splashes of light, making it easier for us to take untouched bread and corn pone off the plates. But now it is as if the lady has conjured the sun in the foyer, as every candle flames before streak-free mirrors, and the light burns through the crystal of the chandeliers. With her husband here, she orders us to give fire to every candle, enough so that the house blazes with light and heavy wax smoke.

"You waited too long," she said. "You should have left the city sooner."

I half listen to their conversation with Esther and Mary as we stand with our backs to the foyer's walls. We gather the husband's hat and bags. He tells his wife that his business partner developed yellow fever; summer has been simmering the city for months, and whole families are falling sick in New Orleans.

"You dallied," the woman warbles. "And what if you take ill?"

The lady insists on feeding him, claims he looks poorly without her there to take care of him. We follow them up to his bedroom, where he sheds his traveling clothes, and Esther and I carry them downstairs. They are damp and smell of congealing milk. He sweats like my sire.

"He got a plaçage woman," Esther says the next afternoon when me and her and Mary are elbow-deep in washing all the clothing the man has bought back from the city.

"What's a plaçage woman?"

"A woman like you: light skin, silky hair." She ducks her forehead, wipes it on her shoulder. "They all over in New Orleans."

I remember the women, crowned with wound cloth, who walked the streets of that selling city, who did their best not to look at us as we walked, bound and bleeding, meant for market.

"He got children with her," Esther says.

I can't help the sharp huff that comes out of my mouth.

"The lady can't have none," Esther says.

The heat of the water and the sting of the soap burn my hands, but I scrub with my arms, my shoulders, my back. I took a mouthful of beans from the blind mother's lunch plate, and it quieted my belly. I think of Safi. What I wouldn't give for the sweetness of her. How it would fill me. I swallow a sob that wants to leap out my throat. I blink, and I lean into the washing.

"How you know about his other woman?" I say.

"He don't empty his pockets. Had a picture of them he forgot to take out his vest."

Mary wrings out one of his shirts.

"She pretty. Got big, dark eyes and a mole on her chin. She bore him a son and a daughter. Both of them look just like him."

I wrench his underpants. They still smell sour to me. I'm dry inside, chalky as soil around the roots of a wilting plant. Starved and wanting.

"What you do with the picture?" I ask.

Mary grunts. Esther laughs.

"Had to think on it. If I put it back and the mistress find it, we would've all been in trouble. She like her overseer; she punish to punish. If I put it back and he find it, then he know we know. So I washed it. Ruined it and left it in his pocket. It turned to gum." She smiles at Mary. "It was Mary's idea."

Mary grins a thin stitch and rolls her eyes. They love each other, Mary and Esther. Maybe not the way I loved Safi, but they do. *Good*, I think. *Good everyone here ain't starving.*

"Mary's smart," I say.

"Yes," Esther whispers. "She is." She straightens and lets the laundry she was wringing run streams down her apron. "Better to work together," she says, "now with him back. If he come across you alone . . ." Her skirt turns dark with the water. "Chew cotton roots," she says, looking at her soaked front, voice barely a huff. "It will stop a baby from coming."

I stretch his clothing, and the fabric sounds like it tears.

"If he don't come for you himself, he meddle. He pair men and women together, make us lay with each other in the cabins, hoping we'll fall pregnant and bear babies. *She* work a pregnant woman 'til the moment they bear and then put them right back out in the fields. Chew and swallow," Esther says. "You don't want that."

I want to ask how she knows this, but I don't.

"Mary taught me that, too," Esther whispers, her words closing the door to the conversation.

THE MAN EATS HIS share at dinner. There are no scraps because he leaves none; he wipes his plates clean with bread, with his knife and fork and spoon. As he drinks, he burns brighter and brighter, turns red as the heart of a fire, but his hands and the edge of his scalp still gleam pale and yellow. The mistress reaches out over the corner of the table every so often, touches his forearm, his elbow; once, even, his face. How easy she is with her affection for him, how sure she is of its reach, its life, its return, because he touches her, too. She squints and laughs when his hand finds her; her sallow cheek shines with the peach shimmer of the underside of a bird's wing. Safi touched me just so when she kissed me, making a bird-cage of her fingers, a careful enclosure of my visage. How I loved being her kept bird, clipped and settled: I preened for her, leaned into her, heart fluttering. How I wanted what this woman has: to touch Safi in the light of day, outside the nest of trees, the buzz of the hive. To be safe in love—but I could not.

Mama Aza was not safe, either. She had her perimeter guard, but she could not love him openly. Mama told me this in the after-work darkness, once.

"She said they tried to stop. That when her and her muster of women came up on him and his men, she turned her face away, her eyes down. She stopped looking, but she could feel his regard, she said, buzzing around her like a swarm of gnats. She had tried her whole life not to want nothing for herself, but now she wanted. She wanted to stand in the circle of his arms. She wanted to kneel with him in the cool feet of the trees and hunt antelope. She wanted to breathe like this"—Mama pulled my head down to her chest as we lay there with Nan's children murmuring in their sleep—"head to heart. But they couldn't. So they ran. It wasn't until they was caught and marched to the boat that Mama found out I was in her, all her love and his, born to a tiny seed."

I touched the skin over her sloshing heart.

"The king sent their families after them: Mama Aza's sister-wives, and the guard's perimeter brothers. The wives and guards tracked them. They had one night of freedom together, out under the sky, in a bed of their own making. One night of holding each other. They got up and ran the next day, but the wives could track big beasts and small, and they found them on their second night running. They circled them. Surrounded them. Mama Aza and the man she loved stood back to back, spears and swords out. She said she could feel the jump of his muscles against hers, every strike, every parry. She said she couldn't help but cry when she saw how they were outnumbered, and she knew the slide of his muscles against hers would be the last touch she would have from him."

Her heart the hum of wings on my cheek.

"Mama Aza said ever after, she felt like a piece of her was still there, would always be there, with him in that moment, fighting, weapons in her hands, the last time she had a piece of what she wanted."

Mama was quiet then, letting tears leak out the side of her face, until she reached up to wipe them away.

"Mama," I said, and I looped my arm around her stomach, pulled tight until I could feel her ribs creaking, protecting all the tender parts of her. "Mama."

She sighed, and the dark ate it up.

"This our moment, Mama," I said.

She breathed a broken breath.

"Yours and mine, Mama."

She squeezed until I felt my own bones creak, and we didn't talk no more that night.

AFTER DESSERT, THE MAN asks for more wood on the fire. He says he has a chill even as the warmth from the hearth, the lingering summer, and the burning of the candles fills the room and fogs the windows. The woman quiets and eats another spoonful of sweet cream, and I let myself go, out of this humid, close room, back, back, to my mama: her hand at my neck, sliding down to my shoulder blade, rubbing in circles. Me: enclosed, loved. A knife rings on a platter, startling me back to the dining room, to the way the mistress's look done turned from little bird to falcon. The husband is sweating, plump as a night-feeding mole.

"What ails you?" she asks. The heat has glazed him. He is looking at me as if I have an answer for his flushing, for his red-sponge face. I look down and away, anywhere but at him.

"Darling," he says.

Esther and Mary are staring at the floorboards we've cleaned and polished smooth over the last week. The husband blinks at them, at his wife, at me again. I squeeze the cloth I hold and look out the window. Aza is not there.

"Leave," the lady says. "All of you."

Esther and Mary and I walk quickly from the dining room, almost running down to the kitchen. The lady's voice rises. She yells at her husband, but her words are muffled through the walls and floors. We help Cora in the kitchen until the lady's voice rings down the stairs, calling for Mary to clear, and for me and Esther to build a fire in their bedroom. We haul wood up, and Esther lights the fire, but it will not take, the wood still green with the wet of late summer.

"More," Esther says, so we run downstairs for more, try to pick the driest logs, try to walk lightly past the sitting room, where, judging by the blaze of light and the conversation between the lady and her mother, they have gathered after dinner. But when I make it to the hallway outside of the bedroom, the husband is leaning against the wall with one forearm, his chin sunk into his chest, his hair a damp cap on his head. I stop with the wood, and he looks up at me.

"I need water," he says, and steps toward me, reaching, knocking the wood to the floor. It thuds. His fingers are long, his grip hot and firm, as he grabs my shoulder. "Damn the wood."

"No," Esther says, slipping out of the doorway to their bedroom, and I wrench around to see the lady standing behind us.

"No," the woman says, and I can't hear anything over the panic rushing through my head like a rain-heavy stream overrunning its banks. The lady's mouth is moving, and I catch corners of words. Her voice rises and rises, and she is invoking God, morality, and sins of the flesh. I hear that word, *flesh*, and then nothing, and then she says *ground* and I back away, stumbling into the wall. The man says *No, no*, and tries to wipe the sweat away from his forehead again and again, and I slump, letting the wall hold me up, even though all I want to do is run, run clear down the stairs, through the kitchen, out of the door, and into the riotous night.

The lady sends Esther downstairs, leaving me stranded here, until minutes later, two hands enter and grab me by my arms. Esther frowns and breathes quickly, watching my face as they haul me down, mouthing: *Sorry, sorry! I'm sorry.* The woman strikes out at the man, but he catches her wrist. They whine, struggling face to chest in the hallway. It is too wrong, too raw. I sink like Emil did to resist the hands' pull. I hear the woman's jealous shriek as the pale men haul me through the kitchen. There is a burning in my throat, a blaze in my head. I reach for my mama, our moment, but I can't hold it, I can't hold her, can't feel the lukewarm damp of her skin, the heat of her breath, the callus of her hands that night in the cabin. Can't feel any moment but this.

THE HOLE: A WEDGED coffin. A long fall. The bottom packed hard from all them who come before me. Air dense in the dark. A black night. Wooden stakes bristling the walls. No rest in this slick clay tomb.

I yell and reach up.

The door thuds shut.

I CAN'T STOP CRYING. My face split with sound. It comes up from my stomach, unceasing, buffeting the narrow tomb of the hole before beating back to me. Still, I wail. I scrabble upward, slicing arm and calf and the side of my face on the stakes the hands have driven into the walls, row upon row, from the bottom to the top. The same men stand on the latched door and laugh. I swallow my keen, shocked still, and squeeze the gash on my arm. Panic flits spastically inside me, turning from bird to bat and back in my chest. I hug myself hard and whimper softly. The hands' laughter scampers and disappears. This hole is as high as the windows in the lady's high-ceilinged house; I would need a tall stepstool to reach the locked grate. The stakes crowd me. My blood thumps in my head.

"Aza," I whisper.

I close my eyes to see the darkness behind my lids, to know a more familiar black.

"Aza, please."

The beat of my heart dims to an insect's tick.

"Mama," I cry. She who loved me without end. I cover my face with my hands, smear salty blood across my mouth, push hard at the bones of my face, wanting to mash my sorrow to nothing.

There is a quiet crumbling. I can't breathe, afraid the earth is closing over me, the ground smothering me, killing me. *What if I die in this hole*, I think, and the crumbling grumbles to garbled words.

She—not—here, it says.

I dig my fingernails into my forehead: *Anchor*, I repeat, *anchor*. Aza speaks with the whistle of wind. The river spoke with the gurgle and swish of water. These words are the patter of soil in a grave.

That one be—of the air—but you—in us.

"Who," I pant, "who you?"

There's the sound of field dirt being scraped into rows, being gathered to receive seed.

We.

I whimper and taste mud, tonguing grit in the seams of my cheeks.

We speak.

Blood on the wet raw of my gums.

Because you hear.

"Who y'all," I say, swallowing and coughing.

We—we take all. Bones of the large and small. Chitinous wings, paper-thin backs. Filaments from a tree's heart. Roots sunk to seek water. Wisps of streams. Burnt leaves. Bald moss. Most desiccated. We take all.

"Why me?"

Rocks blunting each other, edge against edge.

You came. A sharp crack. *We take.*

My legs burn from standing, sore from the long hours of work to prepare for the husband's arrival. I squeeze my head between two of the stakes, rest it against the cool soil.

"I can't breathe," I pant.

Fecund dirt presses against me in the close dark.

You offer. You gave the blood of your feet to the riverbed.

The scent so strong it reaches down in my chest, pushes inside me, insists on my inhale, my exhale.

Your toes fed us over the long walk.

I grab stakes with both hands and start to pull, but there is not enough room to maneuver. When I yank harder, twisting with my whole body, the wooden knives jab me in my back, but I feel a little give, so I keep pulling.

Even now, you feed us, they say.

I jerk and wrench.

Blood. Sweat. Tears.

The mud sighs.

So many of you, over the long earth, offering. From the teeth of our old mountains to the belly of our plains. From the lashes of our bays and inlets to the fingers of our deserts, the toes of our swamps.

"No," I say. "I ain't offering nothing."

I half crouch in the all-dark.

We take—clumps of dirt patter my arms—*to birth. We thought you were a hare, but you are yet a rabbit. Born blind.* I pull again. *In this burrow.*

Clay slides down my back.

"You a grave," I huff. "Mama Aza and Mama and Safi and me, we ain't give freely. Yet you"—I yank, and one of the stakes stabs me in the back of my thigh—"still take."

I wrench out one of the shanks of wood. I drop it and work at another. Hope I can pull enough wood from the walls to clear a space to sit, my knees to my chest, and rest. The earth rumbles, silt sliding to loam sliding against rock. My coffin shakes.

We transmute. We take corpse and piss and blood and break it and break it and break it and press it to its smallest self.

"Y'all greedy: you and Aza and the river and She Who Remembers. All y'all do is take. Y'all don't give nothing." I'm shaking, voice a grated whisper.

Be still, the ground grumbles. *We embrace until the offering bears seed in our body, and then, it bears itself. We eat to transform. You become stone and trunk, sap and grub. Mushroom and pollen. Dust rises, and after many turns, we let you go into the darkness. And turn and turn and turn after and beyond, your hair and skin and blood burn to a star.*

I half hang, half twist on one of the stakes, and it slides from the earth like a knife through warm butter.

She that you call Aza, she rush and blow.

I drop.

That is one who never gives, the earth says.

I wrench at another stabbing piece of wood.

That one take and eat and bathe in offering, fool you into thinking that storm means water, means life, but it does not. We devour but we bestow.

The stake I am wrestling with slips, and then another drops without my pulling at it.

They drop from the wall on their own, splattering like hard rain.

You worship wind, the earth says. *But we give.*

I stand with my hands bunched to my sides, clutching the last stake I yanked from the soil, a heap of fallen wood at my feet. The earth, They Who Take and Give, has rendered them to me.

Be still. The last of the stakes around me give, and I fall against the wall and slide down, loose and burning. *You may be blind and wet and red, little one.*

The floor of the coffin begins to undulate in waves, and I yelp. The earth swallows each fallen stake and pushes up sand soft as a pillow before firming again.

You may be raw to the world, They Who Take and Give say, a rustle of worms through mulch. *Some rabbits build in bad ground. They burrow in loose sand. Their litters smother when the caverns collapse.*

My body is a cluster of bruises, from ankle to head.

But you the one who snuffles. Smells. Wiggles. You the little one who jerks to a crawl. The little one who breaches the dirt and breathes. Your littermates still and stop breathing, their parts becoming down, scilla, smoke.

I curl to a slump in the sandy dirt.

But you, you would fight your way to the surface.

This grave: my bed.

And when you found your way out, you would lick the soil from your paws.

And me with no mother in this burrow.

Swallow it, little one, and then bear it again.

I swipe at the blood on my face, then give up and lay my head against the wall. The earth bathes me in the musk of mushrooms and the wilting flower of worm castings. Through the wood of the bars and the stakes still bristling around the door: stars.

You of us, They say.

They fold me in their hands, their arms, their laps.

You of us.

CHAPTER 8

Salt and Smoke Offerings

When the hands pull me from the earth, I am striped with red blood and clay, and drowsy as an oak-leaf rattler roused from a deep winter nest. They drag me down the wagon path, around the outbuildings, through the insect-studded evening to the house because my legs buckle beneath me and will not stand. For days I called to Aza and begged for rain, but she gave nothing, and no one poured water down the grate. They throw me on the pantry floor, and I roll to my side, trying to open my eyes, to be fully awake from the sleepy stupor I sank into, but I cannot. I struggle, counting the seconds by the clanging of Cora's spoons against the pots, but the sound of her work and the smell of pork fat from her stove is not enough to pull me back to the waking, upper world. The earth has me still. I sink back down into the dream of the hole.

When I was in the hand of the earth, I rose, slipped through the door, and ascended into the air. The smell of smoke enveloped my body. I was over the plantation: high, high up, looking down. The people enslaved by the lady were stripped bare, bending in the fields, the house, the sugar refinery, the barns and outhouses and sheds. They bent and gave, bent and gave, yielding to the earth, shedding flakes of skin, rivulets of sweat, blood from nicks and gashes, vomit from their mouths to the earth.

Kindling, I thought, *ripe for burning*.

Be still, They Who Take and Give said, and I looked down on those who toiled again.

As I hovered over the fields in the dream, all-seeing as Aza, I saw that despair wittled away at those who crawled through the cane and through the hive of the house. But I also saw a vein of green running through the center of every man, woman, and child: a vein that would push its way to blossom. A vein my bees would know for the verdant hope of honey. I wondered if this was why the earth told to me be still, wondered if They Who Take and Give wanted me to understand this: my people could take all that bedevils them and use it to cement seams, to sow and reap, to armor themselves in fat so they could resist, hope bristling in the coils of their hair, in the sable dark of their skin. Their hearts buzz in a great whisper: my people singing in the fields. Is this what Aza meant when she spoke of my people rising?

I curl into my knees on the cellar floor, dreaming, and swallow ashes.

• • •

MARY WAKES ME IN the morning: a hesitant touch to the middle of my back. I roll away from it, covering my face in my hands. All the broken pieces of me, crusted rust red and purple with ache. I feel every bruise, every cut, every wrenched muscle today: residue of my offerings to the spirits of this earth.

"The lady ordering everyone to the cane," Esther whispers. "We clearing the fields."

I lurch up on an elbow and stumble to standing. I am shaking all over as I tie my skirt tight. I am hollow with hunger. After the walk south, I thought the river of jarring steps had etched me to nothing, but now, in this place, I find that there is more to lose to the lady, to the house, to the fields. From the line of my thigh to the cave of my belly to the indents between my ribs to the spoon at the bottom of the head, the back of the neck: this place is paring what little was left of me. Safi loved my legs: sometimes when we walked into the woods, she would crouch midstride and caress the backs of my thighs, the dimples of my knees, down to the lines of my calves. *Look at you*, she would say, grinning. *Look*. My skirt swings against my legs, and they are thin, thin as fallen branches under a sheet of water. She will hardly know me—if I ever see her again, Safi will hardly know me.

Sorrow turns its face up to my throat and chokes.

I don't want to be blind anymore. I don't want to be a baby hare scratching lost at the earth. *See*, They Who Take and Give said. I will see. I hobble to the kitchen and grab a pair of shears from a table before lurching out the door. Mary and Esther run after me, holding each other's fingertips.

"Annis?" Esther asks.

The shadow of the house is icy, like being dipped in cool water. My hair has grown long, coils like rope over my shoulder and down my back. There are small bits in the back that have taken to matting. I grab a great chunk as I trip and run, and I saw. As I sprint away from the big house and the outbuildings, I grab hank after hank of my hair, part linen here, part silk here, a puff of cotton at the crown, and I cut.

"Annis?" Esther asks again as she and Mary trot at my elbow.

"I have to offer," I say.

I grab all my chopped hair, every fine, spiderweb-thin strand, and I trip through a stand of trees and past the cabins, row after row of them, to where the forest begins. It is a long, uneven jog. Every other searing breath, I have to save my weak legs from tripping. I ignore Esther's entreaties, but she and Mary follow anyway. The forest bows, jungle thick, over me. I kick to a stop and search until I find a cypress, tall and heavy with seed. Its bristles are beginning to brown like the trees where I come from, heralding the approach of autumn. I dig in the dirt with my hands. The soil is rich here, and soft, and I cup worms and bugs and feathery cypress needles rotting black, and throw them over my shoulder. I dig a bowl so deep my arm almost disappears up to my elbow.

"What you doing?" Esther says. She and Mary squat behind me.

Mary sighs.

"You going to have to do plenty of that in the fields," Esther says.

I put my hair in the bottom of the hole.

"I'm offering," I say.

"To what?" Esther asks.

"To remember," I say.

You take, I tell the earth. *You give. Take this and give. I need to see more. Show me more.*

Two memories come to me from the black mulch in the seams of my fingers, from the rot under my fingernails. The first blooms in my head, ripe and redolent: Once, when I was very young, a tall man courted my mother. When he sang, his voice carried over the fields, over the woods, all the way up to the house, running like a river from his mouth. After a night of hunting, he left a bloody gift for her before our cabin door: a heart, wrapped in burlap. My mother breathed quick when she saw it and let a little smile hook her face. She bought me to the clearing, started a little smoky fire, and roasted it. I do not remember what the heart tasted like, only that it was chewy like any muscle. But I do remember how when she cut it in two, its chambers bisected, it looked beautiful: a red honeycomb. I knew that the man had wanted to feed my mother rich, chewy food to tell her of his own hunger, that thing that went gaping when she pulled away from him, flinch after flinch, in the worn paths of the quarters. How my mother would walk at least an arm's length away from the man, never trusting the hand of the world enough to settle into that courting man. What rent them apart was when he told her she was making a helpless babe of me when I fell and skinned my leg and she comforted me. He told her she was too tender. She looked up at him and rumbled one word: *Get.* Her breath fast, shallow.

The second memory is less a flowering than a piecing together, a sewing of one moment of time to another. This happened after the courting man showed my mother he couldn't protect the both of us, after he showed my mama she had to seek safety for me and her on her own. I was small in this memory, small enough for her to hold in her arms, for me to rest my chin on her shoulder as she jogged.

Mama, I said.

Hold on, baby, Mama said. *Hold on.*

"Annis?" Esther disrupts my dreaming.

"Hold on," I say, grasping at the next patch of memory, but nothing comes. "Hold on," I say, but I don't know if I'm saying it to Esther or to the earth. "Please," I whisper. What remains of my chopped hair falls over my eyes, over my face, to brush the bottom of my chin. I offered to the earth. "Please," I say.

I put my forehead to the roots of the tree and beg, and They Who Take and Give accept. The scrap of memory comes. I grab on to the thread of it and swallow, and the memory of what happened all those years ago up north tastes like salt, like tears. My mama was tall, and I was a round-legged, soft-tummied child. My mama was running. She carried me for such a long time—on her back, on her hip, clutched in front of her—but after days and nights passed, she put me down. Her grip on my wrist was desperate, and I tried to keep up with her jog, but she dragged me through the dirt as we ran through one evening.

Run, little one, she said. *Run.*

Aʒa, Mama called to the sky. *Aʒa, which way?*

Far off, we heard the hiccupping loop of the hunting dogs. My mama pulled my arm so hard it felt like a great bruising in my socket. We were sprinting as fast as we could.

Yes, They Who Take and Give say. *You have offered. Now see.*

The memory fills my world, blots out Mary and Esther. My mother and I had been running for days. Mama kept saying: *When we get to the swamp, the Great Swamp*, carrying me for miles and then, when she was too tired, begging me to run. The rain seemed to follow us, and the wind of the storm was a driving and drenching cold. Mama asked the wind, *Aʒa, Aʒa*, again and again, *Aʒa*, she asked, *which way*. Aza didn't answer until she did: the dogs' whooping was getting closer, and my mother swung me up to her chest, clutching me to her. Aza said: *Down through that valley beyond, many days hence.* How the spirit's voice wrapped around me and my mama. How it came from everywhere in the dark. My mother tripped along with me in her arms. *Too far*, Aza said, and then my mother and I fell tumbling down a hill to lie, bloody and bruised, where we looked up and saw men with lanterns and dogs leaping down toward us.

Remember, They Who Take and Give say.

"I remember," I say.

We ran. My mother called Aza. We fell. Through a curtain of blood, I saw my mother punch and kick the slave patrollers' dogs, fight them so they couldn't savage me. My head throbbed and throbbed. I fainted at the bottom of that hill to my mother half screaming, half growling, wrestling with the dogs. When I woke up, we were back at my sire's place, back in the cabin with Nan, who only had one child then. I woke up and crept outdoors into the dawn, but my mother was not there. She was gone, gone for days, and when she came back to our cabin, she was swollen and broken in some places I could see and other places I couldn't. There was so much blood, so much terror, that I had forgotten; I didn't remember. *Remember*, the earth says. I do. My mother ran to find safety for me and herself, and the slave patrollers caught her, and then my sire spent years punishing her until he sold her. He walked her ropeward and traded her to the Georgia Man, to this hell of a water-riven underworld. *Run, Annis*, Mama had screamed. *Run*, when they set them dogs on her, and she swung her arms and legs, using the only weapons she had. *I love you!* She cried out, even as the dogs buried their teeth in her and shook, one on her arm, another on her leg. *Aʐa!* she screamed.

"Annis?" Esther says.

I sob into the earth. I offer to They Who Take and Give until I'm a hollow gourd: dry of sorrow, spiked with the dregs of memory. The chorus of bugs that welcomed us to this place is dying to silence with the last kick of summer, so it is the rushing clack of leaves, empty of Aza's voice, that hushes me.

EVERY MAN, WOMAN, AND child who can walk is in the fields. Hundreds of us hunched over the earth, smelling the sharp bite of the cane, the fibrous weeds at the root, and the molder of manure. I follow Mary and Esther as they bend and hoe, grasp and pull. Some of the weeds are so tough they bite back when we yank at them, tearing into the skin of our hands. The sky grants us one mercy; clouds shield the sun and then hide it altogether so that the day cools to tepid laundry water, but my head and my hands crackle with pain, and my back clenches as I work down the rows of full-grown cane. Songs begin and die, wisp and drift away over the fields, dampened coals under the stares of the hands. One of the hands barks at two older men and a girl for weeding too slowly; the girl walks unevenly, one foot turned inward. I ignore the soft pulse of my heart, the thought that flashes through me to help her, to help them. It is only midmorning, but my stumbling from hunger and the fatigue from the hole have gotten worse. Even though I can see the trees at the horizon, how the jungle of the forest stops the cane, leans over it, intent on reclaiming the land, even though I rip evidence of it from the soil, the rows of sugarcane seem endless.

"Why you cut your hair like that today? And buried it?" Esther asks as she struggles with a deep-rooted weed.

I swipe dirt from my palms by brushing it along my skirt. It sounds like another whisper from the earth.

"I was trying to remember something about my mama." Esther wouldn't believe me if I told her about Aza, about the earth, about the rivers. "My hair was distracting me." I light on a lie. "And if cutting my hair make me more ugly to the husband, all the better."

Esther squats and points with her chin past a small cluster of cabins at the edge of the fields to the tangled forest that stretches far into the distance.

"At first I thought you was chopping off your hair to bring it to the border. That's the border," Esther says.

"What?" I say.

"Where you ran this morning. That's the border. But I couldn't understand what good hair would do there." She shrugs and digs. "I guess you could make rope out of it."

"Who could make rope?"

Esther yanks out a thorny weed by the roots. She wipes blood on her waistband.

"Folks who run."

I yank at my own plant.

"That's where some of them live, out there, on the border. In the forest but still close enough to trade and see family here."

The plant seems to pull back and then give, and I sit in the dirt, then kneel to a shaky stand.

"That's the place we leave food or clothes or tools for them. Out there."

I slide the weed in my sack.

"I thought that's why you ran that far, but then I realized you ain't had nobody run from here."

"People live in there?" I ask.

"Yes, in the wild all around us," Esther says.

I swallow, my tongue a water-swelled biscuit in my mouth, and recall the two memories I was given.

"Was a place up north called the Great Dismal Swamp. Word was that they had whole families, whole communities, living there," I say.

Esther shoves her roughage down in her sack.

"Got swamp all around here. Full of snakes and alligator and bear," she says.

Mary whistles to the steel-gray sky.

"Some people," Esther says. She speaks out the side of her mouth, under her breath. I can barely hear her under the shuffle of the people around us, the ripping of roots from the soil, the drag of sacks, the thud of feet. "My mama's mama came from a place called

Terre Gaillarde, south of here, in the swamp. It was strong land. Good land. They ran there and lived off that land. Turtles and fish and such."

The day is overcast, but we are sweating so much it is hard to breathe.

"You had to swim through water up to your neck to get there. It was in the middle of a marsh," Esther says.

The sky boils. I eye the rows, the lines of us weeding.

"But it was hard living. The people there was hungry. Had a man named St. Malo there. He was their leader; he got them tools and guns and bartered work from the plantations."

I won't look for Aza. I won't look for her gathering the sky in her skirts, spinning her way to thunder and threat, to rustle and blow.

"They was free. A kind of free. But the law found out; they called the cabildo. And you know the law couldn't let it stand, not a whole village of people that done run living in the swamp." Esther hoists her bag on her shoulder and steps through another row before squatting again. "And then St. Malo and his folks went to Mississippi to trade and killed a white man who threatened them." Esther shakes her head. "My grandmama said they knew it was foolish, but they figured that white man wanted to cut them down, so they did it before he could do it to them."

I'm sweating in the chill. Little threads of blood drying around my fingers from the pull, the wounds, the work.

"The law hunted them and found them in the swamp. My grandmama and them fought back, but they was all caught. The law burnt everything they built, and then they hung St. Malo. Some they tied up and branded a M on they cheeks, for *marron*. My grandmama and my mama wore that M on they faces for the rest of they lives. Some they lashed three hundred times. All them they didn't kill, they sent back to this." Esther stumbles at a patch of cleared dirt between the rows before bending again. "This a slower death, is all."

We moan. All us moan, and it carries up on the wind. This is a living dirge, building under the toss and swish of the trees. It rushes under the pain of our crawl through the reaching cane, through the fields, violent with growing. How it boils.

"Where you buried your hair? We leave corn took from animal feed. Machetes and knives. Bind chickens by the legs and tie them to trees. And them that done went away, that's out there in the swamps, they leave fish and coons and boar for us that ain't got the courage to join them yet. For us that can't leave babies or mamas. For us that fear what stalk the swamp more than what stalk the fields, or fear the cabildo that come root you out the swamp if enough of you gather in one place. If you dare live free," Esther says.

Esther rips a stubborn plant from the earth, one with roots long as a pitchfork. Her face twists like a wet rag bunched to dry. She fighting not to cry.

"My brother out there," she says. "He sneak and visit sometime."

Mary pats Esther once, a flutter of fingers on her back, fine as the brush of a crane's wing.

WE WEED UNTIL THE sun collects all the color from the day, and the night pours over the sky. After, we rinse the mud and grit and little bits of rubbery green from our faces and arms and hands before serving the woman who eats nothing and the man who eats more than his share. The man shivers through dinner, clanging his spoon and fork on the ceramic. As we clear and walk up- and downstairs for courses, Esther passes the lady's full plate to me, and I gulp the leftover food down so quickly I begin to hiccup. We strip the supper table, turn down their beds, clean and stack the grates with wood, and lay out clothing, the whole time exhaustion knotted like a fishing net to my middle, dragging me to my pallet in the pantry, but I cannot sleep. Instead, I wait until the others slumber and sneak outside the kitchen door, where I sit in the garden. The moon is high and blue and full. I wonder at those who have stolen themselves away, even here. I wonder at them wandering the swamp-ridden, waterborne wilderness. I hold my hand up, blot out the moon, let its beams slide through the web of my fingers. I am waiting for Aza: I whisper her name. This time she comes, trailing a cool breeze like a scarf. How easily she comes and goes in this world. She stops before me, muting the moon.

"Yes," Aza says.

The dark in the moon makes pictures: a rabbit, a fish, an elephant.

"Why didn't you come before?" I ask.

Aza circles her winds.

"I did not hear," she says.

"They buried me," I say. "I called."

"The earth," she sighs, "enclosed you. Hid you. For themselves."

Aza sinks and the moon is clear again, and I figure the stories are wrong. There are no animals on that silver orb. That's water. Those are seas, dark seas flowing one to another by thin rivers, all the way from here, from the earth. Maybe it's the Water Aza talked about, the Water between us all, the Water that connects us. I wonder if that Water sometimes drowns.

"Esther told me they got people out there." I look down and back up at Aza, her eyes dark as storm clouds. "People who ran. People who live in the swamps."

"Yes," she says. A chitter of lightning over one of her shoulders, down into her skirts.

Aza stills. All of her calms: her, a great eye.

"You didn't tell me the truth," I say. "It wasn't Mama losing Mama Aza that made her turn from you." I brush my shorn hair away from my eyes. "It probably didn't make her care for you anymore, but that wasn't what did it. You was supposed to get us to the swamp."

Everything is silent. The trees arc over us, relieved at the absence of the toss and boss of Aza's wind.

"Your mother asked the impossible," Aza says. "You could barely run. That swamp was miles and miles away, over great distances."

Their limbs reach up, up to the moon and her seas. They reach toward the Water.

"She was doomed. I knew when she asked," Aza says, listing side to side.

"You got power," I say. "More power than Mama Aza or Mama or me. You could have done more."

I put my cut hands on my burning knees and stand, every bit of me, from the bulb of my head to the toes of my feet, grinding and resisting.

"My mama deserved sparing. I remember," I say, before I walk into the dark mouth of the house and shut the door behind me.

WE WEED FOR DAYS, but I cannot sleep. I spend my nights staring at the slats of the ceiling, thinking on my mama and how she ran. Recalling the wire of her arms, the way her breath sounded like a ragged groan. So I am awake when Aza slides, ribbon thin, into the pantry, a cool draft inches above the floor.

"Annis," she says.

I stare at Esther's back. The day has flattened her and Mary: they fell asleep as soon as we entered the storeroom. The floor is hard through my moss-stuffed sack. Bruises mottle my arms like dark leaves shaken loose by a scouring wind. Aza pools to a mist, laying like a cool blanket over me and the other women. Her touch chills me, gives me a little pleasure, and I hate it.

"There is much I would say to you."

I ignore her whisper.

"To explain."

I shut my eyes.

"It can be difficult to navigate this world. This place is glutted with people, with beings, with spirits. There are so many, here."

I rub my cheek into the sack; it still smells of the corn flour that filled it.

"We spirits are not bound to this world. We are of it, but we are not bound to it."

"I'm tired," I say to her, low and hushed, but pain clutches my shoulder and I remember the work we did today, and I know I ain't got to worry about waking the others. "Leave me be."

Aza's mist curdles.

"Listen." Her wind soothes. "Please, Annis."

I put my chin into my chest and see my mother, see the dimples marking the edge of her smile, see the dusting of moles high across her cheekbones, a smattering of stars there. Loss sizzles through me, lodges in my chest as her death circles afresh. How she would put her chin down, raise her eyebrows at me, and sweep her thumbs up my temples, and she would say to me, out of nowhere, in the bubble of a laugh or in the low sling of a tired moan: *You going to find a way, little one. I see it in you. You move like her. That way you swing your arms, the way you lean in when you run. Soon as you learned to walk, you moved like you knew how to fight.* How she would curve her hands around the V of my jaw. *You carry my whole mother in you. You going to find a way, Arese.* I don't like that I can imagine her, too, as she must have looked to Aza when she left her: a sickness eating up from her feet through her legs, her limping in another coffle of men and women bent to sorrow. I wonder how long she walked before she fell, if anyone knelt beside her and held her hand as she probably breathed her last in the dirt. I wonder if Aza felt pleasure in being able to abandon my mother in turn.

"I'm listening," I say, even though I have to speak over the sorrow lodged in my throat like a piece of dried and smoked meat.

"The place I came into being is a far place. It stretches from horizon to horizon. Under it all, the Water. Lined with silver, black blushed. I was a breath, first. A huff where there was none." My breathing frosts in Aza's shine. "The Water knew me," Aza says.

"What you mean it knew you?" I ask.

"I felt it," Aza says. "It was an embrace. Wafting up like a mist from the Water. Telling me I was part of it and it was part of me." Aza shimmers. "When you were a baby, your mother would watch you sleep, love for you so strong it was a draft in the room." I sniff. "Love so strong I felt it," Aza says. "That's what I felt from the Water."

She gathers her tendrils, folds her arms in a cotton fog.

"It gave me that regard. And then," she says, "when I knew who I was and where I was, it didn't. Just smoothed over to Water, all-reaching. Silent." Her mist gathers the burn from my bruises. "I blew and flew over its face. I thought if I blew, I could speak to it. Rouse it. Thought maybe it would speak back to me, show me that regard again. But there was only the Water and the darkness and lights far off. Other stars. Other worlds. I swept and blew, but the Water would not call back." Aza's lips darken, blacker than inky trees against a sky. "I grew small. Breezed to a sigh. I wanted to slow the rush of myself. To be still as that Water."

"Like a dying." I mean it to be a question, but I say it like a statement, like it's a fact I was born knowing. And in a way, I do: I know what it means to lie down with despair, to sink with it.

"Yes," Aza says. "But then I met one like me. Another wind. She bought me to the places where we gather. She danced. She taught me to spin, faster and faster, tighter and tighter. And I did what she bade, spinning to a storm, and when I did, I heard a murmuring, a snatch of a murmuring, and knew it for the Water's voice. There, but different."

Aza is shrinking dense.

"That little echo of the Water's voice when I spun to storm? It open a way to here, to this world, where I spun out over your oceans, your earth." Aza is condensing. "Here, there is so much regard, so many people looking up at me. So many calling for mercy."

Aza's touch is warming.

"I go back to the place I was born to blow over the Water, but it is still quiet. We wind spirits see it from the cliffs of our sheer cities, from our streets of fog, etch its story into rock. We spirits make noise. We gather in our birthplace and blanch the world with lightning. Our music: thunder. We dance. We spin, but after so long, we feel it again. The urge to return to your oceans, your land, to this place."

Aza is smaller now, smaller than I have ever seen her. If I reached out a hand to her, we could be sisters. Sometimes, when I am cleaning the mirrors ringed by candles in the house that stretches above us, I study myself: see my mother's eyes, my mother's hairline, the jut of her chin. Aza could be me now: slim, sylph arms, long neck.

"We want to be seen by you."

She is growing ever smaller. The room is growing hotter.

"It's a common hunger. All of us born from the Water, all of us wind and water and fire and earth and green spirits, even with our cities and our worlds and our ways, we all want to be seen by you."

Aza is as short as a child.

"We want your beseeching. We desire your songs. They echo of the Water, too."

She turns slowly, and a humid breeze blows through the room.

"I told your mother the way was far. That it would be nigh impossible to reach that Great Dismal Swamp with you." Aza's voice is quiet as a tear. "But I'd told her about what it was like to move through worlds, and she was intent on bringing you to a new one."

She tilts and spins faster.

"She should have trusted me."

Tendrils of Aza's hair ascend first, whipping away from her to disappear. The throbbing in my shoulder has turned to a searing ache.

"It hurt to fail your mother. She who tried to touch my face, sometime, who looked at me like I was the woman who bore her."

Aza's fingers, her forearms, her skirts, lift and vanish next, until only her wind-wreathed chest, her wind-blasted face, remain, until she spins so fast, she blurs.

"When I only took her form," she says.

The bottoms of my feet cramp all at once.

"The memory of your mother's regard . . ." Aza trails off, her voice a light patter of rain.

"She forsook me after," Aza says. "You going to forsake me, too?"

The last droplet of Aza evaporates. I put my nose into my thin blanket and breathe in the smell of old flour. I know what Aza doesn't say, could read it through her story. The trust she wants is a kind of worship, our dependence an offering, our regard a kind of love. She wants us to be her children. She wants to be our mother. And just as my mama turned from Aza for not giving her what she needed, Aza turned away from my mother, too.

• • •

THE VOICE IS A string, thin but strong, threading through the darkness, calling to the dawn, which walks toward us over the horizon. But when I open my eyes, it is still night. Someone is singing. Cora sleeps on her back, closest to the door. Esther is on her side, facing me, and Mary is behind her, propped up on an elbow. Esther's eyes are closed, and she moans, low and pained, in her sleep: it is Mary who sings. The sound coming from her mouth a honeyed hum, liquid and warm at the heart, crusted with sharp sugar crystals at the edges. How the notes rise and fall, sloughing on the nooks of her throat, her usually silent mouth, to sweeten the air, to make that which is unbearable, every waking, walking moment, weightless.

"Come, make lament: for poor St. Malo in distress," Mary sings. The moon is a half-shut pale eye through the small window, and for one breath, it seems to sway with her song, to shiver in the sky.

"They chased, they hunted him with dogs. They fired at him with a gun. They hauled him from the cypress swamp. His arms they tied behind his back," Mary sings. "They tied his hands in front of him; they tied him to a horse's tail. They dragged him up into the town. Before those grand cabildo men, they charged that he had made a plot to cut the throats of all the whites." Esther has stilled, Mary's song gentling her.

"They asked him who his comrades were: poor St. Malo said not a word. The judge his sentence read to him, and then they raised the gallows tree. They drew the horse—the cart moved off—and left St. Malo hanging there." Mary rubs her hand over Esther's hair, smoothing it to her scalp, and Esther rolls over onto her back and into Mary's chest. How the rumble of Mary's song must caress Esther's cheek. How I miss the tenderness of touch, the brush of those in this world: Safi's shoulder, Mama's palm.

"The sun was up an hour high, when on the levee he was hung."

The whisker kiss of my bees.

"They left his body swinging there," Mary murmurs.

My mother's grip on mine, the jarring jog. *Run, baby. Run.* I lay my head back on my sack, feel the push of the floor against my bruised bones, but Mary's song eases like Aza's cool fog.

"For carrion crows to feed upon," Mary intones, leaning down toward Esther and twining the word that began the song around Esther's face like a ribbon. "Come," Mary sings, and she places her hand over Esther's heart. "Come." I half expect Mary to get up, to pull Esther awake, to disappear from the innards of the house and out of the door, tugging Esther with her, away to the offering underbrush, the swaying swamp. Mary leans in close, so close to Esther, until she is mouthing the word against her cheek: a breathy plea, a command. "Come."

Mary sings the last of her song of St. Malo, the man who led some of us to other worlds. Her voice lingers in the air: the crust of pie around the edges of the pan, the pan that we scrape to savor in the hot corners of the kitchen, the buttery crumb rich in our mouths, but only enough to hint at the cinnamon, the nutmeg, the sugar we are sowing and watering and bludgeoning to green, to bristle skyward in the fields, the sugar one can smell, smell when leaning in close to the verdant stalk, rich in the fiber, and how the stomach feels full for a moment with a quick inhale, full and ragged, over leavings, so I do it now, breathe in deep to pull that leftover sweetness from the air down deep into me, to cull Mary's honeyed song from the darkness into me, so that for one blink in the bowels of this rotten house, tenderness is a touch in my bones.

CHAPTER 9

Burning Men

As summer slinks away and mornings cool, I half expect Mary and Esther to be gone when I open my eyes in the near dawn, but each morning they are still in their blankets, spooned together. Cora coaxes the stove to light, fanning and feeding the heat in its belly. I roll and slide my own blanket into our hiding space, and then I grab a handful of corn flour and bring it to cook. It is all we allow ourselves these tepid mornings of the descending autumn: just a handful of powder, a lick of water, a dab of fat, all to yield four thin flat corn cakes. A whisper of a meal to avoid the lady's accounting. Still, my mouth is wet as I squat next to the stove and wait for Esther and Mary to rise, and watch Cora, measuring and mixing for the food upstairs. She moves like a woman who knows this kitchen inch by pinch: flour, sugar, oil, and salt. Not one reach of an arm, not one step around the iron mouth heating in our midst, more than she needs.

"Coming up on harvest time," she says, half to me and half to herself. "It make the lady crazy, make her count every bean, every pea, in the garden. She act like ain't nothing to spare."

Cora hands me a dab of fat, nothing more than a shimmer, and I rub it over my knees, before sticking a finger in my mouth and sucking the idea of it: salt and smoke. Mary's voice sounded rich as that flavor.

"Mary sings," I say.

Cora drops a pot. She coughs into her apron and then shakes it straight. The skin on my legs stops its incessant itching for one moment. The oil on the griddle sizzles.

"Yes," Cora says.

I trace a circle on my greased kneecap.

"Her voice ain't like nothing I ever heard."

"She come here as a child, same season as Esther. Small, both of them, with little bellies and skinny knees. I snuck them food. Tried to put some meat on them, but the lady got hawkish eyes." The cakes smell buttery and salty, and my stomach drops, ravenous for one. "Ain't no abundance here."

I wrap my arms around my stomach and squeeze, hoping to ease the open mouth at the heart of me. Cramps skitter around my ribs, lance up my spine.

"When the lady walked them down here, she said Mary was simple. But I knew by the look of her that there was plenty more inside of her." She scoops one of the cakes out and hands it to me, and I toss it from hand to hand, blowing on it to cool it. It will have to last me the day.

"Most people can't see all the layers in a person, just like they can't taste all that goes into a pot. They chew and pick out one, two flavors. Cooks know every one."

There is a rustling from the storage room. Esther and Mary drift out of the dark, smoke thin, to crouch next to me, rubbing their arms and legs in the warmth from the oven with hard brushes. Cora ladles out the rest of the cakes, and all of us blow on the plates of our hands. I wait to take my first bite, cooled at the edges, but Mary eats her corn cake in great, hot gulps. Esther touches Mary's shoulder, and Mary stills for a moment before chewing slower, but the look on her is still ravenous.

"This cool air in the morning makes me hungry for my mother's squash," Cora says around a mouthful of silty cake. "We'd roast them in the ashes. They grew big as my head in Virginia, and they melted in the mouth like butter." Cora swallows. "My mama came to me last night. Cooked one and blew it cool for me. Watched me eat," Cora says, halfway done with her little cake. She digs her fingers into her jaw and takes a long blink, lost to memory.

"Some would say that mean something." Esther pinches a piece of corn cake and drops it in her mouth, as proper as the lady upstairs. Cora shrugs. She doesn't blow on her cake, even though it is steaming; instead, she watches the steam waft and disappear. My oiled knees begin to ache, but still I crouch and know the luxury of stillness. I count it with my breath, in and out. Resigned, Cora eats the rest of her meal in three big gulps as Mary and Esther stand and grab buckets.

"I could taste it in my sleep," Cora says. "Clear as this cake."

I stand and shoulder my own bucket.

"I wish she would have said something," Cora sighs. We leave her like that, standing before the stove, placing every bit of meal, every fat, every vegetable, just so. Her and the stove talking to each other. Her eyes still far away, tracing the dregs of a dream.

WHEN WE COME BACK from collecting water, Cora is setting a bunch of biscuits to cool, but she fumbles the pan she is holding when she sees us. A pot of water boils on the stove.

"The man has a fever," she says. "He done got sick everywhere. The lady say she need linens, hot water, vinegar, and brown paper." I've avoided him since the hole, run from him and her. I've looked only at my hands or feet, never up to their faces. *Breathe*, I think, *breathe*, as I walk up the stairs with fabric draped over my arm, a bottle of vinegar in one hand. I'm shaking, and the vinegar sloshes. I wonder if Mama Aza's hands shook, too, the first time one of the other wives handed her a weapon, a real weapon, on the hunt. I breathe like Mama taught me, let my grip slack on everything I hold; this a different fight.

The blind mother waits in the hallway outside the room.

"I can smell it," she mutters, to no one.

There is no breath in the couple's bedroom. It is hot and close from the fire that burns in the hearth. The man is rocking in the bed. He is shaking so hard the bedding bunches around him: he is a tunneling worm, shifting the earth above him. He mumbles, asking for warmth: "More heat."

"Yes, my love," the lady says, "we will sweat it out of you," and then she tells Esther to put more wood in the hearth.

"Yes, ma'am," Esther says as she bends. The woman takes the vinegar from me, holds it in her thin, pale hand, and sloshes the liquid over the brown paper before placing it on his head, gingerly. She hovers. He gags, and she calls for the chamber pot, which sloshes with sour. I hold it underneath him as he empties his insides into it, and the smell is sharp and strong, so pungent I hold my breath until my lungs spasm to avoid the stench of him and of her doctoring.

"You," the lady says, yanking the pot from me. "You said you know herbs. You find something to help him, you hear me? Go," she says. The man's sickness spills over her clawed hand, white with her horror, with her disbelief, all of it plain as any story in her wide eyes, deep black in the middle, her mouth, slack and open, teeth a jumble of knives thrown into dishwater for cleaning. "Please," she says, and it is light as a breath, but when she looks at me, looks at Esther, looks at all of us, for that one exhale, she sees us, plain people, standing there. In her bewilderment, in her terror, she sees.

"And you: send for the doctor." The lady nods at Esther before passing the bucket to Mary, whose arms are full of slimy cloth and soap.

"Esther," the lady says.

Something in Esther balks. It sticks her to the spot, the hard wooden floor. In Esther's refusal, there is another moment I imagine so clearly I see flashes of it: the voracious blond husband, in days past, risen from his slumber, broad chested, red cheeked. I envision him as clearly as I see Aza, as I hear They Who Take and Give. In the vision, the man corners Esther, bends Esther, muffles her mouth, bears her to the floor, and digs into her soft parts.

Esther has not told me this, but I know that this memory makes Esther stick and stare at the lady. Know it is this memory that makes Esther look like she might walk down the stairs, through the bowels of the house, past Cora in the kitchen, and instead of sending one of the hands for a doctor, she would walk and walk until she found her brother, somewhere out in the great green spread of the swampy borderlands.

"Go," the lady says. I wonder what she knows of Esther's experience, whether she has read it in the hang of Esther's shoulders, the set of her mouth, or if in this, too, she has blinded herself. Esther turns from the burrowing, sweating man, the panicked lady, and I follow her down to the kitchen. She stands for a moment in the doorway leading out to the garden, head bowed, eyes closed. I leave her and go to the woods, to find medicine for the man's fever. I hold that thought of Esther's close to me as I bend into the shadows in the underbrush, half wondering how I seen it, but half knowing, too.

This is why Aza said the women of my line sing. This is why she says we are special. We whistle; we regard. *See*, the earth said. All our lives been an offering, and this seeing is what's been given back.

JUST AS THERE ARE mushrooms that grow on trees, there are mushrooms that sprout from insects. Mama said it was one of the most surprising things Mama Aza taught her. These mushrooms are small specks in the air, light and tiny as dust, and they float until they land on a bug or the worm of a bug. If the insect is alive, they kill it, and they send flowering stalks into the air. Sometimes they arise from dead moths in long, pale trunks with little yellow buds at the end. Sometimes the mushrooms rise from the bodies of beetles in fluffy cotton clouds, dense and ivory. Sometimes the mushrooms rise from moth caterpillars in tiny ghostly trees with yellow limbs and white branches as thin as yarn.

I sink to the dead leaves. They Who Take and Give whisper just below my knees. I breathe in the pepper of decay, the rooted, moss-crushed scent of earth, and look for orange. *Orange club.* It grows from moth worms and looks like a club stained orange-red with rusted blood. It will work to heal the blood, to cure cough and weakness, to bring a person back to health after a long sickness. Collect it with the whole body of the husk of the moth worm and give it to the ill. It will cut the wheeze from them, get them walking again.

But there is another orange mushroom, and this one grows from wood. It is flatter, circular, looks wrinkled and wet as a bull's nose. This one does not make the ill healthy: this one makes the healthy ill. This one swims through the body, licking its fingers, pinching every wick, darkening every candle, every burning part: that which sees, that which hears, that which breathes. Both these mushrooms grow in the wood, in the rot. I wonder if Aza knows about these small offerings, these tissue carcasses, these paper wings, these whispers of animals that once crawled, once flew, these leaves that once swung fat and twisted from stems. I hunt on my knees, my hands, my face close to the dirt. The clouds are heavy in the air, but the rising light and heat as the cane fattens to October harvest tells me the day has fanned itself across the sky. I know the lady is waiting.

"What I'm going to bring her?" I ask the chipped brown leaves. I search through the flat, full brightness of the day. I find dead-man's-fingers, good for sleep. They reach up out of the earth, clustered in a black-purple hand: a man resisting offering, a man scrambling his way back to the living. I find pecan mushrooms at the bottom of an oak tree, and I dig them up and brush the soil from them before dropping them down my blouse, where they rest in the soft concave of my belly. They tickle me, feel almost like a caress. My mother would lean in close and smell them when we found them, say: *These a gift, Arese.* And then she would dig, jabbing the ground, and find more until we had handfuls, both of our shirts stuffed tight: enough to feed us and Nan and her children. I grab a stick; it breaks, moss eaten, turns to dust in my hands, so I find another and dig more, dig until I have a clumped band of mushrooms ringing my waist, climbing up to rest at the bottom of my breastbone.

I find the health-giving orange club first. The body of the moth worm at its root is half black, half purple, overlain with white hairs where its flesh has turned to rock. I put it in the waistband of my skirt, sliding it into the pocket between my skin and the cloth, and it lodges there. Strings of mosquitoes drift through the gloom under the trees, settling on my shoulders, around my neck, bringing red beads. I find its cousin, the deadly orange cap, as the sun fills the sky. The orange cap is one of five, and they rise out of the earth like another hand, this one with brunt, broad fingers; this one intent on grabbing what is living and pulling it below. I gather them and wonder at how my hands look even more like my mother's, after this journey to this place, after this time of starving. Sorrow falls like a fine rain. I scrub my fingers against my skirt, marvel at myself, kneeling in the lengthening shadows. How am I with none of the people I belong to? How am I here, life on one hip, death on another?

"Which," I ask the air, "which one?" My voice wending its way through the dusk makes me feel less alone.

Somewhere, my bees fly in this same sky.

"Which one," I ask. One of the damned in the Italian's journey to hell said this: *But please, now reach your hand to me down here. Open my eyes for me.*

"Open my eyes for me," I say.

Somewhere, Safi breathes under this same sky.

"Safi," I ask, "which one."

I can nearly see her, somewhere, cloud haired, long necked, standing in a clearing, like this, under a closing palm of oak and pine. I can almost see her there, turning to me, grinning with one side of her mouth.

"Mama," I ask, "which one."

My mother, who marched to New Orleans, who limped off and died. She could be here, invisible. Even if her spirit ain't, her eyelash could be in this stem, her soft brown eye in this bird's wing, the velvet skin of her inner arm in this pillar of light.

"Which one?" I say.

Above the trees, I hear the cut of a great fan through the air, a steady cleaving, then a faint honk, and another, until a V of migrating birds flies into view, their heads pale cream, their beaks pitch, the undersides of their wings a sable black: the moon in eclipse. I imagine it is warm there, where the feathers of their wings meet the down of their bellies. I wonder if they feel the pull of the South in their bones. One lags. She flies a little slower, her wingbeats un-measured, haphazard. Her honk is the last to sound before she dis-appears over the trees.

"Yes," I say, and I crouch again to look for another moth worm. My knees pulse with the hours.

The leaf-choked, needle-spiked ground hides so much. I search with my hands, sifting. When I look up, the sun has spilled in the West, spread yolk yellow through the forks of the trees. I've wandered. The wood is thick here, tangled with vines, with un-derbrush, with animals working to find their way to food, look-ing for the same mushrooms I am, for acorns, for shelter from the winter they know drifts toward them. The mushrooms in my shirt are warm and silky. I tuck them tighter and walk on until I see a bundle of broad, green, waxy leaves, wrapped around something. I done wandered further than I thought, all the way into the wild, beyond the wide spread of the plantation, into the stretches of what Esther called the borderlands. I unwrap a corner of the leaves and find pink flesh, white at the joints. There are five rabbits, splayed like a bunch of flowers. Somebody has washed them, dunked them in a river, maybe. They smell like innards and musk, and under that, a little sweetness.

"I cleaned them."

A half man stands in the shadows. He is tall like all the men on the plantation, all the men who bend in the fields.

"I cut the stomach. Didn't want to."

I step back, away from the flower of meat and leaves. The man raises a hand.

"Please," he says. "My sister works in the house."

I step back again. Fear scurries down my spine, hot and quick. If I run in the next breath, I can sprint faster than him, out of the woods, back to the lady and the burning man. From unknown danger to known.

"Esther," he says. I stop midturn to look at him. He is a whole man now, in the last dregs of light.

"I don't mean you no harm," he says.

"I don't know that, or you," I say.

"Can you carry those to Esther?" he asks. "I know she hungry."

"How you know?"

The man laughs, a low, rolling sound. It comes from the bottom of him, and it lifts nothing. I can see Esther in him, in the straight line of his nose, and something about the stretch of his lips is Esther's. He's slim as her, but the tendons don't show in his neck like hers, and his cheeks aren't as hollow. He's not starving. He's finding food in the borderlands. If he was eating better, he would be even bigger, even thicker in the neck and across his chest.

"I was there, and then I wasn't. I took myself away."

"Esther told me about you. Say you live in the swamp."

The man shrugs. The dying orange light catches in the hollow of his neck, his forehead, and he shines, pecan glazed.

"She say she scared," I say.

I step toward him, wrap my arms around the mushrooms in my waistband. The man nods, but he doesn't move. He shows me his palms, shows me he has no weapon, but I don't move closer.

"Esther say that, but when we was little, she wasn't scared of nothing. Used to stomp and hiss at alligators, pretending she could talk to them. Got us chased by one, once, and her laughing the whole time."

"Esther?"

"Yes," he says. "It ain't the swamp she afraid of."

He turns his head to the side like a crane and smiles a little. He looks so much like Esther that I step forward and catch myself, digging my feet into the roots, the pine needles, the rotting leaves.

"You having a little one?"

"No," I say. "These mushrooms."

"You got to be careful. Got poisons in some."

I balance on my toes. He ain't smiling no more. He's frowning, looking at my stomach.

"Lot of us got sick from eating some. Made one of the women see things that wasn't there."

A bird chirps. The air shines like honey.

"How you know what she saw wasn't there?" I tuck my shirt tighter into my skirt. "I know good eating and not. My mama taught me, and her mama taught her."

The man's eyelashes are so long they bristle gold. He flashes Esther's smile again, and his cheeks dimple; his jaw is as sharp as an anvil.

"I don't mean no offense."

There's a hot whirling, dense as Aza, behind my breastbone. I look away from his eyelashes, his neck, but the whirling stays.

"Harvest coming soon. Tell Esther to be careful of her hands. To watch." I nod. "You too," he says, and then laughs: "What's your name."

"I got to go," I say. "I been gone a long while." I pick up the rabbits and wrap them tighter in the broad, glossy leaves. The bundle is light. I feel behind me with one foot, then another, walking backward. Esther's brother's eyes are black and soft, as black as his hair that curls up and away from his head: purple clouds in a heavy sky. The whirling in my chest clenches, and I stumble. The man tilts his head the other way. "Annis," I say. "Call me Annis."

"Careful," he says, and one big hand reaches up like he would catch me.

I turn and run.

• • •

THE UPPER FLOORS OF the house are dark. When I slip into the bottom, the hallways are chill, and the air raises the hair on my head, my neck, my arms. But the hole of a kitchen is damp and warm.

"She came down here, asking after you," Cora says.

"She sent me to gather," I say.

"What for?"

"Medicines," I say. I put the rabbit on the counter and then untuck my shirt from my skirts and release the mushrooms we will eat, those that taste of gravy and butter when cooked.

"The rabbits from Esther's brother. And I found these," I say.

Cora makes a small sound in her throat and rubs her hands down her apron.

"How did you find them?"

"My mama taught me," I say.

Cora brushes her finger across one cap, flaking off the dirt, before licking a fingertip.

"Leave me a handful and hide the rest," she says, "behind the shelves in the storeroom."

"Esther and Mary still up there? He ain't no better?"

"They still there. I don't know. The lady look panicked." Cora grabs the next mushroom and sniffs it. "You think you can find more?"

I nod. From my waistband, I pull an orange club.

"This for him," I say. "The man. I got two to cut and let simmer. Can you give me something for them?"

Cora pours water into a little pot. The knife she gives me is sharp, as long as my palm, and dull gray. Her grip on her knife is light and loose, but I can tell by the way she hands me the blade, the little tilt of her head, the way she watches me like I might run off with it, that she is careful about every tool in the kitchen, that she is aware of how each sharp object might turn on her. I rinse and cut the healing orange club, drop it into the pot, and watch it roil to a boil while Cora sautés lard and mushrooms. My stomach clenches at the smell: sweet, savory soil. I move the mushroom tonic to a cooler rack of the stove and let it steep; I wait until the water darkens and then pour it through a sieve, and then I divide it: half in one rough cup, half in one of the lady's fine. I take the rest of the eating mushrooms and wrap them in a sack before sliding them behind the blankets that make up our pallets. When I come back to the stove, I take the rough cup and swallow a big, bitter gulp.

"Here," I tell Cora. "Sip."

Cora takes the cup but doesn't drink.

"For strength," I say, looking at the shallows beneath her eyes, the stretch of her skin. Even she is thinner than she was when I first came. "Go on."

She stirs and sips, and her face puckers.

"I could have spared some honey," Cora says.

"Naw," I say. "You got to know the taste of what heals you."

Esther backs into the kitchen, a pile of soiled cloth balanced on her chest. She waves me away when I reach out to her.

"You had yellow fever?" she asks.

"I don't think so," I say.

"You unacclimated. They think we can't get it, but we can. Me and Mary done had it."

"I ain't," says Cora.

"My mama had it," Esther says. "It killed her. The man hurting all over and feeling cold and getting sick—that's what it was like for my mama. You found something?" she asks me.

"Yes," I say. "A mushroom good for helping you heal after long sickness. But you can't tell her it's a mushroom; she think I only know herbs."

"She been asking after you. If she ain't need the help, she probably would have sent one of us after you."

I hold out the cup Cora and I have drunk from, and Esther sips.

"You and Cora drink the rest," Esther says. She disappears and returns with a stack of sharp-folded cream linens we sweated over for hours in the laundry. "Cover your nose and mouth," she says before handing me an armful. "Come."

I take a deeper sip of the orange club tonic before setting it on the counter for Cora and tying a scrap of fabric across my nose, under my eyes. I grab the linens and the cup I've prepared for the man and follow Esther. We ascend the steps slowly, me careful not to spill the medicine, and Esther plodding, exhaustion written in every bit of her: the slope of her shoulders, the knots of her spine, the loose string of her legs.

"I saw your brother," I whisper.

"Where?" she says.

"Out in the woods. He had rabbit for you."

"Bastian?" she asks over her shoulder.

"He asked after you. Talked about wanting to take you away."

Esther sighs, and the stairs echo her in creaks.

"I found more mushrooms. Good for eating," I say.

Esther stops outside the man's room, and it's only then that I see she was crying while we were walking. I know some of why she cries silently, just a dripping of water from her eyes: know it's because she's tired, mired in the drag of work and hunger and uneasy, slipshod sleep, in the days coming and going bearing more of the unbearable same, and her with only Mary to cling to, Mary who will not speak but sings. I bump Esther with my hip, and she sniffs.

"We eat tonight, Esther."

She nods and gathers herself upright: a needle pushed through cloth in a clean dotted line, pulled tight to cinch a band.

"Yes," Esther says.

It's not until we are in the room that I realize the other orange bit, the bit that holds poison in the little waxy rooms of its heart, is still in my skirt. I set the linens down on a settee in the corner of the room, outside the wash of the fire. I could do it. I could pinch a bite of orange out and drop it in his cup and let it steep to bitterness: I could finish what the yellow fever hasn't. The man moans. I stand there, the room loud with crackling. I am still because I know making that choice would lead to some other vengeance: some brand on my cheek, some metal shackles on my ankles, rope around my neck and my legs kicked asunder.

The lady, her face narrow and glazed, grabs the cup. The tonic sloshes over her hand, runs down her fingers to the floor. She steps in it and slaps me so hard the mask falls to my jaw. She hurries to her husband, and I retie the scrap of fabric tight over my burning cheek, my throbbing nose. The blond man is on the floor, on his hands and knees, moaning into his forearms. She sinks to him and murmurs, putting the cup to his lips. He won't drink. He rubs his forehead into the floor. The lady wrestles him onto his back, and we hold him down so she can feed him the tonic, which, in the end, is only a dribble. The room smells of smoke and soot and vomit, and his skin is hot.

We hold him until his moans slow. We hold him until he is silent and still and pale, and then we fumble him into their bed and pull the covers up to his neck. The lady wets and folds a fresh compress and leans into him, murmuring again, chirping, her mopping soft and hesitant. How quickly her hands turned to talons, how swift her strike that would drain my face to numbness. The lady's violence washed all my feeling away. We mop. We gather the vomit-soiled, the blood-wet, the vinegar-soaked. When we leave the woman and man to their murmurings and moans, I feel again: a prickly wave of hate. I wish I had given it to her, the other orange club, so he could have drunk it from her hand. So she, not knowing, could have killed what she loved.

IT IS ONLY AFTER the little bird has collapsed to sleep in her husband's room, with him breathing shallow and wet, that we go down to the kitchen to eat. The sun has been gone for hours, and all of us are tired. The wood is damp and cold when I fetch it for the fire, and Cora fusses with it before finally getting it to blaze. We sit in a row against the wall while Cora cooks. She roasts and braises the rabbit until the meat is brown, glazed, and dripping, and then she tosses the mushrooms with the game. It sizzles and I swallow, again and again, in anticipation. When she spoons the meal onto plates, my share of meat is half the size of my fist, but the mushrooms make up a whole hand. Cora cooked only one rabbit; the rest she salted and set to smoke so we can eat of it piecemeal during the winter, after the harvest in October, in the short hungry days. The food smells of the lard it was cooked in, and when I lick my fingers, it tastes of salt. Tears spark in my chest, rush up my throat, but I blink them back. I have never, never felt so hungry, never felt so much relief at knowing the grinding spike of starvation in my stomach will soon still, will soon be eased. I pluck the rivets of meat one from the other.

"You think he'll heal?" Esther asks.

The meat in my mouth tastes of wild onions and water-thick grass eaten at dusk. I shrug.

"Sometimes you think they heal, and then they get worse," Esther says.

"What I gave him is for healing. For strength," I say.

The mushrooms taste of butter, of morning sun and warm wind.

"My folks was worse when they came down with it," Esther says.

"Worse than that?" I ask.

Esther snorts and chews. Out in the cool dark, a hound barks.

"They bleed," Esther says to her plate. She looks like she wants to say something more, but she shakes her head again and eats another mushroom. "Thank you," she says. "I ain't never had these."

Another hound answers the first, and then another, and there is a circle of them somewhere out in the dark, baying. I wonder if they got somebody treed.

"I can teach you how to find them," I say. "You gotta look close."

Mary has cleaned her plate. She swipes her finger over the little bits of mushroom and meat, the flecks of food, and licks her fingertip. She is watching Esther and frowning.

"My brother is better at that," Esther says. "Better at finding that what hides."

"There's white ones. Them's easy to see," I say.

"Them's good eating, too," Cora says. She is plucking the meat in petals, eating it delicately.

"My brother, Bastian . . ." Esther swallows. "He hunt with traps. It takes waiting. He's like our PaPa. When they got sick, it was the first time, the only, when I could sit like him, watch like him. Notice all the little things." Esther picks up a mushroom, holds it in her fingers like the man who fathered me held his pen, but then Esther puts it down. Mary elbows her to eat, but Esther shakes her head. "Notice the way MaMa and PaPa sweat. How them turned yellow around the eyes."

"I'm sorry," I say, and recall her caught in that memory when the lady bade her run.

"I—" Esther pauses. "They gums started bleeding. They pissed blood. They cried, and it was blood, too."

Esther passes her plate to Mary, who frowns at her and tries to give it back. Esther palms it away, so Mary eats her leftovers and watches Esther, and with each bite, Mary leans closer until her nose almost brushes Esther's shoulder. She leans until Esther puts her arm around Mary and cups her ear, and Mary finishes Esther's food like that.

"I don't dream about them as much as I want to," Esther says. "When I do, I cry, and it's me crying blood."

My food has turned to mud in my mouth, mud cracking in the sun. I swallow it anyway, and I eat until my plate is clean, too. I lick the detritus from my finger like Mary did, wishing I had hoecake. Whenever Nan was pregnant, any time her belly began to grow, me and my mama would startle her at the creek; Nan kneeling in the sand, putting bits of clay in her mouth, as dainty as any of the slavers I've served. Now, sitting on the floor of the kitchen, with the smell of game meat and fat and mushrooms lying over us like a fine sheet, I understand. This stolen hour, stolen food, stolen time, this brief respite in the belly: I know why Nan ate earth.

I would give anything to taste more salt on my tongue. I would grind my knees into a riverbank, eat sand pinch by pinch. I would let it pebble in my mouth and then suck down the brine of clay. I nod with want. I swallow and feel the memory of a spring onion, bitter and biting, the sharp cold of a frosted morning—my haunches dew wet, whiskers to the air, and the predator above, ever circling.

We clean the kitchen, and it is only when we are all settled on our pallets in the storeroom that I feel something like satiety. It lasts a blink. I lie on my side, burlap abrading my cheek, and think about Esther's brother: see the strong arch of his nose, the bold bone of his jaw, the way the sun set the hair on his face to glittering. I am relieved when Aza does not come, because all I want is to stop snagging on Bastian's brow, his shoulders. I want to slide into sleep so I can forget these hungers. I wonder if Bastian's hidden skin would be as soft as Safi's, and I carry that wondering down into dreams.

WE WAKE TO A wailing.

"What?" Esther says, sitting up in the dark. Cora stumbles to the stove to light a candle. Mary looks up at the ceiling.

"The man," I say.

We wrap our heads, tighten our skirts, and run up the stairs. We rise with the wailing. It carries us up and up to the man's room. The chimney is ashy black. The candles before the mirrors gutter, but we see. We see the woman holding the man's head in her lap, rocking back and forth, her mouth open and open, the sound twisting around her: a bad wind muddying a clearing.

The man is muddied, too, but when we get closer, it is all red: the man's eyes, his nose, his ears, his fingers, his toes, all the small parts of him blotted with blood, but the sickness has not stopped there. It has come from his mouth, maroon puddles splashed all around him. The room reeks of vomit, harsh and burning in the nose, in the throat, so much that I have to swallow down the heave I feel in my own stomach, my own throat, my own mouth opening to answer him in kind. To say: that is the sea in you and this is the sea in me, the salt of saliva and mucus and blood.

We hold hands, our fingers cold and dry. The sound comes out of the lady in a great rushing tide, and she looks up and through us.

How loss blinds. His mottled body, an offering: her sorrow, hers. The house creaks. Mary's nails pinch my palm. Esther flits a smile before blanking her face. I swallow my sick and taste dread because I know the woman's yell. Done heard it every time one of us been stolen, separated, sold. I know that siren is a door opening to sorrow, and that sorrow never comes alone.

✳

CHAPTER 10

Sweet Harvest

The lady sits with her husband well into the cool, sharp hours of the afternoon. She cups the man's head in her lap beyond the last wisp of ash, the final bite of embers. She strokes his face, again and again, leans down and whispers, her mouth to his forehead. We cannot hear what she says. When we leave and return, bringing fresh linens upstairs, we find the lady has locked the door. We leave food for the mother, who walks in circles from her daughter's fastened door to her own room and back: a gray vulture.

"The harvest," the lady's mother mutters. Her hair falls in a limp wing. "The harvest!" she calls through the door where her daughter whispers to her dead husband. The blind mother takes her meals in the hallway, huffs bites between wandering and calling before the sorrow-quiet door.

"Ma'am," Esther says. She attempts to steer the grieving

215

woman's mother back to her bedroom, to herd her like a lemon-kneed goat, but the gray lady shrugs her off, turns back.

"I know," she says, scratching at the wood. "The harvest," she hisses. "The cold!"

When the old mother nests in her room, the bosses come. They smell of smoke and sweat, of burning pine and rotting hay. Their shirts hang loose at the neck. They knock, but the lady is silent. They smooth their hands down their pants.

"What ails her?" they ask.

"It's him. He had the fever." It is only when Esther pats her bloodstained apron that the bosses understand, that they work their mouths as if to call out to the lady in her mourning room.

"We need her," they say, "we can't start without her say-so," and then they turn and lope away.

We scrub and wash and wring and dry. We sweep and mop the floors. We polish and scrape. When the woman unlocks her door, we do all this around her as she slumps over her husband, cold stiff, death swollen, on the floor. She sleeps on his still, stone chest, wakes to worry over him, and then slumps to sleep again. The day drains from the sky, and night fills the horizon. We bring the woman dinner, and then we take it away, uneaten, and we share her supper in the kitchen, cutting the meat in even slabs, mouthing the pickled eggs, sprinkling more salt on the roots and greens before swallowing them. We need not touch the salted rabbit or our withering mushrooms.

We wake to do it all again. To clean, to haul water, to tend the house and feed the garden, to corral the old mother, to deflect the bosses, who are nervous with waiting. "The harvest," the blind mother says. "The harvest," the bosses say. Emil watches us grind corn for meal, and he worries the stump of his missing forearm with his fingers. The smell of the corn rises, earthy and sweet, and I let the scent wash down through me, over my throbbing shoulders, my sore back, until it rests in my tender feet.

"She run the harvest," Emil says. "Them bosses can't do nothing without her."

"What happen if they do?" I ask.

"She get rid of them," Esther says.

Mary grunts over her pestle.

"His body," I say. How do I describe the smell of his body, which has turned on the second day, bruising black, ripe for offering—his flesh that should be softening in the ground?

"I know," Esther says.

The stink of his decay suffuses the narrow hallways, the capped stairwells, the small, high-ceilinged rooms. The old mother circles worriedly, a handkerchief clutched over her nose and mouth. She scratches at the door and gags.

FOR THREE DAYS, THE lady locks herself in the room with her husband's rot. On the morning of the fourth day, we walk up the stairs, our hunger sanded to a dull throb by our filched morning corn cakes, our mushrooms, our feasts of the lady's rejected food, to find the door to her bedroom thrown open. The man waxes foul. The woman has done her best to wash him and dress him, but he has started to swell, the meat of him pushing against his clothes so that the shirts, the pants, his sock-clad, shoeless feet, seem bound in a too-tight sausage casing. He has gone gray around the mouth, all of the red that bloomed in him leached elsewhere. It takes all of us and Emil to carry him downstairs to the front parlor, where she insists we lay him on a sofa, but he is too large, too unwieldy, so instead she directs us to lay him on the carpet on the floor. The woman goes red in the face, all the floridity of him finding her, and she curses and damns us before caressing the man's cheek and hurrying upstairs. The man is still crusted maroon around his bulbous eyes, his nose, his ears, so we bring water to rub his face, clean the muck she couldn't, and I take this liquid refuse to dump in the garden, which is browning, wilting, all its showy life receding into the earth. Fall is here. Aza makes herself known: a shadow across the weakening cast of the sun, even as I trickle the dead water over the plants, give the offering to the earth, whisper: *Here, offering for you. Here,* and the earth sounds a sigh: sand brushed by wind.

How ripe, They Who Take and Give say.

Aza stirs the stalks of corn, setting them chattering.

"You said Mama Aza went to the Water," I say.

"Yes," she says.

"Do they all go there?" I beat the pan on the earth.

How sweet, the earth says.

"I know who take the bodies." I rest the pan on my knees, watch Aza out of the corner of my eye, wonder what truth, what fiction, will come from her. How will I tell the difference? "Who take the souls?"

The Bible the tutor reads says there is a heaven washed with light, peopled with the righteous. When the old Italian wrote about his descent, he called it going into the hollow deep of a grim bowl. Where would my mama have gone? I dig the pan into me, press it harder into my thighs. What will Aza, who craves regard, love, obedience in her worship. What will she want in return if she tells me the truth?

Aza wisps in a slow circle. She raises goose bumps on my arms, my cheeks. The wind catches my skirts and cuts my aching legs. Her spin around me tosses the smell of the man's ripening offal and tips it, rank and liquid, down my throat. I gag it away.

"Look at me," she says.

I look up and squint, even though this is no bright day. Aza's presence feels different now, as if she is standing in a doorway, obstructing the path from one room to another. She inserts herself like sand in a cog. She breaks what's around her.

"Some stay here. They leave their bodies but they are tied to this place. When their deaths are awful, they remain."

"Awful," I repeat, but Aza knows it for the question it is.

"When a person is beaten unto death. When a person is burned or violated. When a person is pulled apart in their dying."

I blink at her, my breathing loud in my ears.

"Violence begets remaining."

"My mother," I say, but she knows my question before I finish it.

"I do not know," she says, but I know she lies, that she is inconstant and quick as a summer afternoon shower.

"You don't?" I say.

"No."

I let the lie sink into the earth.

More, They request.

"What of the others? The ones that don't die in awful ways?" I don't say it, but I think it: What of the ones who die bad but not awful? Those who die bleeding from the eyes, those who die with their breaths rattling, those who die because their bodies break on them, piece by piece, like clocks come to the end of their circling, those who die from bellies swelling, their eyes turning yellow, those who drown in rivers, those who work and work without rest, who lie down one night, exhausted from the march of days, and never wake in the morning? It's all bad.

"There are lands, other lands, beyond the Water. Some go there."

"Does the Water know them?"

Aza turns in a slow circle, snapping the leaves on the trees.

"Does it speak to them?" I ask.

The leaves drift from the trees. They rock in the wind and then spiral to the ground. The smoke from Cora's stove floats skyward.

"The others told me . . . the Water sings," Aza says.

"Sings?"

"Yes," Aza says. "They could not hear the words. But they said they heard the voices. The Water has many voices. The people . . ." Aza searches for the words. "They sing with the Water. They sing back to it."

"Have you heard their singing?"

"Those older than me have. They say it cleansed them. That it wrecked them. Said it swept them up in a terrible wind. That is why some go out into this world: they search for it. The whisper of that singing that they caught, once. From the Water. From your people."

"Do you hear it here?"

Aza reaches out, brushes my fingers. I grip the pot, my knuckles clawed yellow.

"I have heard something like it from children," she whispers.

"In me?"

Aza touches my shoulder. Chills ribbon up my scalp and tighten.

"It wails from most children. Comes like a ululation from some adults."

She studies my mouth, my neck. Gaze sharp as a barred owl's.

"Most don't know it for what it is. For being able to see from this place to others, speaking to spirit, for hearing the Water."

"Did my mama sing? Did Mama Aza?"

The day cuts cool.

"Yes." She nods. "But you—you howl." She looks past my head, through the house, through the fields, through the woods. "Near to screaming." Aza's eyes are occluded and gray as the dead man's. They see everywhere, see nothing. "When you were up north, your sorrow choked your song. Swallowed it down. Even so, it hummed. But the walk changed it. The further you went, the more it rose, until the woman put you down in the earth. Then it shrieked."

"It's too much," I say. I don't know the truth of the words until I say them. "This world enough to feel without feeling beyond it."

"I would give everything," Aza hisses. "I would give everything to know the Water, to hear it, to feel it moving through me again."

More, the earth says, its whisper rough against the hum of dying insects, the steady chop of an axe somewhere in the distance, Emil off with the horses, calling: "Hyah, hyah!"

Give more, the earth says, and then a sound like water over sand. They are laughing.

"The Water's song wraps around you like a hurricane, child, and you in the eye. That regard is a gift. It's a gift to perceive what is beyond this," Aza bites. She is gathering herself, turning small. Her anger brushes my forehead in little stinging puffs. "The singing is a tide in you, in those you labor with. In you stolen. Did you know your Safi heard the singing of the Water in her dreams?"

I let loose the pot and massage my wrists, my yellow palms. Squeeze the meat between thumb and pointer finger to distract from Safi's absence, the terrible tug of memory: Safi's wide, white smile, the little mole at the seam of her lips, how tender her breath in my mouth, mine in hers. I shake off the recollection like an animal flinging off drenching rain. I ignore Aza's question and understand in a blink that Aza wants more than me flinching from the barb of memory. She wants the pain to gust through me, strong as the singing. She wants me to turn to her for comfort, for strength. That is her taking; that is what she wants in offering. She wears my grandmother's face because she wants me to turn to her for mothering. I see my mother's hand, loose and then tight on her cudgel, and I spit on the earth instead.

"Can you go to the Water to look for my mother?"

"No."

I back away from her, bend to pick up the pot.

"Why?" I say.

"I told you," Aza says. "I cannot see all."

I turn away from the receding storm of her face, from the small tornado of her skirts. I shake the pan, let droplets drift in a faint drizzle. Aza trails a wind, and the wet disappears.

"You could see where we do not," Aza says, her face small and spiteful. "If you open yourself to it, to the singing, you could see your mother. You could see beyond."

I press the pan to my stomach.

"The straits would be open," Aza says.

"What straits?" I ask.

Aza pulls her winds to her, and the air around the house is an envelope of warm water.

"The worlds are oceans." Aza floats limp and long as a rope hanging from a tree. "There are currents between them, that connect them. Straits, like streams. This is how we travel, when we dance." Even the bugs are silent.

Aza thinks she is saying one thing, but she says another. *You could swim out of this life*, she is saying. *Tread the surface of the waters, paddle and kick, and when you put your head up to draw air, you will be elsewhere.* She doesn't know it, but she is saying this: *You could leave.*

"Could I swim them?" I ask.

I don't need you, I think.

"You misunderstand," she says.

"How?" I say, not caring enough to whisper, to fear Emil or Esther coming up on me talking to them they cannot see.

"The straits are of spirit."

"How?" I walk toward her now. My foot catches on a melon vine, and I fall to my knees, head down, on all fours, salt water leaking from my eyes. I am the supplicant she always wanted. Aza raises her arms, spreads them, taking to air in a furious turn, and there is pleasure in how she smiles, hunger in how she gasps. Aza always wants more.

"You are tied to body," she says, "to everything that flowers and grows. You are anchored here, to this place. Your spirit can travel the straits, but your body is bound."

I bite my tongue and taste salt, blood. Swipe the tears on my face and push to a crouch. *What else*, I think to myself. *What else?* Aza would parse out my freedom like the lady parses our food, her slaps, the grinding hours.

"They Who Take and Give say there's another way," I say. "When I was in the ground. They said I could crawl, could burrow, could make my way out through the earth."

Aza spins again, her winds writhing.

"They know better than most what it is to be bound. They are a fool," Aza says.

THE MAN'S BODY IS gravity ridden and awkward.

"Lift!" the lady says. "Lift him up!"

The lady will only allow we women who work in the house to move her husband to his box, when she would have put us in the ground for looking at him in life. We try: we hoist him up under our arms, knee him with our thighs, bear his weight on the length of our backs.

"Careful," she says. "Careful!"

His turgid, rot-heavy weight pulls at my shoulders, makes my knees grind. She directs us to wedge him into his coffin, leaning upright, freshly delivered by the hands. The husband's blind eyes open even as she closes them, so she takes a handkerchief from her blood-dabbed skirt and places it over his whole face. Under the thin white cloth, his skin, his meat, puffs, struggling away from the bone in a great, fleshy cloud. The woman sends Esther out. She returns with a boy who is the color of pecan meat. His shoulders are rounded, as is his neck, and he looks at the ground. The lady directs him to fetch the undertaker. He looks up to Esther and nods at her instead of the lady before sprinting from the room. The old mother is making her way down the stairs, slowly, the wood creaking and moaning with her coming. I catch her and grab her elbow. Her hair is tangled around her head, pins slipping, in a hairstyle days old. She will usually only let Mary attend to her. Sometimes she fights the rest of us, panicked by her blind eyes, the dark wash of the room, hands not her own, but she does not bat me away. She is still in her sleeping gown, and she kicks it from her legs as she descends, smelling of brittle leaves and loamy earth.

The lady is crying soundlessly. She wipes the tears that spill from her eyes, that drip to his face. The old mother shrugs me off at the doorway of the room, so I wait with Esther and Mary. The old mother listens her way to her daughter and stands by the coffin, feeling the man's still chest, his waist, and then up to his bloated, covered face. She plucks at the handkerchief but does not remove it. Instead, she grabs the woman's hands, pulls her forward to whisper: "The harvest!"

"I hear it. It's ready," she says. "We wait, and it will sour."

The old mother caresses her daughter's cheek as tenderly as Cora pats pie dough, then twists back and slaps the lady across the face: once, twice.

"Was one lesson I taught you: this earth be merciless, and us tasked with taming it," the blind mother says. "I told you it wouldn't ever sit easy."

The lady slumps, and the old mother raises her hand again, but the woman shows her palms, the soft white meat of her, like a deer would, like a rabbit would, before darting for cover in a bramble-tied thicket.

"It nor them," the blind mother says, lowering her backhand. The lady gathers herself like Aza, snatching all her power close, bunching her hands into fists in her skirt, sniffing the snot of her tears before turning away from her husband.

"All of you," she says, her voice like raked rocks, fallow land. "To the fields."

WAGONS EDGE THE FIELDS, along with bosses and hands who ride brown and river-red horses. Hundreds of us are in the rows. We women and children are thin as the cane, our skirts and shirts and bindings and pants knotted tight. The children, tender behind their ears, soft skin at the backs of their knees and on the insides of their wrists, stand still as pine saplings in a clearing with no wind. I hold quiet as the women in line with me, who are as stoic as the children. Emil sits at the helm of a wagon behind us, the horses whisking away flies. A row of men advance before us women and children, some wearing shirts, some bare backed. They grip machetes that remind me of the way my mother held her training staff: loose at the palm, a breath away from tightening. The sugarcane shushes as a broad wind ruffles it. I look for Aza, but she is not here. The cane is a green lake: it stretches to the far forest, snapping with emerald waves. Hunger clenches my whole body, and if not for the man atop the horse, his firearm slung across the pommel of his saddle, I would drop in this living tide, let it submerge me. I wonder if my mother felt this urge to kneel, to sink, under a clear harvesting sun, the air high and dry with the cool touch of a brook, but then I cannot wonder at all because the man on the horse yells, and the line of dark-shouldered men raise their weapons at once. We are moving.

A smell, green and sweet, blooms over all of us. For one moment it fills my insides and I can imagine I have eaten my fill, that I am sated on flour and sugar and fat, on half-eaten cookies and slant-chewed cakes I have tasted a handful of times, filched from plates. A taste I can recall easily: sweet and buttery on the tongue. Food made to make you want more, with sweetness that gathers like a dense fog in the mouth: inhaled in a breath, and then gone. Light lances down on the field. I exhale, empty again.

I wonder what the men have eaten. I know they forage: I have heard Emil say that they grab handfuls of the animals' feed, withered corn kernels, hard enough to crack teeth, to break their fast. When the white hands watch, they don't even have that. They try to keep gardens, but seedlings wilt in the heat, wither from neglect with them always in the fields. Once Emil told us in the kitchen garden: "*I don't know how the animals fat as they is: don't nothing eat good on this place except them in the house*," and then he laughed, and the sound rolled over his gums, the strong white teeth that remain, and there was no mirth in it. We all starving.

The men reach their weapons high and slice down to the root of the stalk. Their arms blur; the cane breaks with fat cracks. The men strip the flags of green, cut off the top, and then throw the cane to the ground behind them. Before the stick has struck the earth, they are raising their arms again, whirring, slicing. A woman leads our line, bald and short, grabbing one sugarcane, and then another, and another, and the child who walks beside her, who is as tall as she is, wearing her mother's nose on her face, follows the line leader, gathering. Mother and child push the stalks up onto the bed of the wagon, hoisting the bundles up with their whole bodies. The other women and children on the line bend and lift, and the chopping of the cane, the step of feet through the shorn stumps, the trampling of flags and leaves, echo the waning trill of the last of the insects, quieting as they settle into starvation like us, as they slow like us, as they doze to dream midcrawl, midhop, and jerk to waking, waking to remember that what they dreamt of was stopping, stopping in the cane-drunk fields.

"Hyah!" the man on the horse screams. "Hyah!"

I grab my first stalk. It is so fat my grip hardly fits.

"Move!" the man on the horse says.

I grab another. Emil flicks his reins, and his wagon surges and stops.

"Cane ain't going to cook itself!" the seer says.

I grab another and another until the weight of them pushes my feet down into the sweet, stubby green.

"Fires lit!" the man says.

I trip toward the cart. When I stumble, the people in my line help me stand as they stab into the loam.

"Boilers hot!" the man says.

I shove them up on the pile.

"Rollers a-tumbling!" the man says.

The thorns from the shorn stalks leave white-pink marks on my arms.

"Sweet sugar," the man says, whistling.

I return to the line, and I bend.

"Hyah," the man on the horse says.

The men raise their arms. They hack. They strip. They toss.

"Good," the man on the horse says.

I clutch the cane.

"Good boys," the man says, as if he's kneeling over a hound with a blood-wet muzzle, stroking its velvet sides.

I grasp another.

"Faster," Esther huffs.

I grab another, hand gone slippery.

"Annis. Faster," Esther says.

I hug another.

"The lash," Esther says.

The smell of sap all over.

"The ground," Esther says.

I groan.

"Good girls."

I hoist.

The day burns and burns.

THERE ARE SIX FLAT-BACKED wooden wagons for loading cane. They ring the fields and come one after another. Cuts etch my palms, my forearms, my legs, connect like the filaments of a mushroom, that part of the body that grows underground, webbing through the roots of trees and shrubs and ferns in a great mat: *This hurts*, the mat says. *This stinging wash*, it says. *Enough*, it says.

Enough. But I do not stop. I move. I see the hole, its wall of spikes. Feel the sinking mud beneath my feet. I will not go there. We are all glazed with sweat. I try to wipe my face on my shoulder, to clear my eyes, but everything is sodden. My skirt drags. The women and children in my line breathe in sobs. The day stretches open its bright mouth and swallows. The hours, the bosses and hands on horses, the women in the house; they are all hungry for more. We cut and strip and haul until the sun sinks over the edge of setting, beyond the darkening brush of the trees.

"Come on." Esther says, grabbing my shirt, and we follow the last wagon of our shift down a narrow, rutted road that winds away from the fields, away from the borderlands, to the river and the sugar refinery. I put one hand on the cart, letting it half drag me along the narrow path. Dirt clouds our way, and I watch my feet, smelling my own salt, my own blood. I have never been so tired. I blink, and it is a long time until my eyes open, and I realize that I want to fall to my knees, my stomach, my face, in the dusty grooves. But I don't. There is no one to carry me back. I raise my knees, trying to kick off my fatigue, until I smell the river, mossy and silty, and then in a great tide, caramelized sugar and smoke.

The trees fall away, and the refinery looms over their tops; it is as large as the house where the lady lives. The women and children we worked with in the fields are unloading a wagon and placing the cane on two giant belts that rattle and clank, over the cogs beneath, moving slowly as they spin the cane into the building.

Our wagon joins the others. The clearing before the refinery is crowded with bodies and cane and wagons. Esther leans into me, her mouth at my ear. It is very like her brother's.

"We got to unload the cane!" she yells.

I nod.

The fires shine through the tunnels where the belts and the cane they carry disappear. Rollers then turn, great wheels, and smash. They grind, turn it to pulp, a green and white mash. This is how the cane offers its juice, which runs down and below to the vats. This is where the fires simmer, licking and enwrapping the iron bottoms of the pots so fiercely that the heat billows out of the building at its openings. A trickle of a breeze runs past my nape, my cheek, tosses my hair before receding, but this swish of Aza's skirts can't brush the smell of the congealing crystals or the crackle of burning from the deepening sky. And still, the wagons rise like small hills around us, laden with cane.

The mother and the child with the same face appear out of the dark. She has another child at her elbow. The low slope of this child's shoulders tells me she is tired, tired like her mother and sister, but she grabs at the cane as they do.

"Helen," Esther says, and nods.

"Esther," the woman says.

"Your baby here?" Esther says.

Helen reaches out a hand and cups the back of the child's neck. The child shrugs away Helen's hand and gathers three cane stalks at a time; these she brings to the rollers, her arms knotted ropes that she loosens when she lets them fall. She clenches her bottom lip in her teeth, concentrating on lifting, balancing, shuffling through the dirt-scummed air, and then tossing. The way Helen watches the child echoes through me; there is a tender string, thin as fishing cord, from Helen's hands, from Helen's heart, up and through the crown of Helen's head, that ties her to the child, the thin-shouldered child, all sinew and skin. The child stumbles, and Helen rushes to her.

"Mama," the child says, a grimace fluttering over her face, moth quick, even as the child leans into Helen, even as she tightens her hold on her stalks.

"Careful," Helen says.

I want to see my mother. I want to see myself, when I was the same size as Helen's daughter: short, slight, hair a snarled fall down my neck. I want to see my mama walking the path between the shacks, hand at my neck, the V of her thumb and pointer finger steering and saying: *She is mine, here is mine, I am hers and she is mine.* The knots of the shorn cane prod me black and blue, draw red. The fire whips over us, licks the sky, rides the wind. The drain of the day pushes and pulls: an inexorable tide. Helen is singing, low, under her throat, and then her girl takes it up, ties her voice with her mother's, and her older sister's, and all us that toiled in the field, we are all singing, and then I see my mother, and I see me, see the knotted weave of my hair, the red wire of it passed down from my sire, but brighter is my mother's deep hand, her small ears she gave me, the way she looks as if she is swimming when she walks down the dirt lane between the shacks, how she blazes when she hands me her weapon and whispers: *Feel it, feel the balance—you move with it and it will do for you, little one, it will do,* and then the tide and the singing carry me back, back to the mill and the smoke and the sweetness. Aza gave me the truth—I can see, I can see, I can see.

THE LADY AND HER mother sit eating at a small table in the front room: Esther and Mary dragged it from the corner and set it, crowding its face with spoons and forks and knives and plates so that the saucers and cups hang over the side like flower petals. With each clink of the women's silverware, the table trembles.

The man's body stands across from them, sandwiched in his solid, smooth-edged wooden box. His head brushes the top of the box. Death continues to swell him. He is almost a stranger, all the red leached from his face, his features spread flat and pale as a pancake. The smell of the creep of black silt below the surface of him, beneath his tightly woven clothing, clots the room. The air is a wet towel; I inhale in hot, fetid sips.

"He looks well," the lady says. She places a tea strainer over her cup.

"The harvest?" the blind mother asks.

"We cut in time," the lady says. "Barely."

"I felt the cold coming," the older mother says. "Felt it in my knuckles, my knees."

"They still need my hand," the lady says.

"Kept me up all night," the blind mother says.

"They're slow," the lady says.

"That and the wind, rattling the windows. Too much," the mother says.

"Too slow." The lady pours. "You have to press them." She raises the pot and an eyebrow at her mother, who nods. She pours.

"This house shifts. It rise and settle." The mother laughs. It titters to a cough, and she sips. "Sugar."

The lady spoons sugar from a small white porcelain bowl, edged in blue. There are gold dots all around the rim. A headache blooms behind my left eye.

"They'll bear with some prodding," the lady says.

The old mother sips and hums, and the pain in my head simmers.

"Your father said the house move faster than the slaves," the mother says.

The woman dips the spoon in her cup, stirs, and then points it in the air, level with her eye. She looks over the spoon at the man.

"He wants sugar in everything. His grits. His coffee. His eggs," the lady says. The lady slides the spoon in her mouth, sucks the sweet crystals from it. She swallows slowly. The sound is loud in the room. She sets the spoon down on her plate and it shivers. "I only ever want it in my tea," the lady says.

The blind mother laughs at the lady's joke, and the sound of it tumbles in a roasting grind over my eyeball and through my skull.

"He loves it," the lady whispers.

I close my eyes and gold washes over me. *Little one*, my mother said. Pain hammers me. The dead man reeks of chitlins and water-starved mouths. I wonder what They Who Take and Give will do with this sugar-loving man: make him into an orange club, sweet gum, stiff red clay? If I could just turn my head quickly enough, I think, I could see beyond the pain, these women, this room, these bodies bent on decay.

I could see me and my mama again.

CHAPTER 11

✳

Thin and Smudge

The days smudge. The harvest presses one morning into another. I blink, I sleep, and then I am awake again. The lady orders Emil and six of the men to brick a mausoleum in a small clearing visible from the lady's bedroom window. After the mortar has dried, she makes the men paint it white and then directs them to haul the man out of the parlor. The mausoleum has their last name etched across the top, and it is wide, wide enough to fit the husband's casket and, one day, the wife's. The lady's neighbors journey from their plantations. They ring the husband's grave, sniff into their handkerchiefs and wrists, their faces waxen and grim. She demands us from the house attend, but the hands and those who work in the field continue to toil, a multitude of backs. The lady stands as near to the mausoleum as she can without crawling into it, crow-still, tears slowly leaking down her face to pool around her neck, and when the men slide the casket in and begin bricking up the opening, she collapses to her knees. When her neighbors try to pick her up, she sags in their grip as I did, as Emil did, in the arms of the hands on the way to the hole. Her mother whispers to her, tries to coax her up from her staggering sorrow, but she remains on the ground. I wish the earth would give her what she wants: that it would open beneath her and swallow her with its multitude of mouths. She kicks the dirt and sobs.

After the funeral, we settle into harvest, and it is endless: we serve breakfast before the sun slathers itself across the sky, we gather and load cane, unload at the mill, serve dinner late in the night, the candles flickering and smoking at the mirrors. The lady, like a queen at the center of her hive, does not sleep. We don't sleep. We crawl through the fields. We gather the sweet sheaves. We crush them. We burn the nectar. We collect the sugar. We pack it in hogsheads, large wooden barrels, and send them downriver.

I shrink: the work wrings me to ropes. The walking, lifting, throwing, washing, clearing, and trudging pare my face. I am less. We are all less. The bones of Mary's hips jut from her skin in a bowl. Esther's cheekbones are overturned spoons. When I open my eyes to this morning, I know with a sinking of my stomach that part of me will always be here, in this endless place, mired to the neck: held tight in the grip of these bristling green fields, this black earth, this perpetual burning of my body, the open petals of my hands, the bruised stems of my feet, this hunger that hollows me from the inside as the land hollows me without.

Today we gather wood for the house's fireplaces; there is nothing to spare from the trees nearby. The mill's fires have eaten it all. We walk farther away, where the forest is still, the coming cold casting a faint brown on the leaves the same way illness blanches the faces of the sick. Three egrets alight in the cypress; they nod and bow to one another, settling on their haunches. This day, I decide, I will move slowly; the lady is not here, not in the woods. She has no claim here. There is pain in every part of me: up the long muscles of my legs, across the band of my back, on the caps of my shoulders. I look for mushrooms and find one, pale with skin of the softest leather. The dirt in its stem crunches. My teeth are daggers in my gums. I look at Mary and Esther, find another, and give it to them.

Esther looks up from her crouch.

"Brother," she says.

Bastian, his hair pulled back and braided, creeps into the clearing. He picks Esther up and hugs her, hard.

"You ain't nothing," he says.

"Bastian," she says.

He frowns at me before turning to Mary, who stacks branches and half-rotten logs in a pyramid.

"It's harvest up and down the river road," he says.

Esther lets her arms loose and steps back.

"No," she says.

The light of the day passes in a shadow-dappled beam between them: a golden emptiness.

"Esther," he says again, and the slope of his shoulders, the way his voice drops like a trickling fall of water between them, makes him smaller.

"I know her," Esther says to the pine straw, to her feet. "She will chase."

"Wouldn't no harm come to you," Bastian says.

"No," she says, stepping away from him again. He raises an arm to her, his fingers splayed wide, but she is too far away from him to touch.

"Come," Esther says, turning to Mary. "Slim pickings here." But she stops before she leaves and leans into his chest and mumbles to him so quietly I can't make it out.

Mary picks up her bundle, holding it against her: one of the limbs scratches her chin, etching a white welt, a red line. She nods at me and follows Esther over the stumps, both of them slow and then stumbling, lurching to trots before they disappear into the forest.

Esther's brother's nose is a fin in his face, his eyes the bottom of the deepest part of a river, the black cool where the current cannot reach, where driftwood, whole trunks, sink to silt. His neck, even though he is almost as lean as us, is solid as a young pine. This is how he stands in the clearing, but he lists like a tree, too, rooted in place but for the twisting of the wind that pushes him one way and then another. To walk toward me, or not.

"We say the same, every time," Bastian says.

I wonder if his hands are still callused to leather coins from his time in the fields. I have not bathed since harvest started, have had no time to detangle and twist my hair, to soothe my skin with water and fat. I know I am cut-ridden, fulsome, my bones poking out from my skin like the spines of feathers from a thin pillow. Know that my tongue is large and cotton-heavy from thirst in my mouth, but if I go to him and put my hands on his shoulders, wait for his assent, I can be soft when I lean forward and nuzzle his neck. I step over gnarled black-oak fingers, the sea of mushrooms, the insects riotous in their eating, their storing, their hoarding for the cold. Pine needles crunch. I clench my hands in my skirt and lean toward him, and his list stops still.

"She scared," I say.

"I can keep her safe," Bastian says, but his voice rises at the end of it, and I wonder if he doubts it even as he says it, if he knows there is pine in the column of his spine, that the center of him will only bend so far before he snaps. That he is a sapling and this world a hurricane.

"She ain't scared of that. She know you."

"Do she talk about it?"

I shake my head and sniff without sound. Bastian smells of bayou sulfur, salt, the char of wild game roasted over an open fire. There is a core of caring at the heart of him, given to flowering in his rabbit bouquets, in the leaf-wrapped meat he pulls from the sack slung at his side.

"It's coon," he says. "Miserly eating, but it'll fill."

Bastian hands me the leaf-wrapped meat. I hold the loose coil in my hand. I wonder if the man who loved Mama Aza looked upon her like this big, even man looks at me: with the alert, careful hunger of a hunter. He stoops toward me, and the line of his collarbone, the bow of his arms, calls Safi to me, bending over me as I sat on the lip of the doorway of our cabin, fanning air at a stinging, weeping scrape running down my shin. How she leaned over me, picking the grit from it, whispering: *Easy, love, easy*. My heart clangs. I step back, hoist the leaf-sack, feel the phantom wound tingle on my leg.

"She scared of all the harm that could come to her. The devil here? She know the devil here," I say.

"I would protect her."

"She don't doubt you," I say.

"Then what?" he says. I can read the frustration in the slant of his brows, black and thin as soot-burned sticks, in his crumpled mouth, the way he looks from me to Esther's trail, then back to me, where he stays.

"It's the rest of the world she don't know about," I say.

The wind moves high in the trees before sweeping down, brushing us both. The touch is soft.

"What about you?" he asks.

The wet embrace that falls in the spring and presses through the summer has been lightening over the past days. How that liquid hand of the air feels as if it is pushing me in the earth, month after month, so that on a morning like this, cooler and lighter, the absent touch feels strange. Makes me feel my whip-thin arms, my dry tinder, even clearer.

I would have another touch. Another hold.

"Me?" I ask.

"Would you go?" Bastian asks.

I set the leaf-wrapped meat onto the ground. I take a short step toward him. He swallows, and his skin flutters at his throat, its wave as soft and hesitant as one of my bees alighting on a flower.

"I could protect y'all," Bastian whispers. His words glance along my face.

I blink at the tender wisp, remember the last, when Safi laid her fingers on my cheek before she ran at the waterfall.

Bastian skims his fingertips over the bridge of my nose. I swipe my thumb along his lips.

"Why me?" I ask.

He angles his head to one side. His glance a fishing line anchored with rock, dropping deeper and deeper into me.

"You careful when you gather. You take enough mushrooms for y'all, and you leave more for them that comes after. You watchful: you read my sister and Mary. You help me know them in ways I can't, because you can." He touches the side of my neck. "You sad," he says. "And beautiful. Same way a lean fox is. How the beating the world give you can't make it less."

"You do," I say.

"You should have more," he says.

I grab Bastian's shirt and pull him to me. Stand up on my toes, but he has to stoop to meet my mouth. He tastes of moss and game and ash. I lick his teeth, lean into his arms, and I am in two moments now. I am with Safi, soft Safi, her arm looped around my shoulders, her fingers in the crook of my elbow, her mouth soft, so plush, each brush of it waking flutters, pulling honey from my chest and out of my mouth, and I am with Bastian, too, his arms like great branches around and under me, the touch of his fingers hesitant, cotton fluff, his facial hair the fine filament of an insect's wing, the press of his nose along mine, the lick of his mouth firm and present, and we breathe each other in before I step back and sit. I raise my palms, waiting, and he crouches before me. I kiss the knobs of his knuckles. He touches my neck, my chest, my stomach. Everything slows. I drag my skirts up. I will take these caresses, these thin pleasures, for myself. I will devour this tenderness, but I want him to hear me before I open to him.

"I see you," I say.

At my back, the earth hums. Aza is there, toeing the high tips of the trees, sending browning leaves down in a dead shower, and they settle on Bastian's back. I warn her away with one hand and wipe the dead leaves from the living bridge of him with the other.

●　　●　　●

I DON'T LOOK AT Aza when she descends to my side on my walk back from the forest. One of the hands, seeing me walking with my bundles of wood and leaf-wrapped meat, stops me on the trail. I glance at his mouth and his yellow beard stained brown from chewing tobacco, and then off into the underbrush as he tells me to head to the levee, that the canal needs clearing for the barges that carry the hogsheads of sugar to float. Aza waits, circling me in a misty drizzle. A buzzard flies overhead before sinking like a spear over the tops of the trees. Great geese fly south in raucous triangles.

"You would go with him?" Aza asks. Her hair moves in a fine spray around her.

"I might."

"Your grandmother—"

"I know," I say.

The spray of her hair peppers my face in little stings.

"She trusted him, and it led her to the dark gut of that ship. He couldn't protect her."

"Last person protected me was my mama," I say, and I don't understand the truth of it until I say it.

She stops before me, and I dodge her, but her robes, the streams of her arms, still feel real, and they cut in stinging, cool lines.

"I protect you," she says.

Aza blows into the sails of my skirt. How Bastian touched me with kindness, I think, just as Aza's whispery spray burns the scratches on my back, on my legs. I stop in a little copse of cypress trees when I see the river. The trees' leaves shrink red and thin as feathers, falling to the ground. I lay down my bundle of wood and coon.

"Not from this," I whisper, and run my hand over the welts and wounds of my arms. I sink to my knees, thinking about rest, about whether I can snatch a handful of minutes now in the underbrush to sit for one breath, two, to watch the river, swollen from storms in the north, bubbling white and roiling greenish brown. The banks are clogged with splintered trees and fan-shaped branches.

"I am spinning another storm," Aza says.

"I know."

I know what happens when people escape. The thieves gather their men, their thick-saliva'd, hang-toothed dogs, and run after them to steal them back. When the men find them that fled, they wrap the ropes around their hands and feet and necks. They beat them with leather, with boards. They heat steel orange hot, and then they brand the people: their cheeks, their backs. They collar them with spiked metal. They encircle their ankles with iron and chains; they make pregnant people shuffle their way to delivery. I want. I want to grow my hair long, to find food and feed myself without hiding, to sit in the sunlight and scratch the worry out my scalp, to breathe without fear and terror choking me, to choose my seconds, to choose my minutes, to choose my days. I done suffered enough. Aza wavers next to me, pin fine and shimmering wet.

"I could dig a cave in the riverbank. They Who Take and Give could make it hold," I say.

"You trust them?"

I nod.

"Them who give chase would find your fire one day." Aza flutters darkly. "And you."

"I could cross the river. I could journey a ways," I say.

"That water has no mercy."

I know the river's hunger. I clear my throat and swallow just to swallow something.

"What you want, Aza?" I ask.

A late gnat wisps my ear.

"Run. Run in the storm," Aza says.

The swampy wood bristles to brown around me.

"I don't know."

"I'll smudge your tracks. Blow your scent away," Aza says.

"Where?"

"North, Annis."

I've heard stories of them that will ferry one from this under-world. People talked about it in the cabins when I was a child, how the ferrywoman would come in the middle of the night and take you up and out, and the coin you gave was your desire to be free. But I don't know if anyone ferries here, and I don't want Bastian's kind of freedom, his half liberty living in the borderlands, carrying stories along the river road, trading with us, still bound, witnessing those he loves ground down with the seasons; he is a ghost in the gray lands of the dead, too. Another thought startles from me, a small, watery-muscled, downy-haired idea: *I want to walk through a world of my own making.*

"If I don't?" I ask.

Aza drifts and drizzles next to me. A squelching noise rises from the muddy bank beneath me, and I know it is They Who Take and Give, that the hiss of the sediment of the river as it comes to rest on the bank, along with the soaked rotten wood, makes them sing with pleasure. *Yes*, They say. *Here*. Aza frowns, her displeasure crackling. When my first queen bee died, the workers began feeding grubs, one of which would be the next queen, bathing them in opaque cream. The grubs grew and surfaced from their sticky wombs, all black bodied and furious, and they fought mercilessly until only one shivered in the midst of the swarming, caressing workers; this new queen sang to them, battle drunk. These spirits want worship, want succor, want adoration, want obedience, want children. They want love. We starve, but they are hungry, too.

"Aza," I say.

Her hair creeps about her face, stretches over it until all I see is her electric eyes.

"I will make a way," Aza says.

I could dig a cave, cover the entrance with pine brush and dead wood. I could run tunnels from it, given enough days, that would disperse the smoke so I could burn a fire within it. I could live my days in the dark, in the maw of the earth. The mud sucks at my feet when I stand, but I pull away and walk to the water. Aza drifts and follows. I step into the shallows, into the fast-flowing water that grabs my ankles with sure hands and tugs. I lean against the current, grab another branch, and fling it to the land. Mary and Esther are upriver with more women and children; they see me and begin picking their way downriver, closer to where I am. The women and children are wrapped around trees, around each other, making a human chain to clear the wood-choke of the storm, to wipe the face of the river clean.

I am so full, so full, but I could do with another, another, I could do with you, I would wrap myself around you and we could go far, to the bayou flats, to the bays, to the sea, the river speaks.

I wade deeper into the water and pull a branch from its maw.

That windy one cannot lift you up, but I could, the river says. *Them others would bury you.*

I grab another branch and tug, but the flow tugs back.

I would sweep you along to the ocean and islands yonder, the river murmurs.

The wood rips from my hands, takes skin with it, draws blood. More offering. The river laughs.

I could take you away, the river says.

Grab for another piece of wood. There are men out further in the water. They have tied themselves to trunks on the bank, and they are pulling downed trees to the shore to dry and burn in the sugar mill fires that smoke and singe the throat on waking, on sleeping. I trip. The current is strong, and it claws me a few feet downstream before I can dig my toes into the sand and stagger out of the water. The current laughs, chilly and burbling. Esther and Mary walk down to the edge of the river and Esther holds out her hand.

"Here," Esther says. "Come on."

She hauls me up the bank. My clothes weigh heavily, and my legs ache with the struggle of walking to the tree line.

"You grab the tree," Esther says.

I choose a slim pine to wrap my arm around. Esther grips my skirt with one hand and holds Mary's skirt with the other, all the muscles and tendons in her wound tight as yarn. Mary walks out into the shallows and grabs branch after branch, throwing them to the banks. She takes one halting step and then another, further out into the river, stretching our thin line tight.

"Mary," Esther calls. "Stop."

Mary does not listen. She takes another lurching step. Esther has leaned so far out that her hand grasps only a small handful of my skirt, and another small handful of Mary's. Mary steps again, and her skirt yanks from Esther's hand. Mary sinks to her neck. She has walked off an embankment.

"Mary!" Esther shouts.

Mary turns and tries to grab at Esther, but Mary is already beginning to bob and flail in the current. The giggles and hiccups, drunk with storm.

I, stone cleaver, the river says.

Mary sinks, then surfaces and screams.

"Esther!" Mary sings.

Esther lets go my skirt. She runs and leaps out into the water, shining in the air, long and lean and beautiful as a deer startled midfeed. Mary sinks and pops up again. Her eyes wide, her mouth wide.

I, city swallower, the river says.

Esther swims, pulling with her palms, kicking with her legs. Debris batters her sides, but she cuts through it, sure and straight. She grabs Mary's hand and hauls her up, clutching her. The girls grip each other. Their heads bob along the warp of the water. They speak into each other's mouths before raising their faces to the sky.

What will you call me? the river asks.

The last of the insects scream. The light cuts the air in blue knives. *Go,* I think. *Go,* I wail in my head. *Go!* A rolling log startles Mary and Esther in their frantic swim, and they scramble at it together before grasping it tight. The men are shouting at them, shouting at each other, shouting for someone to jump in to save them.

"Go," I whisper. Mary and Esther twine their arms together around the log.

What do I care, the drunk river says, *when I eat the world?*

The brown churn of the water whips Mary and Esther downriver. The log spins and then spins again; the water carries them faster and faster until they cut cleanly down the center of the river. They approach the river's bend. Esther links one arm around Mary's shoulders and under her armpit, and she lifts her hand in what could be a wave as she looks back at me. I hold my own out to nothing, to Aza shimmering into being next to me. Esther clenches her raised hand into a fist, and then they are so small I have to squint to make them out. The girls disappear around the bend. Leaves cascade from the trees. I hug myself, and my stomach burns. Sorrow is a wrung rag in my throat. *Please.* The prayer rises in me and I don't know where it goes, but not to any of these spirits here, this merciless river, this grinding earth, this waiting storm. *Please*, but even as I say it, I don't know where Mary and Esther could find safety.

"Can you help them?" I ask.

Aza whips another gust over the water. All that is left are the cries of us on the bank.

"My purview is you," Aza says.

I am shaking, my teeth rattling one against the other, my jaw opening and closing. *Please*, I breathe, and then I know who I am praying to, who I am beseeching: the Water, the water beyond this water. All of a sudden, I am blind to the world, to the men and women and children on the shore, to the bend in the river where Mary and Esther have gone, Aza, sullen and still at my back, my aching, hunger-struck body, all of it gone, and all that remains is a waterfall. It runs through me, blinding me, and there is a great presence at the heart of it, all-seeing, all-knowing. I am small and afraid and aghast at it; I am embraced. I am. It rushes through me for one second more, and then disappears as quickly as it came, and I open my eyes to the world, tears streaming down my face, and I know, with each breath, that if I reach out to that Water, I will know it, and it will hold me.

"Annis?" Aza asks, but I crawl back up the bank to crouch near a tree and wipe at my cheeks. I can still feel the echo of the Water through me; it is a murmur, slow, inexorable, light, *there*. The hands will be here soon, are probably scouring the riverbank, interrogating, plotting how far they need to go downriver to find Mary and Esther, but I will sit until they come. I will sit until they demand more: more loss, more offering. The river growls. I sniff a ragged breath and wait. The memory of the Water holds me like I ain't been held since my mama clutched the whole of me when I was a baby, her baby, too white, too red at the mouth and ears, wet with afterbirth, the dirt in the seams of the midwife's fingers streaking my skin, but against it all, how my mama held me.

"I'm here," I tell Aza. "I am."

WALKING BACK TO THE big house, I wade through a high, moon-driven tide; entering its bowels, I submerge myself in a sable lake. I am watching my feet, so I don't see the lady in the kitchen, white and thin as an unburnt wick. Cora burns brown and tall; she stares at the floor, her hands folded, and it is the first time the room, and everything in it, doesn't yield to her. The lady's mouth is a crooked slash, her forehead a wrinkled fall. I stop in the doorway, the wood and leaf-wrapped bouquet of coons waxy and slippery in my hands.

"Come," the lady says.

Cora hums, and I make to hide the bushel behind my back, but the lady looks at it square, and I stop.

"Come here," the lady says.

I walk toward her until I am a little over an arm's length away. The racoons are gamey and musky, and the lady covers her nose.

"You take," she says through her fingers. I shake my head. She shushes me with a low whistle, with the flutter of one thin arm.

"Whose game you hold in your hand, girl?"

She brings her other hand up, folds the two in prayer.

"Whose leaves?"

She brings her praying hands to her mouth and speaks around them.

"Whose wood, girl?"

The lady picks up a poker Cora uses to rouse the fire.

"The two that fell in it?"

She swings the poker at me but I step back and lean, all the lessons my mother taught me singing through me in that dodge, in the parry, raising the sticks and the limp bouquet of coons to block her, and the meaty mess splats on the floor.

"Mine," the lady says. A tremor shakes her, whipping her tight.

Her a clothesline snapping in a gusting wind. I wonder what spirit moves her, what spirit shakes her down to blood, sinew, bone. It must be a massive, whiteout storm. It must bear the creamy stink of maggots, of bleached bone. I know it: I seen it in my father's teeth. I seen it in the Georgia Man's knuckles. I seen it in the doctor's palms, in the wrinkles of the seller's skin. I seen it in the roll of this woman's husband's eye. That monstrous spirit binds her, blinds her.

"Stay!" she hollers, and swings again.

No, my body says. *No.*

"Stop." She stabs. It has been too long since I learned this dance with my mother, too long since I stepped in, stepped out, ducked and twisted away from a weapon. The poker catches me on the arm, and it is a spiking, fiery sizzle. The woman lets loose a razor-sharp shriek.

"You!" She whips the poker at my head. I lean away and block with the kindling, but the wood splinters, and the metal catches my temple and pain explodes, sizzling hot. Cora and the woman disappear. I fall.

CHAPTER 12

Ferrywomen

I wake in the black fist of the earth. I am in the hole. Above the roof of soil, the sky is storming, and in the rooting of thunder, I recognize Aza; she is howling outside, spinning, shaking her skirts, clapping her hands, and lighting the sky. My head pulses with each flash of her lightning. Rain gathers and runs down the walls of this pit; it finds glee in puddling at my feet, reminding me of the river's drunken promise to whisk me away from this place.

This, the red marbled earth hisses, *this is how you escape. Find the red clay and dig, dig a tunnel, dig a cave.*

I touch my head. Hot blood in the seams of my fingers.

I will hold you, the earth rumbles.

I will bear the mark of this night into whatever nights I have left.

I will hide you, They Who Take and Give groan.

Silty blood in my mouth.

You could make a life in the dark, They say.

Aza calls me to the surface.

You could bear children there, in the dark, They say.

With who, I think. "With who," I ask.

They are silent. The gathering pool murmurs at my feet, licking and sloshing at my ankles. The mud of the bottom softens and oozes.

There is life in the sinking, the water at my feet says. *Life in the descent*, the aquifer's whisper intones.

"Naw," I say. "This ain't living."

I dig my hands into the rifts in the mud wall. Some of the spikes near the top of the hole have been replaced, but the rest of the hole is nude. I can't breathe with the rain streaming over my eyes, down my face, with the mud sucking at my feet, anchoring my legs. I grip the wall and drag myself, my whole body, up. My fingernails rip and the earth slides loose, and I fall. I can't breathe for sobbing, for choking. I suck mud and blood from my fingers, suckling to ease the hurt, before jamming my hands back into the wall. I kick my toes into the clay and pull upward, crying. Everything burns, but I am crawling up, up toward the grate, the flashing storm. I grab two of the spikes near the door and try to hoist myself up, but Aza shrieks, and I lose my toeholds and grips, jerking the spikes from the wall and sliding back down to the wet muck.

"No."

I stab one spike into the melting clay at my shoulder, reach as far as I can over my head with another and ram it into the earth, jab my toes into the wall again, and I strain upward. I wrench one spike out and stab again, imagining the lady's face, her soft-jelly eye in the socket, and pull. I am crawling upward. I am eating mud. I am stinging and crawling. I will always sting, always crawl, to free myself from this dark womb, this eternal offering. I feel one of many, feel as if all them that done been in this hole, bled into this mud, all them bound with ropes, hacked with hatchets, burned alive, buried alive, are all here with me. We swallowing rainwater, gulping mud, wailing against the wind.

"What you give us?" I ask. "What you give?"

I don't know I'm speaking until my nose hits the grate of the door. I fit one foot in the wedge of one wall and the other foot in another. I lace my fingers into the grate, and I stab at the soil at the seam around it. I jab through the earth. I am the weapon. Aza howls and I twist my shoulder and chest as much as I can, draw my hand back, gathering power, gathering movement, that which could be a killing jab, and I punch with the spike. I hack at the rain-melting earth, digging and digging until there is a hole at the seam of the door, and still I hack. The grate door catches my skin, peeling it from my arm.

"Go," Aza says.

Go, the earth says.

Go, the water says.

There is a rushing through me, the rushing of the Water, and I am blind with rage, with pain, with the witness of the Water. I jab and jab, reaving soil from soil, mud from mud, clay from clay. My arm a spear, knifing through and up into the storm-wrung air. The mud of the earth slops from the hole, a hole the size of a large melon. I stab again and again, widening the opening bit by bit until I can fit my shoulder through, and then, I can feel the rain on the side of my face. I hack the hole wider before dropping the stake, grabbing the top of the grate with one hand, and heaving and pulling myself through the ripped seam between earth and door all at once. I push my head through the mud, crowning in the dirt, but I am stuck fast. The hole is not large enough for my collarbone and torso to come through. I half wail, and Aza screams back. I yank at the grate, but there is a lock holding it shut. I keen, wrenching the metal, trying to loosen the earth's grip, but it holds tight.

You your own weapon, my mama said. I am my own weapon.

The needle, I think.

I slide the ivory awl from my hair and stab the ivory needle into the lock, jab and twist, feeling at the small metal parts, searching for the give. I teeter on despair as Aza rips the sky, drenching me.

"Please," I say. "Open." I fiddle and jab, and the mud begins to slide. I push myself upward with my legs, knowing I will not last for long. "Please," I say. "Please!" I yell, even as despair runs into my mouth with the falling rain, even as my body begins to sink.

My own weapon, I think, and I stir the awl, desperate, breathing fast, panicking, until there is a small give, the most infinitesimal of settling clicks, and the lock opens. I fumble off the lock, duck back into the hole, bend my knees. I slide, the soil eating my wedged feet. I angle my shoulders just so, and piston up, slamming the door open, even as I am losing purchase on the melting, muddy walls.

The door swings wide. I grab its frame and pull myself out into the air, flopping onto the ground next to the hole. Aza's wind peppers me. I am newborn raw, lurching to a crouch, chin on my knee, my heart beating so hard I can hear it in my ears over Aza's rushing yell. I swipe uselessly at my mud-caked face.

"Come," Aza says.

Come, the earth says.

Come, the river says.

"I'm here," I whisper. Far off, toward the house and quarters, an orange light bobs: a lantern held aloft. They are coming. I crawl away from the cage in the earth, shuffle backward on my hands and knees in the mud and grass until I jam up against a bush, where I hide. Snatches of words carry on Aza's wind, flung with the rain.

"Here," men say. "Here," the hands call. They walk to the pit and lower the lantern into the prison hole, and there is shock in the jerk, shock that I am not there, that I have escaped their hold. The light shakes and recedes back toward the quarters, to rouse Emil, I bet. To call the men who are not still under the jungle-choked cottonwoods, the moss-wreathed oaks, searching for Mary and

Esther, to search for me. I can see the old woman's light is on, as is the lady's. They will want what they believe is theirs. The storm screams. The night is wide.

They brand you, Esther told me. *They brand you with the fleur-de-lis on your face,* she said, *so everybody, every person who sees you, knows you done fled and got caught. They put chains on your feet, make you walk with steel bracelets 'til they grow into your skin. They put collars on you, metal collars that eat your neck, make little neck-laces of sores. And that's if they don't shoot you, if they don't hang you, if they don't slit your throat because you had the gall to take yourself back.* I can hear her voice, her whispered words at my ear, as clear as if she's crouched next to me in the dark dirt, in the wrap of wind and rain. Fear curls my back and sizzles down my legs, makes me want to stand, to shout, to surrender to the hands so after they beat me, they will bring me back to the dark kitchen, to Cora working some miracle, surely working some miracle to feed herself, to feed Emil, to feed others come to the kitchen, driven there by hunger to beg for scraps in the flour-scented dark.

I half stand to wave, to make my way back to the hell I know, but a tide moves in my guts, moves in the soft part of me that would rot first if I died. It stirs and rises up the nest of my chest, the branch of my throat, to my head. The Water is here, too.

"You," I say.

I open my eyes, and I let the great net of the Water pull me to a crawl, low and hidden in the night rain, until I reach the ring of woods around the house. This instinctual run, steady as breathing, steady as my heart throbbing in my chest. Rain washes my eyes shut so I can't see, but still I trust the Water's current, how it curves with the bustle of Aza's wind-etched skirts, steering me toward the rushing murmur of the drunk river, its beckoning keen. The Water clears the burnt-sugar blaze of the mill, guides me toward the under-dark, the under-bush, and sends me sliding and falling down the riverbank, vines flicking, small trees flaying, the hand of this world wanting to lay me flat, but the Water's tide does not yield until I am knee-deep in the shallows, standing, on my own.

Come, the river says. *I can take you to the sea.*

Dig, They Who Take and Give say. *Dig.*

"Run, girl," Aza gusts. "Run."

Swim, the river laughs.

Burrow, the earth says.

"Mama," I say, her name licking up my throat, a whimper in this bruised abrasion between moonlight and dark. "What I do, Mama?"

I can't breathe.

"Mama."

Little one, my mama says. I jerk tight and tall. First her voice comes from without, a diffuse chime in the night, but then she speaks again, and her voice is everywhere.

"Little one," Mama says, her nickname for me ringing in my ears. It's been more than a year since the Georgia Man dragged her away, but I hear her now. "I was miles from it, miles from the swamp, from the water. When we fell, I knew I was too slow. The run too long. Aza no help. But I had to try, Arese. I had to fight. I thought I could make you into a Moses if I got to the swamp. Thought I could put you in reeds, in rushes, in a log, and you could float. Float, my baby. Float," she says, and then I feel it, feel my mama's love for me as clear as I can feel the rush of the Water when it comes. I can feel her love all around me, stronger than Aza's storm, than the sink of the earth, than the drag of the river. I am alight with it.

I lurch down the shoreline, against the beat of logs, the trees we couldn't clear from the clogged water. I will find a bed of reeds. I will find it. I will. I catch myself on a thatch of floating trees, bound together by their branches, all tangled to one another. I don't think; I rip my shirt over my head and loop the sleeves under the branches and over, pulling them tight, even as I hear a hound's grinding yip. The hands have loosed the dogs. I tie the knot and fumble my way onto the sodden trunks and branches. I push off from the bank, but the thatch is so heavy it will not move.

"Aza!" I yell. "Aza!"

"This is not the way," Aza says.

"Aza, push!" I say as I shove again with my legs and lean, lean into the vortex of river.

"You ask me to give you over to one such as that river!" Aza spits.

"I won't never speak your name!" I say. "I won't never look for you, and my children, my children, they won't never know your name! They won't never call your name, Aza, if you don't do this."

I lurch against the thatch of trunks and branches and it budges, barely budges, before wedging in the earth again. "Let go," I yell at the muck, the sand, the clay. "This my way," I say, flopping on my stomach on my nest of floating trees, my quick-tied shirt, before pushing off the bank with my feet.

"Go," Mama says.

The dogs yip, high and excited.

"Push, Aza. Push!"

The dogs' barks spike like the teeth of a saw. There is no mercy here. If these spirits fail me, I will bare my throat. I will throw myself at those dogs, and I will fight them and lose, and I will go anyway—to the Water, to the singing place beyond the Water, to Mama Aza, to Safi maybe, to my mama. I will be free this night, by doorway or window, by keyhole or dormer. I will be free. The truth bursts in me.

"Go," says Aza, and she flicks her skirts.

Go, say They Who Take and Give.

Go, says the river.

"Go." I kick again, and my toes slip from the bank, and for one second, all is still until I am skimming along the surface of the river in my nest of trees, in my makeshift boat. I am arrowing down the center of the water, straight and true, with a hissing rush. My face cleaves the wind. When I look over my shoulder, lamps set the water's edge aglow, light the lunging barks of the dogs. Their hackles gleam in the yellow oily shine; men's arms flash in the dark, worms rising from muddy earth. They struggle one against another on the bank, the dogs pulling the men, the men pulling the dogs, all of them looking toward me, where the dogs are scenting, but none leap.

"Go," I say. "Go."

I do not know who I say it to, whether I say it to everything and nothing, or only to myself, only to my own hands buried in the pine boughs, my own legs jammed between the trunks, my own head, my own heart beating in me, hope and terror flailing about.

"Thank you," I say, mouthing the branches. "Thank you, thank you, thank you."

I close my eyes to Aza's storm, the gibbering murmur of the river, the swishing of the trees. My mama does not speak. The love that enveloped me, thick as night, is gone. All I feel is the cold of the rain and wind, scratches and gashes burning my stomach and arms and legs and chest. I am alone. I wonder if this is how Safi felt when she ran away from our roped line out into the darkness. I wonder if Mary and Esther are somewhere before me on the river, still clinging to each other and their log. Or have they been dragged down to the river's silty bottom, pale and airless? Or have they escaped the river, the storm, and are they on the shore, hearing the far-off bark of the hounds, their hands clenched one to the other, fleeing?

"Mama," I say.

But my mother does not come. The dogs and hands call from the muck, scrambling after me and Mary and Esther, their voices tearing through the air on a ribbon of wind. I close my eyes.

"There is a story," a voice says, echoing about my head. I do not recognize it. "There is a story you must know," the voice says, and then this voice is everywhere. It is deep as my mother's, but her words rise at the end. There is a singing beneath the sentences. I look out of the corner of my eye, and I see her, misty as Aza, who dances above, pelting and pushing. Mama Aza is next to me: my grandmother. A dog yelps.

"I knew I was carrying your mother when they led us through that carcass of a fort, that last tomb of a room, the door of no return, and down into the bottom of the boat," Mama Aza says.

Another dog screams.

"I knew her in me, and I wondered how she would grow in that dark hold, under the press of the living and dying, in that rocking, salt-scored underworld," Mama Aza says.

Another hound bays. Mama Aza is slim except for the jut of my mother inside of her.

"I slept to despair. I woke to despair. I wanted to die. There was a girl next to me who went to sleep one day and did not wake up. I envied her, even when she began to swell and turn gray."

Another dog answers, farther off. Mama Aza is long limbed and lean.

"We whispered in the dark. We shared names, stories of overbearing mothers, of kind mothers, of absent fathers, of prideful fathers, of little sisters, of big brothers, of dutiful cousins. We rolled, trying to keep sores from opening on our legs and backs and arms, from turning green and black."

Another hound hacks, closer now. There are muscles etched in Mama Aza's shoulders, in her neck.

"I thought there were better ways to die. I thought that if they let me up on the surface of the ship, I would leap over the railing into the water. I took the rope that bound me and worked it loose, and I looped it around my neck, and I tried to cut off my breath. I found a nail jutting up from the floor, and I pressed my arms into it, pressed my legs into it, tried to work my throat against it, but the cuts were not deep enough. The slashes crusted over, slowly, slowly. My stomach full with your mother. I thought of the man, large and gentle, who I made her with, and I wept."

I lick my lips. There are faint lines running from Mama Aza's nose to her mouth from the strain of the hunt, from her endless running.

"When the storm came, for one moment, I thought: *Now, now the boat will be tossed end over end, and we will all die. We will all sink.* The ocean roared so loudly I could not hear my prayers, nor the prayers of those with me. The ocean was all. The sea wormed its way into the hold, and we swam in the salt water, in urine and feces and blood. I prayed but our offal choked me quiet, and I coughed and coughed and coughed, curled around your mother, who swam within me."

Far off through the tossing trees, lanterns wink in and out like summer-soaked insects. The river ululates my raft along.

"That is when the storm answered, when she made herself known to me."

The hands' cries slip by: their heat-heady whoops.

"That is when she took my face. My form." Mama Aza's eyes are even sadder than my mother's. The memory of this sly storm who stole from her even as she pled for her life, even as she honored it with calling, with beholding, weights Mama Aza's gaze. "Yes, the storm spared the boat. And yes, she spoke to me. But when I was choking on all of it, my throat closing like a fist in the fight for air, I knew something then: I wanted to live. That even though I leaned toward dying, toward taking my life from myself, I didn't want anyone to do it for me."

But now, Mama Aza is golden.

"That spirit spared me, spared us. And so did the ocean. And so did I." Mama Aza nods at me, straight. "I spared myself, Annis. Every day I woke, I spared myself."

There is a spark, a flash, at my right, and now, my mother glows to light: young as I've ever seen her, hair braided and fastened about her head in long loops, what must be her father's eyes in her face: large and soft as my grandmother Aza's are small and sharp.

"I knew what sparing was before," Mama Aza says. "I saw it in the eyes of the elephants we stalked. How, until the last moment, they wanted life, even covered with hundreds of cuts."

My mother lays her shimmering hand over mine, and it is no more than a touch of cool air.

"Even bound by pain, they bellowed for it. Bayed for it," Mama Aza says.

I drink my mother with my eyes. I cannot stop looking at her.

"Take it for yourself, child. All of it," Mama Aza says.

My mama: my moon. Her smile the open flutter of a moth.

"Fight for it all," Mama Aza says.

Mama touches my cheek: a cooler rain.

"I knew," Mama says. "I knew before you came."

I hear and know her voice all at once, just as I know her: Mama sewing our clothes, letting out and taking in; Mama cooking rice for us, flavoring it with mushrooms and wild herbs and filched pig drippings; Mama braiding my hair, her thigh soft under my face. Mama telling one of Mama Aza's stories, laughing, waiting for my smile. A great snake squeezes in me, grounding grief, that I would have forgotten what her voice sounds like, how it is gravelly at the bottom and smooth as a river running up top, because I haven't had the hearing of her in so long.

"When you walked, when you slept, when you ran. You wreathed in your bees. You with your staff. You scratching my head."

"Mama," I say.

"How you shone," Mama says. "How you shine."

"Mama," I say. "Mama."

I cannot say more.

"You your own weapon," Mama says. "Remember."

Crying jags through me.

Mama Aza puts her hand to my back, but it is nothing but warm glow, recalled heat, and then she nods and shimmers away. Then there is only Mama and me on this bed of reeds, this loose raft. She looks at me as seriously, as calmly, as she ever did. Her nose spreads. Her cheekbones dim. She is disappearing, but the black velvet of her eyes stays.

"It ain't forever, little one. It ain't forever."

She will always be with me. I know it through my gasping. Know it through my grasping. I know that I will see the gleam of her in the pocked glitter of the moon, in its embered shine. Know I will see her in the shattered stream of stars across the molasses-dark sky. Know that I will see her in the wrinkling of my hands, the whitening of my hair. After my last breath, at the end of my toil and hours, know it will be her who will ferry me across the Water. *Mama.* I know it sure as I know the far-off hounds, rooting through the underbrush at the water's edge, raising their noses to bay all at once, their calls trailing up to whip off in the air: frenzied and starving. Lightning lights the river, the tunnel of forest overhanging the water, twisting over me and my raft, beckoning me along. Thunder thumps the sky and rolls around me in a great circle.

I cry and mouth the pine needles. Taste the bite of resin.

THE STORM SEEMS ENDLESS until it isn't. The wind and rain drain, and in their absence, the river murmurs like a drunk nodding off to sleep. Aza descends, coalesced into her human form, and floats at the back of the raft. I see other aspects of Mama Aza in her: Aza has mimicked the long reach of Mama Aza's limbs, the fine lines of her arms and legs, the leonine set of her face, even the small roundness of my mama in her stomach. I swallow.

Aza wants more than worship. She wants love. I read envy in her mimicry of Mama Aza, envy for my grandmother, who breathed in spite of all that would choke her; who carried the fruit of her embrace of her lover in her womb; who knew what it was like to sit with her sister-wives, her sister-warriors, after a long run, wind cooling sweat to salt; who knew what it was like to tell jokes, to watch joy overtake her sister-wives' faces like a green shivering of underbrush, and for them all to laugh, dimples carving tadpoles in their cheeks.

Aza coveted when she descended to that boat. She coveted when she left Mama Aza in this strange land and returned to behold her, again and again, to watch my mother being born, and later, me. She saw a mother's love in Mama Aza's will to live, in my mama's running with me to the Great Dismal Swamp, and she coveted that relationship for herself: Aza wanted to be a mother to the women of my line. Our beseeching, our begging, was never enough regard; Aza desired more. But she was foolish because she could never know us in our fullness.

I have to look away from Aza when I realize that even in the giving, this spirit took, too; even as Mama Aza's work in this awful place withered her, broke her body, this spirit remained, a mocking image of Mama Aza's younger self. Aza tangles a breeze around the lashed logs. The river has slowed, and my ramshackle raft eases to a drift, from one side of the water to another. The swamp rises thick around us, enclosing us in a green curl of leaf and pearly-white light. A fog simmers over the river, but I stay low in the raft and hope that the brown of me bleeds into the brown of the lashed trees.

"This river will empty into the bigger river, the one that cuts through the city. We should stop there," Aza says.

Birds chatter through the tops of the trees, flutter from limb to limb, following us.

"Why the city?" I ask.

"My children there," she says.

They are cranes, slim and long legged, pale as the morning fog. When I bought water to those who toiled in the rice fields, the cranes moved slow as dancers, nodding and bending.

The cranes glide from one tree to another. They alight, light as paper on wind. They stop as my raft snags on the bank, and Aza's winds still.

"You can disappear. Become one of many," she says.

The birds study us with black-rimmed eyes. They ruffle their feathers and settle. They watch.

"You could find my children." Aza looks away when she says it, but I know she's watching me. "The ones who call to me." What she doesn't say: *You could be my child.*

The snag of my raft echoes the catch in my chest. I don't want to hide in the city, live my days like a rat, cleaving to walls and corners, averting my face, surfacing at night to beg, filch, steal. I don't want to give over the tender parts of myself to men like the lady's husband. And I don't want to settle on the enslaver's borders, either, even with Bastian, even with Mary, even with Esther, if they are alive, if, with Aza's help, I could find them. I could never sleep, never laugh, for listening for the baying of the dogs, for the excited shouts of the hands. How the dogs would howl. How the men would file into our clearing in the swamp, guns cocked and wedged in shoulders, teeth bared and jaws unhinged. Given enough fire, even green will burn.

"No," I say.

Even men will burn. How the black of the roiling fire and the smell of them, cloying as roasted pig, would rise to the sky, yielding more offerings to the gray cotton press above us, the many-voiced earth below.

"What?" Aza says.

How we dissipate for the gods.

"No," I say again. "I want to go beyond the city."

The birds hop from leg to leg down the limbs of the tree before fluttering to a stop. The forest overhangs the water, dropping orange needles and brown leaves to pock its eddies.

"I want to find a swamp so thick even the Georgia Man can't walk through it."

The cranes raise their shoulders all at once and shrug.

"One so thick, only spirits can find me."

Pleasure blooms on Aza's face. I know I flatter. I know I feed her hunger for worship, for mothering. Me: her wayward, duplicitous child. I know that given another choice, I would starve her right out of Mama Aza's body. Starve her to her true face, her true form, but I need her to stir her skirts. I need her to shove me from this shore, to hide me in her mist through the city. I need her to steer me around the steamboats and slave ships to solitude in the far wilderness. I flounder out of the raft, sinking to my thighs in the river, the skin of my chest crawling with cold. I grab a big broken branch, thick with leaves, and clamber back onto the raft. I dig the end of the branch into my stomach and heave against the pull of the water. The silent cranes shiver. I wrestle the branch over me, lie faceup under the lace of the twigs and wide oak leaves.

"Please," I say.

Aza rises and smooths her skirts. A breeze blossoms. The cranes settle and watch, stretching their necks so that Aza's movement ruffles scruffs, easing some itch they didn't know they had.

"On?" she asks.

I nod, and Aza pushes.

I WAKE TO THE punctured darkness of New Orleans. The river has broadened to a silent, glistening murmur. It is a watery boulevard, a wide humming, clogged by tugboats and barges carrying cotton and cane and stolen men and women, who cry and plot and make families in their dark holds. The people speak under the lilt of the river. Tall buildings rise along the shoreline, lamplight shining in their blind windows. Women and men cuss, smashing together in the dark, on cobblestones and plaster, loving one minute, scratching and slapping the next. Horses whinny at their posts. Overlaying it all is Aza's fog, gray muslin shot through with gold, peach, and silence.

The earth deep beneath us groans, sinking under the weight of the silt washed down this ruined earth, over the miles of river. The plate of Aza's face is brown in the night, but she is not the only spirit who moves through this city. She Who Remembers burns over the docks, etching the names of the enslaved on the scroll of her skin as she watches them stumble from the holds of the ships, blind even to the light of the city night: their tongues thick, their scalps itching, the rot of the southern voyage turning their stomachs. Another spirit, white and cold as snow, walks the edge of the river; it hungers for warmth, for breath, for blood, for fear, and it, too, glances against the stolen and feeds. Another spirit slithers from rooftop to rooftop before twining about wrought iron balconies outside plaçage women's bedrooms, where it hums, telling the bound women to portion out poison in pinches over the years, to revolt, revolt, revolt. Another spirit lopes through the streets, black hat askew, grinning. Another spirit beats drums, furious drums, their thump the sound of herds of horses, swarms of feral pigs, stampeding their way across the earth, rooting through forests and denuding plains. Another spirit sits at the foot of a bed where an infant screams, and she guides the little brown fingers to the mouth, bids the baby to rub its feet one against the other, humming to give comfort. Another spirit sits on a mountain of blades, sharpening machete after machete before sheathing each into the earth between the cobblestones; when I float by, she grins and points a blade at me. I nod, knowing the salute for what it is, and she returns to grinding metal against stone. The air of the city smells of sulfur.

Aza sinks to me.

"Why not here?"

"No," I say.

I see my place. It is somewhere out there, beyond the wide, deep river, beyond a far, shivering lake. It rustles and waits, thick with trees whose roots rise above the water like knees, thick with meaty cattails and hissing alligators, thick with whiskered catfish and mangrove trees.

"There," I say.

Aza folds the fog of her hair, her garments, tighter around the pines. I turn my face away from the glut of goddesses and gods, spirits and people on their knees, on their walk-weary feet, on their backs in the gutters. I know it is all bound, that the Water runs even here, but this place is not mine. My skin itches with sap, but I rub my face against the bark and breathe in the acrid green of the needles anyway.

CHAPTER 13

*

Once More Saw Stars

Under the first whitewash of dawn, I discover I'm in brown-silver, brackish water at the edge of a vast, hungry lake that has swallowed my raft. The lake spreads so far, I have to squint to see smoke in the distance, where people are waking and setting fire to wood and cooking. Their lives thin to smudges on the horizon, then disappear. I'm shaking, clenched against the cold and the dwindling raft. The lake's waves jostled tree trunk after trunk away so I am left with my arms and legs locked around the two I first lashed together with my shirt. My teeth clack, insistent as the toss of water. I touch my lips to my shoulder, just to feel something soft, something tender, but they are hard as a puddle iced over on the first day of winter.

"Please," I tell Aza.

She huffs me further along the lake's expanse, toward a north-flowing river.

"There," I say, and she follows.

. . .

BREATH BY BREATH, CLACK by clack, the wild rustling that called me here over the miles grows louder. It clicks and rasps, pauses, then takes up again. It beckons. Over the hours, the river narrows, closed on all sides by orange and dull fall green, until the branch of one of my trees digs into the riverbed, bringing my raft to a stop. I fall into the water and drag my craft to the bank. I hold my hands to my head, breathe into the cool of them between shakes. Cypresses bow and shimmer. I try to listen beyond the tick of small frogs in the muck about me, gasping into the cold, dying in the mud. I am so tired. My shaking makes it hard for me to breathe. I lay down with the frogs, and they leap away.

"Annis," Aza says.

"Can't breathe," I say. I hug myself. My head feels pulled apart at the stitching, threads frayed, and I squeeze my eyes against the lash of pain. I am trying to hear the calling, channeled through the Water, which bought me here, but I can't hear for the lashing. My skin burns and pulls tight, ready to slough off. I close my eyes to the grind of pain. Each breath: a shallow dip. Each blink: a beckon to stop. I could drift off like this, under my own reckoning, my own wanting, but there—a tuft of yellow and black, whirring through the air. A bee. I lurch to stand and follow.

I fight to lift my feet out of the mud, squinting against the gray sky, the leaching green of the trees. I duck vines, ropes that grow in dry tangles from tree to tree. I give up and crawl on my belly beneath them. The bee beckons, flying slowly in curls and loops. Aza puffs behind me, and the bee lists with her breeze. The green that called me has quieted now, quieted to a shush.

"Aza," I say. "Please be still."

She whirls.

"I can find a path," Aza says.

"No."

I want to lead. I want to find my own way through this knot of woods, drying toward their winter sleep. I want to choose where to put one aching foot, where to sink into the mud, ankle-deep in mosquitoes, before pulling it out to step again. I want to raise my head to the bee. I want to choose. Breath burns through my chest, in and out. The ache in my head, my limbs, recedes the further I follow. The bugs rustle and call, and the bee wends its way through with a buzz so low it is nearly inaudible.

There are flowers here in the undermuck, in the below dark, in all that is sinking to the undulating mud to rise again next spring. A cluster of purple here, then yellow, and then white. The petals look skyward like me, trying to catch the last shine of autumn, the last turn of warmth. The bee settles to drink from one bloom, then rises to fly again and fall to another to sip. I climb logs. Branches scratch yarns of red over my shins, pull at my calves, say: *Stay here, with us, and hollow.* I kick through them. The bee threads its way along, and I rise and fall with the land. I stumble up a faint hill, drier than the rest, and find the grass shorter here: instead of sawgrass wisping over my shoulders and cattails nodding over my head, here the swamp grass grows to my thighs, and in bald bunches. There was a trail here, once, maybe, leading through the dim underbrush. Vines rise to loop along the branches above me, to fall in a curtain across the path. The bee slips through the venous curtain, so I sink to my knees and search until I find an opening, and I crawl again. The mesh of bleached green has thorns, and they grab at my hair, my skin. I scrabble until I see light, until I wrench through to crouch in open air: I have found a clearing. The burnt husk of a house reaches like a hand from the high, dry ground to the sky. The swamp hums in assent around me, sealing me in its secret heart.

I found a way.

"THERE WAS ILLNESS HERE," I say. I know it. Aza is right; since I opened myself to the Water, it is easy to slip into vision, to see beyond this place into another. This is the past; I see the flicker of a white man, his skin sallow as eggshells, standing in the clearing, pointing, talking without sound as three work-weary, barely clothed brown people unload canoes packed with hammers, stakes, and axes. The white man is pocked with sickness, fallen to his knees in the half-built ruins of the grand house he was forcing on this impossible place; in the next flash, he is bleeding from his eyes, his toenails, his nose and mouth.

"The yellow fever . . . it rooted through the enslaver," I tell Aza.

The people who were left set fire to the bones of the sprawling foundation, the pale man's ill dream, and fled into the swamp, free. "The people burned this." The bees found the black husk of an oak branch that caught fire: they walked through its empty veins and filled its holy hollows with wax and filament, honey and young. The jungle took the ruins then, grew over hours, days, weeks, months, years, over the burnt timber, the jagged brick, up through the soot-soaked earth, to wreath the cabin the people lived in while setting the bones for this hidden plantation. This empty, green-grown cabin, the escaped men did not burn. This, they left for me.

"Why here?" Aza twitches beside me, annoyance plain on her face. "This lonely place? The city—"

"No," I say.

"No people here," Aza says, "and no one to feed you."

Aza flicks her skirts like a cat's tail. I know that she's talking about me, but she's also talking about herself. How she would starve in this place with no one else to worship her.

"I'll feed myself," I say, and I set about doing just that. I am too new to the bees; I can't smoke them, can't coax them. The cabin is littered with rusted tools: an axe, a hatchet, and hammers. I dig and find dirt-hardened balls of string, a quilt sewn from scraps and ossified to a board's stiffness, and an iron skillet.

"Thank you," I whisper to They Who Take and Give, dirt caking my ruined fingernails. The earth roots and settles in reply.

Aza blows out a breath, and it turns the cabin cool. I shiver. She shakes her shoulders, and her skirts billow outside the narrow door.

"I will come back," she says.

Aza spins up from the building, over the ruined bones of the mansion, away into the low-bellied sky.

I follow her with my eyes until I can't, and then I turn back to my hidden, green-walled room. I gather wood sorrel and mushrooms and sassafras, and I eat until my stomach eases, until the spikes of hunger soften, and a small brown rabbit leads me to a thin, clear-running stream where I forage more, finding so many plants and mushrooms to eat that my skirt bulges. I sit at the edge of the water, only sit, and watch dozens of wet green frogs jump from bank to bank, croaking to one another. A gray and white crane with lavender-seamed feathers lands on its banks, and another follows. They step and peck, step and peck, devouring the frogs. I sit as the sun wedges a hand through the clouds and shines golden and full on the birds' black-crowned heads, and on my own: mud caked, thorn woven.

The cranes look at me with soft black eyes, as soft as my mother's, and we sit with each other until I stand and go back to the husk of cabin and set about the work of cleaning. I clear the floor, stack what's left of hewn wood for a pallet, sweep away mole nests and spiderwebs with a pine bough. As the sky lights orange and the insects ring a twilight chorus, I wash in the stream. I gather Spanish moss for a bed. My skin, with all its nicks and cuts, its scabs and scratches, takes in the light and shines. I pick a small well in a nude pine stick, layer it with straw, find the straightest twig I can and wedge it into the well, and then spin it with my hands until my arms ache, until the sun nearly sets, until smoke rises from the pit and sparks spit from the small well and catch the needles.

"Thank you," I say.

They Who Take and Give rustle, and then the swamp echoes and sings, and I let the loneliness and the gratefulness for the first day of my free life leak from my eyes and cut hot trails down my face and drop. I cover my mouth and laugh and cry at this new afterlife, this otherworld.

"I wish you had this," I say to the darkening sky, wreathed with pink and peach, deepening purple. "I wish you had this here," I say to my mama, to Mama Aza. An owl hoots from the murky green turning black with the evening, and a feeling drops through the center of my breastbone before echoing out in circles, and I hear my mother—just a snatch, just a whisper.

"I know," my mama says.

Off in the distance, an alligator hisses.

"I miss you," I say. "I love you."

"I know," my mother says, and then there is a silence in my mind, a stillness.

• • •

LATER IN THE NIGHT, Aza settles into the clearing. She burns with the low fire, the flame lighting her arms, her eyes, the tips of her hair. Her false belly round. No child there: she is fed and full with praise.

"They drum in a square in the city," she says. Her eyes glow orange. "They call me by another name, but they sing to me. They sing to all the spirits."

She drifts closer, stands before me, and reaches out a tentative hand; her finger feels like a spatter of rain that falls in the sunshine.

"They ask for us to sweep down into their lives, to take away all that doesn't serve, all that clutters, all that blocks." She caresses my arm, which is starved to the same roundness from shoulder to wrist. "The women wear white."

I shake her off.

"We dance with them." Aza looks around me, at the hut at my back, at the ruins beyond. "They open themselves." Aza rouses the beehive with her worship-drunk wind. "We dance through."

The bees sound a sleepy, sudden buzz. The flames flicker.

"They would welcome you," Aza says.

I keep my face still, feel the warmth from the fire that covers me like a blanket. I fist the edges of the quilt I found and washed in the creek around my back. It is barely damp.

"Like they welcome you?" I ask.

Aza smiles: a small slip of teeth.

"As one of my children?" she says. "As one who I speak to?"

Pain throbs from fingernail to toe. I am hungry again. Aza moves to the other side of the fire, and I remember harvest season when I was a child, my mama simmering a small pot of rice, flavoring it with some filched lard, some stolen salt, and how I ate myself full, my belly big, and laid my head in my mama's lap. My mouth wets.

"I don't know, Aza."

"You could be my priestess," Aza says. "You could teach them my true name."

I flinch, recalling the story Mama Aza told me on the raft, the reach of her slim arm. *It's not your name*, I want to tell Aza, but don't. Aza rises with the smoke, resin rich, billowing with the stars at her back, the frothy heads of the trees underfoot.

"I'm tired," I say.

"I will return," Aza says, and I know where she goes even though she doesn't say it. I know she whips her wind over the tops of the trees, hurrying back to her city of spirits and worshippers: her children. The frogs sound and I hear the splash of fish leaping from the water to eat night-flying insects before slipping below again.

I lay in my nest of Spanish moss before the fire. I will cut two branches tomorrow and put a third over the flames so I can cook. I will make a tea from the cattail root. I will gather frogs, kill and

skin them, slice off their great jumping legs. I will seek mushrooms.
I will add it all to the pot. I will follow my mind.

THE CALM I FELT on my first day does not echo into the next
morning. Fear, present and prickly, rings me in the night. I sleep
in snatches. My panic ebbs when morning washes through the
swamp, but it returns through the hours, surprising me. I startle
when patching the house. I seal the vines I crawled beneath to get
here, weaving them back together, and then remain hidden in their
tangled growth, trying to slow my breathing, my crackling heart.
I listen for dogs. The next night, exhausted, I fall asleep under the
wheel of stars. The moon hides her face. One morning, one sunset,
one dawn, one day, one evening; the first week, the second week,
run into one another. I sleep in snatches until I don't, until I'm
awake for a day and night, and then I doze off with the sun filtering
through the trees, me cushioned in their needles, gathered cattails
and roots in hand. Later, I crouch in the shell of the burned great
house, heartbeat heavy in my neck, my ears, straining to hear the
coming of saw-mouthed men. Aza's leaving turns cruel.

One morning, I wake and vaguely remember dreaming of my
mother, of Mama Aza, but when I try to recall if they spoke to me,
I don't recollect words and can't see their faces. I only see myself in
the dream, knob kneed and skinny necked, eating bowl after bowl
of salty, rich grits until my stomach bloats. In my waking hours, my

ribs jut like butter knives. In the waking world, the Water is silent.
I patch the cabin and store food for the winter, busy in lurches. The
wind blows cool from the north. It takes me weeks more to parse
the low within me, dry and empty as an abandoned hive, since
I haven't felt it since my mother was taken from me: loneliness.
What will become of me if I don't follow Aza to the city? Will she
return one day to find me dead? Or perhaps alive but mute, knotty
haired, the swamp grown over me?

But then a family of boar slips through the underbrush, and
I watch them go, the bellies of the smallest piglets tickling the
earth, and l think: I am not alone. And They Who Take and Give
squelch under my feet, and the trees rustle their branches, and
I reach out to the Water, and I imagine what my mother would
say: *You not.* I find a cluster of morels. But still, when I sit before
the fire at night, sharpening an axe and thinking about the little I
learned from Emil about butchering, wondering whether I could
build a little smokehouse, how much fat I could render off one
of them piglets, I fantasize about the feast Aza's dancers would
give me if I let her blow me back to the city, to people. If I take
her for my mother. And I wonder whether she wants me thinking
this, and then I know it, know she does, know that her absence is
intended to show I need her, need her rain and her wind and her
elemental mothering.

•   •   •

THE MOON SHINES FULL and fat. I sit before the fire, feeling my sore chest. I've never felt this pain, and I wonder if I'm ill with some swamp-borne sickness.

"Do you know?" I ask the hive. My chest throbs, mimicking the clean-burning flames, and I'm surprised to see a lone bee, golden and glinting, drifting before the fire. It lists and then drops, tickling and downy, on my wrist.

I laugh and see another, which hovers and lands. I look up and there are myriad bees, all awash in moonlight, above me. They drift and land, one after another, to settle on me, and it's not until they wreath me, a bristling, sweet living garment, that I know how starved I am for kindness, and my breasts blaze with heat. I remember my mama sitting with me the first time I bled, teaching me how to staunch the blood with rags, how now she said: *You can carry a child.* How she'd put her arm around me then, hugged me to her, and cried.

Why you crying, Mama, I asked, but she rubbed my ear and muffled my face in her neck, and her tears scalded my cheek.

"This why, Mama?" I ask the night, the bees taking flight from my arms, my crown, back to their hive, in a silent, sweet rising.

I reach across the Water, remembering how my mama wiped her tears, brusque and hard, away. I know now what they were for: terror, love, relief that I had lived long enough to bleed. My sire would sell her three seasons later.

"Mama." I reach.

"Blessing," she says, and then she's silent. I count the days since my last bleeding, and suddenly, I know what my reach for pleasure with Esther's brother has done. I know what the soreness in my chest means. I know that there is a seed, a song, a babe coming to me.

I put my hands on my stomach and rock.

I SWALLOW DOWN NAUSEA through the days and hunt mushrooms for strength and healing. At night, I feel the press of my fingernails growing back into their beds, the itch of my skin stretching at my hips. I build a small lean-to for smoking meat, and I kill squirrels, a raccoon, and a piglet with a sling, but I can't stop thinking about rice and grits, especially in the mornings. I try to let the thought, the memory of grains, go when I drink my mushroom-and-meat broth. This is what I am eating the night Aza returns.

"You been working," Aza says, descending into the clearing with a gray fog. The fire dims with dampening, and I rouse its embered heart with a stick.

"I have," I say, surprised at the feeling in me, the gratefulness at her return, the pleasure of company, which is warm and thick as a swallow of corn cake with honey. She is even more flush than when I last saw her, her arms round and plump, her face lit by lightning, awash in pleasure. Mama Aza probably never had the luxury of this fullness.

"You healthier now," she says. She's appraising me, and for one breath, the look on her face is the thin, white-faced lady's, wrenching wealth from the people, the sugar, the earth. I feel a quick stab of panic.

"I been eating," I say to cover it up. "More than what I could being stolen."

Aza nods and hums. Her skirts darken with the sound. She is gathering power.

"Build a raft." She smiles and threads a strong wind through the tops of the trees. They toss and murmur, obscuring the moon. "You ready."

I look down at They Who Take and Give. My bees, the swamp, Aza, the earth: they are all silent, waiting. I cross my arms and look up at Aza, her sharp beauty, the roil of her magnificent hair, the spirit inhabiting my grandmother's memory, and think of the seed, the song, the secret in me.

"No," I say.

I raise an arm to the room of the clearing, the shivering trees, the animals that slide through the night, the bones of the great house, the husk of the little shack that I have scratched and swept and patched into my own home.

Aza rumbles to stillness. Thunder beats through her breath. Still, her words are quiet.

"I delivered you here, to this place."

"No," I say.

I hold up my hands. I marvel at my arms, little more than bone wreathed in skin when I came here, but now wormed through with muscle. "I delivered myself."

"No," she says.

"Yes," I say. "You was a help, Aza."

She tosses her winds over her shoulders.

"I'm here because of me," I say.

She whips the wind again, and I crouch closer to the earth. I have to close my eyes to the gust and then squint up at her to read the words on her lips when she speaks.

"Without me, you would have died on the trail."

"And Safi," I say.

"Without me, you would have died in the markets."

"And Phyllis," I say.

"Without me, you would have died in the sugarcane."

"And Emil."

"You would have died in the hole."

"And Esther."

"You would have drowned in the river."

"And Mama Aza."

"You would have turned over in the lake."

"And my mama," I say.

The wind twists the clearing like a great screw. The sky is a deeper black. It flushes with Aza's face, and where her feet would be turns dark as soot. She rolls her head on her neck, and she spins.

"You would not know this dance?" Aza asks. She turns again, her skirts a smudged blur. "This love?"

I dig raw fingers into the earth. Grasp roots and runners. Aza's air blasts. It pushes me to bow. To worship. I lie belly-down in the earth-stirred sand I sweep clean every day. My fire dies. I flatten myself as low as I can, cringing from Aza's turning, her storm frenzy: her chest washes and spreads, her arms rise and whirl, her hair writhes to a cone. She has danced herself to a tornado. I huff in what little breaths I can.

"You helped me, Aza," I say.

The moon is gone. My mouth is pasty with grit.

"But I can't give you my life," I say.

The browning swamp sank to Aza's flaying wind.

"I will always see you, will always be grateful for you, but I ain't yours," I say.

Aza booms, loud as the grinding ocean in storm. I shut my eyes to the salt world.

"You ain't my mama," I say.

"Your mama?" she asks, her words whispered into the low place where I crouch. I gasp in sips. I open my eyes and they burst black. She would take even my breath, especially that.

"You not," I choke.

I mouth the mud. Aza's winds rise to a song, a song sung with feet in dust, coffin digging into the soft meat of the shoulder, the weight of the box light as an eyelash under the press of sorrow.

"I am," I say. "My own."

The trees whip through the air. They nod their heads to the sulfur-scented earth. I hold fast with the little, the small hearted, the quick limbed. I hold low with those who still, eyes shining in the night, and pretend to be dead to foil the lank coyote, to dumb the yellow-smiling wolf. The frogs protest, the bugs dissent, and my moans come quick and sharp, but Aza does not hear the whine of small beings. She is too flush with fury, twisting and tossing sap-wounded limbs in her wake.

"You forsake me," Aza sobs as she cuts, machete-sharp, through the night swamp. As she spins away. Even with the seed, the secret, the babe in me, Aza's leaving hurts. It breaks something in me. *Mother*, I almost want to say to her. *Mother*, because that is the name she wanted from me and my mama, the true name she covets. I could give it. I could give it and she would turn back. If I called her now, she would return. I could lash a new raft, could pin myself to it, could let her ferry me back to the people-choked city, to the children who call her by another name, could take my place among them, hide in the throng, pray that I never see the sharp-faced lady or her handymen ever again. But no. No. I don't want that chase, that hunt. I want this green room, this bed padded with moss and cypress needles, this turtle soup, this smoked boar, this honey that will come with spring. I want the seed, the secret, the babe, to be born here. I want the first breath she takes, the crack of her cry, to ring the clearing, to rouse the spawning tadpoles, open the possum kits' eyes, raise the piglets rooting.

Aza rends the sky. She rips the book of the air. She ascends and spins, and I know I have wounded her greatly because she is not returning to New Orleans, which is westward. Instead she travels east, bound for the heaving slate ocean where she first found Mama Aza. She will spin overland up the long road we walked, back over my sire's house, back to the nursery of her sea. She will dance herself from torrent to trickle, and she will dissolve over the water, wring herself dry over the skeletons of Mama Aza's sunken people, and then she will pass through a strait to return to her own mother: the Water. Aza has offered: she escorted those who were bound south, bore witness to our drowning, our burning, our bleeding, our descent into the bellies of the rivers, into the black mouth of They Who Take and Give. The first time Aza came to me, spoke to me, how cool her touch, how soothing: a mother's hand bearing a chill rag in fever. And now her leaving: the warm rag falls. When she returns to the realm of storms, to their airy cities, will that be enough? Will she know the Water, and will the Water regard her?

With Aza's leaving, the swamp night unfurls its minutes. The insects cry, weeping their broken breathren. The seething dark smells of sap and rotten eggs. I climb over debris to kneel in the stream to rinse my mouth, my face, my body, clean. Wipe my soft parts, looking for blood; I'm relieved to find the seed in my belly remains. Tufted branches and torn leaves blanket my dead fire, overlie the moonlit clearing. I search for my quilt and wrap it about me, kick the clutter from the doorway, and lie across the doorjamb. My mouth tastes of the dense root of earth. I suck the flavor away, gazing up. Aza's storm has wiped the wheel of the sky clear, and the great river of stars shimmers.

I hope my mother helms a tight-seamed boat with a large white sail on the celestial waterway between worlds. Her vessel one of the resurrected fleet navigating the Water. I hope she stands wide-legged on her deck, Mama Aza beside her, their sashes snapping in the invisible dark wind. Sure-footed, farseeing women. The wide byways open and glittering to them, seething with ice and light, water and spirit. How the whitewash of starlight would buoy them along. How they dance with the rocking deck. How them sing.

Acknowledgments

I'd like to thank my editor, Kathy Belden. This book was particularly difficult to create, and I am ever grateful to her for asking the necessary questions that led to the metamorphosis of the novel in the big revision. She saved me in the writing of this book and in life, because she held my hand through my grief and helped me find my way back to my voice. Rob McQuilkin, my literary agent, fiercely advocates for me and my work. I am grateful to Rebekah Jett, associate editor, who kept me organized and faithful to deadlines. Jaya Miceli, my art director, designed the beautiful, transcendent cover. Laura Wise, my production editor, assured all the details were right. Thanks to Stuart Smith, associate publisher, who was an early advocate for Annis. Ashley Gilliam Rose and Brianna Yamashita worked tirelessly to get this book to readers, as did Georgia Brainard. Kate Lloyd has been my publicist for a couple of my novels, now, and she is fantastic: a firm, inventive firecracker who has ushered my books and my kids into the world with the same thoughtfulness. My thanks to Nan Graham, who has chosen to champion my work and invest in my career, and who also offered helpful notes with this novel. I would also like to thank Miriam Feuerle, Hannah Scott, and all the staff at the Lyceum Agency, who work tirelessly to bring my work to readers.

I'd like to thank my colleagues at Tulane University, who have been flexible and supportive in the making of this book, especially Professor Michael Kuczynski and Professor Thomas Beller. President Michael Fitts and Dean Brian T. Edwards have also made room and space for my literary career at the same time they support my academic one. My students at Tulane are exceptional, and they inspire me to show up for creative writing and to push boundaries in my fiction.

I could not have found my way out of the fresh dregs of loss without my friends, chief amongst them Dr. Veronique Robins-Brown: my eternal thanks to her. My fellow writers always inspire me, and they are ever gentle with me, even when I disappear: Elizabeth Staudt, Natalie Bakapoulos, Sarah Frisch, Justin St. Germain, Stephanie Soileau, Ammi Keller, Harriet Keller, and Rob Ehle. Special thanks to Christian Kiefer, who became my friend in the thick of the pandemic, and also to Regina Bradley, cousin of my heart, both who spurred me to finish *Let Us Descend* when they completed their own works in progress. My college besties, Julie Hwang and Brenna Powell, have always kept me afloat. All love to the ladies who laugh but don't play: Kimberly McWilliams, Anna Liese, Tatum Wingfield, and Amanda Wood, who love my children like their own, who give me reason to laugh, and who stand with me and for me.

Finally, I could not do this without my family. My mother loves me, feeds me, and ushers me through unspeakable pain. My father showed up and supported me after my beloved B died. My sisters, Nerissa and Charine, are with me day in and day out, bearing me up. My oldest nephew and godchild, De'Sean, was the first to give me some understanding of what it meant to love a child and care for a child unconditionally; all these years later, when we lost B, he cared for me as I did for him. My godmother, Aunt Gretchen, has always nurtured me. My Aunt Judy teaches me the power of a good line of dialogue and induces laughter every time we speak. My uncles, especially Tom and Phil and Jason and Dwayne, are lighthouses. My cousin Nadine has always modeled grace, wisdom, and fearlessness. My little brother/cousin Aldon remembers the stories I have forgotten, the stories Joshua took with him, and he tells them so that I don't lose that part of me that only he and Josh knew. My cousins Rhett and Jill hold me in love, always, regardless of my failures, my mistakes, and my choices. My extended family has always encouraged me. My best friend, Mark, is ever present, ever faithful, even when I am silent for a time. Sister of my heart, Mariah, has pulled me back to the land of the living, again and again. My nieces and nephews keep me open to joy: Joshua B.,

Kalani, Au'laysia, Joshua D., Jhernii, and little Brandon. My kin/ girls help me to remember that life is worth living: Danielle, Bernetta, Robynn, Nikki, Rachel, Blake, Diedre, and Dwynette, and their children are stars to me, too. My new partner, Marcus, reminds me there is more love and more life. My children are wondrous miracles, and they keep me breathing: Noemie, Brando, and Xavier. The specter of losing each of you helped me to understand Annis's descent, and every word I write is for you.

About the Author

Jesmyn Ward received her MFA from the University of Michigan and has received a MacArthur genius grant, a Stegner Fellowship, a John and Renée Grisham writers residency, the Strauss Living award, and the 2022 Library of Congress Prize for American Fiction. She is the winner of two National Book Awards for Fiction for *Sing, Unburied, Sing* (2017) and *Salvage the Bones* (2011). She is also the author of the novel *Where the Line Bleeds* and the memoir *Men We Reaped*, which was a finalist for the National Book Critics Circle Award and won the Chicago Tribune Heartland Prize and the Media for a Just Society Award. She is currently an associate professor of creative writing at Tulane University and lives in Mississippi.